What just happened?

Had it been so long since he'd been attracted to anyone other than Anne that he'd forgotten how to act around a woman as vibrant and caring as Brooke? Had his heart shriveled to a size smaller than the Grinch's? At least the Grinch had a heart at the beginning.

All he had to do was get in the car and wait to make sure Brooke drove off safely. That was the easy option, the option that would keep him from risking loss again. Brooke exited the building, her purse in hand.

Eating crow wasn't as tasty as his favorite chocolate puff cereal, but even he knew he needed to smooth things over with her.

That was the easy part. The hard part would be doing everything within his control to keep from falling for her.

Dear Reader,

When I researched my debut novel, Jonathan Maxwell landed in Hollydale as its newest police officer. I knew then he wasn't the typical rookie cop, and he's inched his way toward his own happy ending ever since. In this first book of the Smoky Mountain First Responders miniseries, Jonathan grapples with the aftereffects of grief while raising two daughters, each with a unique personality, which, as a mother of four, I relate to all too well.

Enter Brooke Novak, who promises her son they've settled in Hollydale. Brooke and I share something in common, as I moved frequently as a child, just as she does as an adult. Moving can be an exciting adventure with new opportunities around the corner and the hope of connecting with a community and friends always in sight.

Brooke and Jonathan have issues to overcome, including the reactions of their children to their fledgling relationship—more to relate to for some readers. I hope you enjoy discovering how they navigate that challenge. I love to connect with my readers, either through my website or on my Facebook author page.

Happy reading!

Tanya Agler

HEARTWARMING

The Single Dad's Holiday Match

———

Tanya Agler

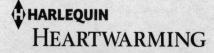

HARLEQUIN®
HEARTWARMING™

ISBN-13: 978-1-335-42643-7

The Single Dad's Holiday Match

Recycling programs for this product may not exist in your area.

Harlequin Enterprises ULC
22 Adelaide St. West, 40th Floor
Toronto, Ontario M5H 4E3, Canada
www.Harlequin.com

Printed in U.S.A.

Tanya Agler remembers the first set of Harlequin books her grandmother gifted her, and she's been in love with romance novels ever since. An award-winning author, Tanya makes her home in Georgia with her wonderful husband, their four children and a lovable basset, who really rules the roost. When she's not writing, Tanya loves classic movies and a good cup of tea. Visit her at tanyaagler.com or email her at tanyaagler@gmail.com.

Books by Tanya Agler

Harlequin Heartwarming

A Ranger for the Twins
The Sheriff's Second Chance
The Soldier's Unexpected Family

Visit the Author Profile page
at Harlequin.com for more titles.

To my older son, Mike. I remember the first time I held you in my arms and the day you were officially taller than me. Your creativity continues to amaze me, and I love the person you are.

To my friend and mentor, TR, who read the first pages of my debut novel and whose advice helped make the book so much better. Your friendship is a treasure.

To all the first responders and frontline workers who give up holidays and important events for the sake of others, this book is dedicated to you with appreciation. To the teachers who take the time to make sure each child who transfers in the middle of a school year feels warm and welcome, a heartfelt thank you.

CHAPTER ONE

NEVER BEFORE HAD the first week of any of Brooke Novak's previous five jobs, all in different states, been quite so exhilarating or exhausting. The air of The Whitley Community Center now buzzed with an energy missing when she and her son, Colin, had carried her boxes to her new director's office, the windows of which overlooked the Great Smoky Mountains of North Carolina.

Brooke halted on the staircase and smoothed a flyer she'd posted this morning for Trunk or Treat, one of two programs approved at her first staff meeting a few days ago. Her Halloween costume for the event hung in her temporary closet in Aunt Mitzi's guest room. Until she and Colin found an affordable place to rent in town that would also take their rescued labradoodle, Daisy, they were staying with her favorite aunt, who hadn't batted an eye when the dog bounded into her small house. Instead, Aunt Mitzi lavished attention on Daisy, who preened, and Colin, who pretended otherwise.

Although her son had voiced his disappointment about leaving his friends in Houston, not to mention his hard-fought spot on the varsity basketball team, Brooke softened the blow with a promise they'd remain here until he graduated Hollydale High. No more moving.

Besides, Aunt Mitzi was winning Colin over through his stomach. Last night he consumed three pimento cheese sandwiches and several helpings of her famous coleslaw. He'd even made a friend at school and asked if he could go white water rafting with Riley's family.

With a smile, Brooke climbed the remaining stairs and entered the computer room where Olivia, the youth events coordinator, led a group of homeschoolers in a coding lesson. Brooke ran her finger over one of the black computer towers in desperate need of replacement with sleek modern equipment and faster connection speeds. Tablets with the latest learning apps were also a necessity.

Everywhere she turned, something needed improvement, and her list of expenditures for future purchases grew at an exponential rate. During her job interview, the primary benefactor and boss, Frederick Whitley, warned her she'd have her hands full considering the extent to which the previous director, Ray Hinshaw, neglected his job in his final year. Her six-month contract gave Mr. Whitley an out if she didn't bring the center up to par.

Instead, she intended on giving him every reason to deliver a long extension, with her promise to Colin that they'd be staying in North Carolina a bonus incentive. Besides, only holding down one job instead of two, sometimes even three, was downright luxurious.

Her vision of this becoming a real community center, a place where residents could earn their high school GED or congregate for exercise, would take longer than six months, and she wouldn't stop there. The town needed a food bank, and this location was the perfect place to help residents survive rough patches. She knew what it was like to want and need help as a kid. If Aunt Mitzi hadn't sent Brooke's mom a monthly check, Brooke would have gone to sleep hungry more often than she had.

Olivia glanced Brooke's way and walked over. With her blond hair pulled up in a ponytail and her oversize striped oxford shirt, Olivia looked more like one of the students than their teacher. Just out of college, she was eleven years younger than Brooke, not to mention *perky* and *peppy*, two words that would never begin to describe herself. "The kids just started their assignment. What do you need?"

Brooke reached into her oversize cross-body purse and pulled out a pen and notepad. "I called another staff meeting for tomorrow morning, and I'm bringing pumpkin muffins from the Night Owl Bakery. What's one thing that would make more teenagers want to come here for programs?"

"Food." Olivia grinned and rubbed her stomach.

Brooke chuckled. "I should have known." Thanks to Colin, that answer should have been obvious. Sixteen next month, her son was an endless pit and resembled a walking beanpole, his tall frame already at six feet. The three inches separating them didn't seem like much, but he could pack away an olive-and-green-pepper pizza by himself and still have room for a salad and dessert. "Any thoughts on innovative programming?"

"I'll ask the group of teens for suggestions when the lesson's done, and I'll also research some ideas tonight."

Brooke's phone buzzed. "Hold that thought."

She checked her incoming text and then read it again. A police officer was waiting in the lobby for her. If that wasn't enough, the desk attendant, Betty Ruddick, the sweetest septuagenarian Brooke had ever met, had included a flame emoji along with a thermometer in the red.

Olivia laid a hand on Brooke's arm. "Is anything wrong?"

"I hope not. If you finish your report before the meeting, email it to me so I can review it. Thanks."

Brooke hurried downstairs, her curiosity piqued. The officer's back was to her, his police hat underneath his arm as he chatted with Betty. From the slope of his shoulders, Brooke didn't sense urgency. Good thing, as Frederick Whitley had made it very clear his expectations of her as director included the center staying out of the news for anything other than positive publicity.

"Ruddick. I knew that name sounded familiar. Are you any relation to Mason, the local paramedic?" The officer's strong voice echoed in the open lobby atrium, the natural light from the skylights flooding the area with sunny brightness.

"He's my grandson." Pride laced Betty's words, and she glanced at Brooke. "Handsome as all get-out, if I do say so myself. I keep telling Brooke she needs to meet him. I'm not getting any younger, and Mason is taking his sweet time settling down. I'd like a great-grandchild while I can still hold him or her."

Brooke laughed at another of Betty's attempts to set her up with her grandson, who had to be a good five years younger than her. The officer turned around, and sunlight glinted off his short brown hair, making it appear almost blond. He was no slouch in the handsome category himself, with his hazel eyes and square jaw. When she stepped closer, he smiled, and the fine crinkles at the edges of his eyes jumped out, making him look slightly older than her original guess of thirty-five.

She extended her hand toward him. "I'm Brooke Novak, the new director. How may I be of service?"

"Officer Jonathan Maxwell." His smile turned into a concerned straight line. "I have a few questions for you about the center. Is there somewhere we can talk?"

"Is something wrong?" *Not already.*

He shifted his hat to his other arm. "I'd like to review some of the center's security precautions with you."

Her gaze flew to her office door, where she was still unpacking the boxes of books from her online college program. Being squished in like sardines with them might not be conducive to a serious conversation. Shuffling noises came from the direction of the gym, where some senior citizens were practicing their chair yoga positions with the instructor's calm voice guiding them through the gentle moves for increased balance awareness. "Hold on a minute, and I'll take you on a tour of the gardens." Brooke closed the gym doors before grabbing her blazer from her office.

Today's cream pantsuit was another of her bargain thrift store scores, and she smoothed the material to gain some confidence before escorting him through the electronic front door. In no time, Officer Maxwell matched her slow steps along the sidewalk. She wasn't accustomed to being outside this time of day, and the coolness of mid-October in the Smoky Mountains would take some getting used to after the heat of Houston.

"Does the center employ a nighttime security guard?" He sure didn't beat around the bush.

"Although I admire your bluntness, can you start over and fill me in on the purpose of this visit? Since I'm still composing the letter to the local sheriff about cooperation between the center and the police department, I gather this is official business."

His gaze swept over the path ahead of them.

"You're right. I need information about your operating hours and your security detail."

"That's a rather broad statement. I'd like a reason for my answer first." She stepped over a large crack in the sidewalk, taking care with her two-and-a-half-inch black heels that brought her eye-level with Officer Maxwell. She added sidewalk repair to the long list for maintenance man Joe, who happened to be Betty's husband. Yet another item for tomorrow's staff meeting, and another expense.

"There was an incident this morning involving a juvenile in a fender bender. He admitted the community center was where he acquired a fake ID. He never actually met the person he dealt with, but this was where he was told to collect the fake ID. I was wondering whether the center has any security cameras. Any footage of the possible exchange might be of assistance in the investigation."

Officer Maxwell's words caught Brooke off guard, and she stumbled. He reached out an arm and helped steady her. She sent a smile of thanks his way before distancing herself. "How long ago was this possible exchange?"

His perceptive hazel gaze met hers. "Within the past month. The center's cooperation would be appreciated."

"I hate to be the bearer of bad news, but I can't release any footage to you."

Those warm eyes cooled, although she received the distinct impression Officer Maxwell would remain friendly unless circumstances called for a different side of him. "I can get a warrant."

She bristled at his presumption she was being difficult. "That's not the problem, Officer Maxwell. We don't have exterior cameras at the present time, and our inside monitors, which are limited to the gym and a few other areas, mainly upstairs, are only on a live feed loop. Betty keeps an eye on the screens behind her desk during operating hours, and we're looking into upgrading the system."

Another expense, but one she'd have to justify to Mr. Whitley during their next weekly conference call. While the center received the bulk of its funding from the state, making it a public facility, the Furniture King of North Carolina turned philanthropist supplemented the remainder of the budget from his millions. Growing up in Hollydale and now living in nearby Asheville, he oversaw the board of directors, and his last name graced the front archway and the pavilion among other areas.

"Is someone guarding the premises 24/7? A

security company?" He pulled a small notepad and pencil from his front pocket.

"No, but I'll look into hiring one." She smoothed her hair, some strands escaping from her tight bun. "If you have any recommendations of where to begin, I'd appreciate it. I've only just started here in the past week, and I'm not familiar with local firms. However, the center will be undergoing some renovations soon."

"What precautions are taken to guard the property at night?" He tucked his notepad under his arm and donned his officer cap.

"There's a padlock on the gate you enter to gain access to the parking lot. It's locked every night." They turned the corner to the flat open space where a construction crew would break ground for a new aquatic addition after the start of the new year. "I unlock the front gate every morning as I'm the first to arrive."

"Besides you, who has keys to the facility?"

"All the exterior locks were changed on my first day here, as well as the security codes and passwords. Myself and Mr. Whitley have the new keys." The millionaire philanthropist was above reproach, and she held up two fingers and then three more. "The local locksmith also made keys for the assistant director, the janitor and Joe Ruddick, who's Betty's husband and our maintenance person."

"Do you also lock the facility at night?"

"Joe locks up every night except for the five times a month when we have late hours."

Officer Maxwell stopped walking and wrote at a furious pace. "When's that?"

"Two Fridays and a Saturday every month. On those days, we extend our hours and remain open late for a game night or a cooking class or some other special program for teens. There are also two Wednesday night adult programs for those who can't make time on weekends or work during the week." Until she could justify hiring additional staff, the current hours would remain standard operating procedure.

"Can I get a list of the teen programs?" He glanced her way, a slight smile curling his lips.

She couldn't shake the feeling that smile had gotten him out of trouble a time or two. "I'll email you the list before I leave today."

He pulled out a business card. "This has all my work contact info."

She accepted it and reached for her cell phone in the inside pocket of her blazer. After snapping a picture of the card, she stored them both away. "I—" She stopped herself before mentioning how she had a habit of forgetting about business cards in her pantsuits and washing them.

"Yes?" He held his pencil midair.

"I was wondering if you knew anything else about the person manufacturing the IDs."

"Ask me that again in a couple of weeks." There went that smile again.

This time, however, determination lurked in his eyes, and she wouldn't place a bet against him tracking down the responsible culprit by then.

He closed his notepad and inserted the pencil in the spiral wire. "Does the center have a computer lab? Any laminating equipment?"

His point didn't escape her. "Are you suggesting the person made them here? I thought you were only investigating the location where they were sold or exchanged. I don't even think it's possible to manufacture them here. Our equipment is in serious need of updating."

Now she wished there was a camera that had captured the exchange so an exact date for the transfer could be established. If news of this visit reached Mr. Whitley, it would serve her better if the transaction had occurred during her predecessor's tenure. As it was, she only had six months to turn this center around, and this wasn't a good beginning.

"Just gathering facts, Mrs. Novak."

"Ms. Novak." She shrugged as they reached the front of the building. "Brooke works, too. The computer lab is on the second level. Follow me."

Noise crackled on his walkie-talkie, and she stepped back while he answered.

"I'm going to take a rain check on that tour of the lab." He glanced at the blue sky, dotted with white fluffy clouds against the verdant mountain peaks, a change from the flatter, brown landscape of Houston. "Not that there's a hint of rain around."

That smile surfaced again along with a glimpse of his appealing sense of humor, and her gaze went to his left ring finger, which was bare. She blinked away any curiosity about his marital status while he waited for her to enter the building. Though the officer had an easygoing manner, he'd transitioned to all business when it came to questions regarding this morning's accident. His trail would hopefully peter out somewhere else. The last thing she needed was for the center to become embroiled in a fake ID scheme.

As much as she wanted to return his smile, not that it was aimed at her as anything other than the director of the center, she couldn't.

She liked her job and intended to keep it. Colin wasn't the only Novak to like Hollydale, not by a long shot.

JONATHAN MAXWELL PULLED into the Hollydale Police Department parking lot and banged his hand on the steering wheel. He expected some days to be harder than others. That was simply the life of any law enforcement officer. The shifts involving car accidents, though, jarred him like no others. He shook out the stinging pain and cut the engine.

He exited his vehicle and headed toward the one-story nondescript brick police station, dwelling on the details for the accident report and the subsequent interview of the director at the community center. Fortunately, the teen driver had walked away, but not before Jonathan caught a glimpse of the future when his twelve-year-old daughter, Izzy, who was growing up too fast, would sit behind the wheel of a car.

It was hard to believe that only this fine October morning, Izzy had exclaimed she couldn't go to school without her lucky soccer ball. Not even five minutes later, his younger daughter, Vanessa, upended the sofa cushions, along with half the house, while hunting for her favorite scrunchie. She kept mumbling she'd fail her math test if she wasn't wearing it. When had his daughters left stuffed animals and tricycles behind for competitive sports and fashion accessories? If life didn't slow down, they'd be asking for the car keys too soon.

The bracing wind buffeted his cheeks, and he hurried toward the back door. The cooler temperatures, along with the scarecrows the elementary school students used to decorate Hollydale's sidewalks, were a sign the holidays would arrive faster than Izzy would outgrow another pair of soccer cleats. Years ago, his wife, Anne, had always transformed their Savannah home into a winter wonderland between Halloween and Thanksgiving. All Jonathan had to do was show up and bask in the laughter and love.

This fall, those holidays and Christmas promised long days at work since he was Hollydale's newest police recruit, although, at thirty-seven, he was by no means the youngest officer. Uprooting his daughters to North Carolina from Georgia after Anne's death hadn't been easy, but any regrets dissipated in the soft mountain breeze once his favorite cousin, Caleb, had returned to Hollydale, with his aunt and uncle following close behind. The only pitfall was saying goodbye to his hard-earned detective badge and some of the accompanying perks, the biggest of which had been enjoying holidays at home unless he'd been on call.

Concentrating on Izzy and Vanessa provided a welcome distraction from this report, as he dreaded his follow-up discussion with the sheriff. Mike Harrison wasn't going to like what Jonathan had uncovered, although he wouldn't be surprised either.

Jonathan entered the station, the familiar scent of bleach and stale coffee mingling in a rather comforting fashion after the day's events. His spotless regulation boots smacked the faded beige linoleum. He waved at Harriet, the dispatcher who kept everyone in line, having done so for the last two generations of police officers.

"Afternoon, Maxwell." She removed the familiar headset, her springy gray curls popping back into place. She extended a mug with a cat lurking among bright pink flowers toward him. "That bad, huh?"

How she read minds like that he wasn't quite sure, but he wished he could read Izzy and Vanessa half as well as Harriet deciphered every officer in the department. He gave a grateful nod of thanks as he accepted the brew. Admittedly, it wasn't quite up to the level of Deb's, who ran the local coffeehouse across the street. It was liquid caffeine. While not the best choice since adrenaline still coursed through his veins, he'd take it and run.

"Seen worse." If someone ran one of the four red lights, that warranted the siren and a mention on the front page of the *Hollydale Herald*. "Mike in?"

"He asked about you earlier. That's why you were lucky enough to get the last cup from the pot. Still hot from this morning." Harriet's eyes crinkled at the corners. "I figured you'd need this since he wants to see you in his office first thing."

"Harriet, if you were ten years younger…" Jonathan sniffed the rather strong brew and somehow stopped short of wincing. "I'd get down on one knee and propose right now."

She laughed and replaced her headset. "If I were thirty years younger, I'd say yes, and then Bert would challenge you to a duel."

Jonathan chuckled at the reference to her husband, two hundred eighty pounds of pure muscle and all heart. Some Hollydale residents were still recovering from Harriet and Bert's fortieth anniversary bash last month.

"My money's on Bert every time." He winked as she answered a call.

Jonathan slipped away and set the mug on his desk. Although the caffeine cried out to him, the dregs of this morning's pot turned his stomach, and he no longer wanted it. Best to get this encounter with the sheriff over and out. While the former sheriff had hired him, Jonathan had spent most of his time on the force reporting to Sheriff Harrison and found him to be a man of his word. He'd had worse bosses, and few better.

After tapping on the sheriff's door, Jonathan waited less than a second before Mike bade him to enter. *Good.* With a report to write and another round of running radar on Timber Road, he could still arrive home in time to eat dinner with Izzy and Vanessa if this were kept short and to the point. Mike closed a manila file while Jonathan settled on the hard oak chair.

"Fill me in on the accident." Mike leaned back and closed his eyes, although that wasn't a sign the sheriff was tired, only his way of visualizing the scene.

Jonathan pulled out his notepad, preferring the old school method of taking notes, although he could have recited the information from memory. "The juvenile ditched school, drove his dad's truck and was involved in a fender bender. When I arrived on the scene, he didn't realize his fake ID had become stuck to his actual license. After I read him his Miranda rights, he muttered something about the 'stupid community center.'"

Mike opened his eyes and righted himself, snapping his pencil in half. He flinched and shook his head. "Didn't mean for that to happen. Go on."

"Remember when the owner of the Corner Grocery called us a week ago?" Jonathan leaned forward and pressed his elbows into his thighs, the stiff navy fabric of his uniform not yielding much.

"When he confiscated the fake ID?" Mike rubbed the bridge of his nose and reached for a disposable cup with The Busy Bean's distinctive logo. He swigged a large sip. "From our investigation, we determined the teen wasn't local."

"Today's juvenile, Eric, had a fake driver's license with his photo on it." And a birthdate to indicate he was twenty-two, which was most unrealistic, considering he looked younger than his actual age of seventeen. "I wrote a citation, and his parents are contacting a lawyer, probably Penelope Romano. I'll go through her office to schedule an interview. Then I touched base with the new community center director."

Although he would have guessed she worked for a major corporation instead of a small nonprofit. Tall and elegant, Brooke Novak looked like she could have stepped off a runway and onto the sidewalks of Hollydale. Her cream suit paired with a coppery silk top resembled something from one of those fashion shows Vanessa loved to watch. Her chestnut hair, worn up in a sophisticated style, showcased her regal neck. Even her calm voice gave every impression of someone upscale and on the move.

She probably wouldn't last long in a small town like Hollydale before some urban job caught her attention.

"Logical follow-up. Did you get any leads there?"

Jonathan shook his head. "Brooke, um, Ms. Novak, just started, so she's still learning the ropes."

"Okay then. Good work. Keep me posted." Mike lowered his gaze to his desk and rearranged some files.

Intent on leaving, Jonathan rose and caught sight of his name on the tab of a manila folder. Was that his employment file? He expected the information to be in the computer, but the paper copy didn't surprise him much, considering Mike's predecessor preferred handwritten reports. After his election, Mike had updated the twentieth-century computers and upgraded the bulletproof vests. Progress took time, though, and he guessed other projects had priority over digitizing records.

The incident report would have to wait a couple more minutes. "Is that my employment file?"

Mike nodded and opened the manila folder. "Degree in criminal justice, several commendations for your service as a detective in Savannah. Hollydale had to be a step down for you. Why?"

What Mike might see as a demotion, Jonathan perceived as a trade-off, if not exactly a full promotion. His daughters had needed a change. He wanted a return to life without pitying looks from coworkers and friends. If he'd heard one more person whisper "Poor Jonathan" behind his back after Anne's death, he might have had a meltdown. Besides, Anne had been the one who'd wanted to settle in an urban setting close to her parents. Personally, he'd enjoyed his summer vacations in Hollydale, a welcome time away from his parents' busy schedule, when every minute revolved around work. Small-town living suited him. That might sound corny to some, and the fact was, he didn't want to say any of that aloud. Even if he did trust Mike with his life.

"Too many reasons to name. Glad I moved here, though. I wouldn't miss seeing Ethel follow Caleb around their yard for all the commendations in Georgia." After his cousin had married Lucie, her menagerie, which included a miniature pig named Ethel, who adored Caleb, had taken Jonathan's family in as well. His daughters loved spending time at Caleb and Lucie's home.

Mike opened his mouth as if to say something but stopped. Instead, he downed the rest of his coffee and threw the cup into the trash can underneath his desk. "Last night I went to the county commission meeting."

Having sat in on a couple of those himself, Jonathan didn't envy Mike the task. "Thanks for taking that one for the department."

"No problem." Mike grinned before a somber expression came over him. "The county commission approved the upcoming year's budget and an expansion of our services. We're reaping the benefits of local growth, but we've also seen a small uptick in crime over the past several years."

Nothing like the crime Jonathan had encountered in Savannah, though. When Jonathan moved here a couple of years ago, a series of burglaries had rocked Hollydale. Mike had found himself in the middle when the former sheriff formed a definite opinion about the main suspect, namely Mike's best friend and now wife, Georgie, who'd been innocent. However, that was about the extent of the criminal activity around here.

Jonathan settled back in the chair and kept his gaze on his file. "You raise a good point. Are these fake driver's licenses and IDs related to that growth? Or is the person behind this local to Hollydale?"

"That's what you need to find out. This could be related to the influx of people from Asheville buying vacation homes in Hollydale for a Smoky Mountain weekend getaway. Some of the teens might think we're yokels up here." Mike plucked another pencil from the holder on his desk and began tapping it against the scarred oak surface. "By the way, the county approved the funds for the expansion of the department, including a new patrol officer and a salary allowance for a lead detective for Dalesford County."

That woke Jonathan up more than one of Deb's espressos.

While Jonathan liked Hollydale, something had been missing over the past few years. Handing out speeding citations didn't quite match the thrill of searching out evidence and piecing together the activity in more complicated crimes. "When will the job opening for detective be posted for applications?"

Mike tapped the folder on his desk. "Soon, but I have to warn you, rural detectives face different challenges than you may have encountered in your previous urban position. There's no question about your qualifications. If anything, you're overqualified."

Two years of working in a small town had prepared Jonathan for the more leisurely pace in these parts. There was nothing like having to write out a traffic citation to his uncle, Drew, for speeding. Still, Mike's voice held an edge Jonathan didn't often hear. "What challenges?"

"More local interference and forty hours a week is what's expected and required. More than that won't necessarily be compensated unless it's approved beforehand."

"Sounds familiar." Jonathan shrugged, as that was normal for the department anyway. "You're holding something back. What is it?"

"I talked to the district attorney, Stuart Everson, to finalize details on the posting and give you a recommendation based on what I remembered about your background." Mike gave a sheepish shrug and grinned. "He said we still have to post it online and the usual places, even if someone in the department is qualified for the job. Assuming you're interested, that is."

"I haven't been this excited since Deb at The

Busy Bean started giving first responders a discount."

"But Stuart also told me something else." Mike closed the employment folder. "His niece, who's awaiting the results of her detective's exam, is applying for the job."

Local politics, indeed. Jonathan exhaled a deep breath. "I see."

Mike rose and crossed over to the window. "All things considered, you're overqualified for your present job…"

"But I'm not related to the district attorney." Jonathan finished Mike's sentence for him. "I can't do anything about that at this late date. Pretty sure he and his wife, Kitty, won't adopt me and my daughters."

Mike opened the blinds before facing Jonathan. "If you find out who's behind the fake ID scheme, that would seal the deal as far as I'm concerned. Even Stuart would have a hard time saying no with proven results. Did I mention the detective job comes with a pay raise and extra benefits, like holidays off?"

That made the position all the more attractive. His daughters already missed out on having their mother around for holidays. His extended family and neighbors pulled their weight and then some, but it wasn't the same as having their father present for holidays. He should know since his parents had been work-aholics in every sense of the word.

"Nothing like a little pressure to solve a case."

"Like you'd settle for anything else. That sense of humor of yours doesn't hide your strong work ethic from me, Maxwell." Mike scrubbed his jaw before sitting once more. "I'd take over this case if I didn't trust you to get to the bottom of it."

"Twist the knife a little harder, won't you? There's nothing like a superior's confidence in you to exert extra pressure to solve it." He knew fake IDs could be generated anywhere. Still, Jonathan couldn't shake the feeling this was a local operation. "I'll assume the budget didn't authorize a computer program to write my report. I'll log in the evidence and get it done. Anything else?"

Concern crossed Mike's face. "I have to ask. Will you be okay taking the lead on this one? The car accident, I mean."

Mike was trying to be kind, but Jonathan didn't know whether to be touched or run screaming out of the station at yet another reference to his past.

He brushed his hand over his chin, the slight stubble no surprise. "I'm a police officer. Car accidents are part and parcel in this line of work."

He sent Mike a curt nod before striding away.

Nothing could have prepared him for that moment five years ago when he'd witnessed an accident through the window of his squad car. Within seconds, he arrived at the scene. Cold had descended into his bones when he recognized the mangled metal of one of the cars. He rushed to the driver's door, thrown open by the impact of the crash. There he found Anne, unresponsive, while the other driver stumbled over, rubbing his bleary eyes, in anguish over falling asleep behind the wheel. Jonathan started CPR to no avail.

Anne had died on impact.

CHAPTER TWO

WIGGLING HIS HIPS in time to the hip-hop music playing on his Bluetooth speaker, Jonathan quartered several Roma tomatoes and threw them in his food processor. He reached for the red onion and brought up the knife for some serious dicing action when Vanessa ran into the kitchen. "Dad! You have to see this."

He lowered the blade a tad too close to his thumb for comfort and then laid the knife on the cutting board. "Whoa, Nessie! No running in the house."

His younger daughter caught her breath and waved the paper around. "It's the best thing ever. It won't cost much money, and it's a fabulous, once-in-a-lifetime opportunity."

He lifted his right hand above his eyes and then turned his head like a periscope. "Where's Vanessa Maxwell, and what have you done with her?"

Her giggles brightened his day, and she came over and yanked on his blue polo shirtsleeve. "Daddy, it's me."

He finished cutting the onion into pieces and deposited them in the processor. "Nope, it can't be my Nessie. Mine's like clockwork. Every evening at six on the dot she comes into the kitchen and asks the same question."

Another giggle lightened his mood even more. "What's for dinner?"

He snapped his fingers. "Well then, I was wrong. You're my little girl, all right. It's taco night. I'm making the salsa now." He picked up the garlic press and squeezed fresh cloves into the mixture. "Now, what are we talking about here? A slumber party? Horse lessons? A used disco ball?"

Vanessa doubled over, and his heart all but melted. Izzy ran into the kitchen, paper in hand. "Dad, there you are. We have to talk."

"Well, talk away. My imaginary vacation to Tahiti fell through at the last minute, so you're stuck with me." He added the rest of the ingredients and pulsed the salsa until it reached the consistency he wanted.

Izzy tapped her foot, her short brown hair the same rich toffee color as his. Vanessa had inherited Anne's fair complexion.

Izzy shoved the paper under his nose. "Read this. It doesn't cost much money, and it would expand our educational horizons you're always telling us about."

"And my best friend is going." Vanessa chimed in before Jonathan could skim the flyer.

"Dull roar, okay?" He reached for his reading glasses. Ah, the joys of getting older. Although some wouldn't consider thirty-seven very old. He slipped on his glasses and shook his head at the community center's Thanksgiving break offering during the weeklong school holiday. "It's a no-go, girls. You know Aunt Tina is excited to have you over that week. She has lots planned."

"But we see Aunt Tina all the time." Vanessa narrowed her eyes and smiled, that dimple in her cheek as adorable as she was. "This is Heartsgiving. We'd be learning everything about hearts. How they work and how to draw them, and we'd be expanding our hearts by bringing in canned food so we can help the center start a food bank to help people of Hollydale. That's what the pretty woman said at the assembly today."

Pretty woman? Vanessa could only be describing Brooke. After he'd written out two tickets on radar duty, one for speeding and one warning for a broken taillight, he had intended on returning to the center for a tour of the computer lab. Instead, an urgent dispatch from Harriet concerning a report of a bear spotted near the elementary school required his presence. Fortunately, the bear turned out to be a friendly Great Dane, who was only too happy to make the acquaintance of Jonathan and the animal control officer. Thanks to the dog's collar, the owner came within minutes and picked up his pet, apologizing for the trouble.

How he'd missed Brooke at the school if they'd been there at the same time was beyond him. She was hard to miss. There was a unique air about her, one of formality yet casual elegance, that emphasized her laser-focused personality.

The way Vanessa tapped her foot suggested she was waiting for him to change his mind. He wasn't. "Aunt Tina already asked Lucie for the time off. She's going to teach you how to knit."

Protests started on both sides as he placed the salsa in the refrigerator to chill, swapping out the bowl for the package of ground beef for the taco filling. His cell phone rang, and he thanked whoever it was for the interruption. The screen display showed the power of suggestion as it was, indeed, his favorite aunt, Tina.

"We were just talking about you. Izzy and Vanessa are right here. They're looking forward to Thanksgiving."

The protests turned to glares, and he shooed them away. They retreated with their shoulders slumped.

"About that." Her apologetic tone didn't bode well. "Lucie just had a major company book the retreat center for the weekend before Thanksgiving until we close on Wednesday."

Lucie had married his cousin Caleb Spindler after she renovated her family's lodge and turned it into a health and wellness facility, which now bordered the nature conservancy Caleb helmed. "That's great. I'm glad things are looking up for her. Can you take over hosting duties on Thanksgiving since Lucie's going to be so busy?"

He'd be grateful since he wouldn't be there. Next month's tentative schedule had him working on Thanksgiving. Another sure sign he was turning into his parents. At least the girls would be spending the day with relatives who loved them. Being without a mom wasn't easy. Being without both parents on holidays had to stink, too, same as it had when his mother and father hadn't spent a holiday with him and instead worked.

If he received this promotion to detective, however, he'd be spending more time with his daughters, maybe even as early as this Christmas. Getting the job was a big if. His current case might hold the key to landing the position. There had to be something he'd missed today, but what?

"A purple hippopotamus flying over the center." His aunt's voice rang in his ears.

"Run that by me one more time." Admitting he'd been daydreaming would be rather embarrassing. He switched the phone to his other ear and pushed the ground beef around in the cast-iron skillet, the popping sounds providing a much better excuse for his failure to keep up with the conversation. "I'm making tacos, and it's time to add the water and seasoning. I have one more minute to talk."

"Aha, I knew it. You weren't listening, so I'll repeat myself. Lucie needs me to also work then, but a month should give you enough time to find someone else to watch Izzy and Vanessa since that whole week of Thanksgiving is a school holiday, right? Do you want me to check with Ethan and Mattie's regular babysitter? She might be available. If she can take care of Lucie's twins, she can handle anything."

Jonathan laid down the spatula and picked up the flyer. He wasn't a big believer in coincidences, but this Heartsgiving day camp might be the perfect solution. "I have a lead on something to keep them busy during the first three days of the week. But Thanksgiving is now at your house instead of Lucie's, right? What do you want me to bring?"

"How about those sweet potatoes I love so much?" The smacking sound gave away how much his entire family loved his signature dish.

"Izzy would disown me if I didn't." The meat was ready for the seasoning. "We'll talk more later."

He switched the flyer in his hand for the measuring cup holding the water. Now he had an excuse to visit the attractive Brooke once more.

The water sizzled coming in contact with the hot pan and ground beef, and he stirred in the seasoning. Izzy wandered back into the kitchen. "Did you two discuss adult stuff?"

"Aunt Tina wanted to talk about work."

"Oh." Her disappointment rubbed him the wrong way, and he frowned.

If he told Izzy about the work emergency, it might sound like he'd given in to their demands. There were times he missed Anne's sage advice more than ever.

"She was also checking to make sure we were still bringing your favorite dish to Thanksgiving."

Izzy perked up and rubbed her stomach. "Apple pie."

He shook his head. "Sweet potatoes."

"Dad, that was so last week. You have to keep up with the times."

Vanessa rushed in and skidded to a stop. "Is dinner ready?"

"Not yet." He might as well tell them now. He reached for the flyer and stifled the urge to fold it into a paper airplane. "I changed my mind. I'll stop by the center tomorrow and sign you up."

Vanessa's shriek almost burst his eardrums. She threw her arms around his waist and squeezed. "I can't wait to tell Lily. You're the best dad ever."

One look at Izzy's arched eyebrows convinced him that was wishful thinking on Vanessa's part, but he'd take the approbation where he could get it. "Thanks, Nessie."

She released him, her eyes sparkling. "You don't have to make a special trip to the center, though. You can register us online."

Izzy opened the refrigerator and pulled out tomatoes and cheese. "Vanessa and I can get the toppings ready if you want to register us now."

Vanessa's head nodded up and down like a tightly wound spring. "That's a good idea. That way you won't forget. My teacher forgets where she puts her glasses and then laughs when we tell her they're on her head."

He'd met Vanessa's teacher, who was set to retire at the end of the year. Nice to know Vanessa grouped him in with anyone over thirty. "Thanks."

As quickly as it arrived, there went his excuse to visit Brooke again.

THE NEXT MORNING, Jonathan adjusted his eyes to the dim fluorescent lighting of Mo's Gas and Bait Stop. If only he could adjust his nostrils as easily. The strong odor of night crawlers and other types of bait overpowered him, even though he'd done his best to steel himself before entering.

He nodded at Vern, who returned the gesture before scurrying out of the shop, a bucket of live worms in hand for a day of fishing at Lake Pine. Everyone around here knew he and his group of senior cohorts gathered on the shores each morning as a way of eluding their honey-do lists more than for the sport of fishing itself. A nice catch of walleye was a bonus that provided for a tasty supper.

That was, for people who loved fresh grilled fish. It had been his mother's favorite go-to dinner at nine at night. Jonathan couldn't stomach the taste.

Jonathan clipped his sunglasses to the front

of his uniform and spotted Mo Chastain at the counter.

Mo waved him over, his denim overalls over a blue plaid flannel shirt—his one apparent concession to fall. "Officer Maxwell, I didn't know if Harriet would send the sheriff over or someone else."

"Hope I'm not that much of a disappointment." Jonathan whipped out his notepad and pencil. "What can you tell me about the person who came in here to buy cigarettes?"

Mo scratched his balding head and sat on his stool. "Didn't recognize him, for one thing." Considering Mo knew everyone for miles, that probably meant the teen wasn't local. "I could tell right off the kid thought I wouldn't give a second thought to selling him a pack of smokes."

Not many besides Jonathan knew this, but Mo was a member of Mensa. He often finished three sudoku puzzles in the parking lot of Sweet Shelby's Tea Room while waiting to drive his wife, Belinda, the Pie Queen of Hollydale, home, since iritis had curtailed her driving for the next few months. Mo was sharp as a tack.

"What gave the perp away?"

"If he ever shaved before, I'd be surprised. Fifteen's closer to his real age than twenty-one.

For another thing, the license didn't feel right." Mo tapped his fingers on the battered counter.

The bells on the door jangled, and Jonathan glanced over his shoulder as another older gentleman shuffled over to the wall of flies and other colorful tackle. Jonathan faced Mo again. "Run that by me again. How did it feel off to you?"

"I've handled licenses in this establishment for going on fifty years. You just know how they feel." Mo shrugged and motioned for Jonathan to step aside. He rang up the newcomer's purchases. "Great choice, Norm. Can I interest you in a bucket of minnows on this fine Friday morning? I heard some mighty nice comments on how the walleyes are clamoring for them."

"Two buckets and five dollars of scratch-offs ought to do it." Norm reached for his purchases and left.

"Lightweight. Not the same heft to it. The plastic didn't feel right either." Mo resumed his answer without missing a beat.

"I'll take the license with me, then." Jonathan reached for an evidence bag.

Mo closed the cash register. "Kid grabbed it and muttered something about it being a worthless piece of junk from the community center before he ran out."

Jonathan pointed to the video camera prominently displayed near the ceiling. "What about the footage? Can I take a look at it?" A judge would sign off on a warrant if need be, but Mo's permission would suffice.

"Sure. Come on around." Mo rose and unlocked the small door leading to his alcove. He punched a couple of buttons, and video footage popped up on the screen. "It was about a half hour ago."

Jonathan glued his gaze to the small screen until Mo hit a button. "That's the kid."

After a few minutes, it was clear the kid's hoodie with the logo of Jonathan's favorite baseball team shielded his face. The kid had done a good job glancing at the floor so there was never a clear view, even when he snatched the fake license and ran.

"Sorry. Guess this was a waste of your time coming out here."

"Not at all. You helped my investigation." Somewhat, as it indicated the incidents hadn't stopped yet. "Can you give me any other information about the teenager? Height? Weight?"

Mo scratched his chin and redistributed his weight on the stool. "Lanky sort. About my oldest son's height, so that would make him right about six feet. Longish hair fell over his eyes, which were sort of a mottled color. Not really brown, not really blue."

"Hazel? Like mine?"

"That sounds as good as any other."

"Thanks for your time, Mo."

Only time would tell what would become of this. If these were fake licenses acquired over the internet, there'd be few ways of tracking down the seller with the limited resources of the Hollydale Police Department, which had a smaller staff than his previous post in Savannah. Even then, his former superior would have written this off as not serious enough to pursue. However, this was the second time in as many days someone mentioned the community center. Perhaps there was a way to find out if this was a local job rather than yet another instance of teenagers ordering them online.

Jonathan tipped his cap at Mo and hurried to his squad car, breathing in gulps of the clean air unencumbered by the strong odor of fresh bait. His next step was clear.

It was time to pay Brooke another visit.

BROOKE WOLFED DOWN the rest of her avocado veggie wrap and then organized the last of her books on the middle row of her office bookshelf. She straightened the pictures of her and Colin on the top shelf and went to retrieve her duster when the intercom buzzed.

"Brooke, this cutie of an officer is back.

Do you want me to send him to your office?"
Betty sounded almost giddy at Officer Maxwell's second visit to the center in so many
days, a far cry from the flutters in Brooke's
stomach that had nothing to do with lunch or
the officer's easygoing manner.

And presumably everything to do with his
presence on yet another official matter. Her
boss, Mr. Whitley, hadn't been nearly as en-
thusiastic as Betty when she updated him yesterday about the police presence at the center.
Thankfully, she'd been on her way to the elementary school, where she pitched the idea
of Heartsgiving to the students as part of their
pep rally. That had given her an excuse to cut
the call short.

"Brooke?" Betty interrupted her reverie.

"Be right there."

While her office was taking shape, it wasn't
perfect yet. She brushed Daisy's tan fur off her
blazer and donned it before stepping out. With
his elbow propped on the reception desk, Officer Maxwell acted like he had all the time in
the world to chat with Betty.

"Officer Maxwell."

He stood up straight and clutched his cap
in hand.

"I hope this is a personal call today."

He fiddled with the brim of his cap, and he

didn't have to answer. His face mirrored Colin's guilty expression whenever she asked if he'd made his bed. "That would have been my preference, but this is another official visit. I'll try not to take up too much of your time. Is there somewhere we can talk?"

She glanced toward her office door. Not going in there with a half-eaten apple on her desk and empty boxes littering the room. A crash of thunder stopped her short of suggesting outside. She waved her arm toward the hallway. "The nice thing about a community center is you have your choice of rooms. I suggest we avoid the men's and women's locker rooms, though."

He laughed, the fine crinkles at the corners of his eyes adding to his appeal. She stopped herself from blinking. *Appeal?* Yes, Officer Maxwell was attractive, but she could ill afford a second look in his direction with a center to turn around in six months and no time for a casual relationship. Even if the attraction happened to be mutual, she wasn't optimistic. Her last three dates hadn't gone well. Every time she'd found time to spare an evening away from her online courses and work, each guy escaped as soon as she brought up Colin.

Besides, she was only getting settled in Hollydale. Growing up in a small town, she hadn't been able to conceal her pregnancy forever. The stares from some in her hometown once baggy sweaters or puffy coats no longer hid her baby bump from view were seared into her. Then again, those glares hadn't been as bad as the whispers behind her back once she passed by. *What else did you expect of Brooke with a mother like that?* Those left a bitter taste in her mouth.

While the residents of Hollydale had been welcoming, she had little doubt everyone knew who was dating whom and every detail of the latest breakup. She didn't want to experience those same types of whispers if another relationship drifted away in the wind.

Colin and Daisy and her job had to come before any type of romantic involvement. She wouldn't do anything to jeopardize her son's future, or her own.

"Where do you suggest we talk?"

"The art and music classroom is close." She pointed that way.

"Does the center have a copy room? What if someone, say an instructor, needs to make copies for a class? Do they bring their own or can they use the center's machine?" His hazel gaze left little doubt as to his ability on the job. Detail-oriented and observant, he was making an impression on her, and she'd best wrap this up as quickly as possible.

To Betty, she said, "If anyone except Colin calls, please take a message."

Officer Maxwell fell into step beside her until they reached the stairwell door. He opened the door for her, and she started to protest before one look at his face made her accept the small courtesy. "Thank you."

In the stairwell, her black heels click-clacked on the cement.

"Colin's fortunate to have someone like you in his life." Jonathan winced and halted in the middle of the steps. "If talking about your husband like that came off as unprofessional during an investigation, I'm sorry."

She chuckled. "Colin's my son, not my husband, and you don't have to apologize for asking about him. There are times in the past fifteen years Colin hasn't felt fortunate, but he knows how much I love him. He's looking forward to making friends and graduating from Hollydale High." He'd even applied for jobs so he could start saving for a car. For the first time in a while, he'd talked about his friends, including his new best friend, Riley.

She climbed the next two steps. Then his voice stopped her. "You have a son in high school?"

"I thought I mentioned him yesterday."

"No. I'd have remembered." He joined her in one step, his broad shoulders standing out more in the narrow staircase. "What drew you to Hollydale? The director's position or something else?"

"My aunt Mitzi owns a small business downtown. She told me about this opportunity, and the thought of living near her at long last was too good to pass up, especially since I've heard so many wonderful stories about Hollydale."

"Mitzi Mayfield? Everyone knows Mitzi. She's the sweetest woman around."

Once again, he opened the door and held it for her. She was used to doing everything for herself, but since she'd been in Hollydale, she found neighbors waving her over to their mailboxes and talking to her. When she walked Daisy, a few had even handed her a welcome card. And last night when she arrived home, her aunt had cooked up a feast of fried chicken, still piping hot and waiting for her.

Brooke led Officer Maxwell to the small workspace set aside for the instructors. He cleared his throat and motioned to the corner of the hallway, where there was a video camera with a light blinking. "Is that one of the closed-circuit monitors?"

"Yes, Betty watches over what's going on."

"What if she's away from the desk or is talking to someone?"

Brooke folded her arms and shrugged. "If she knows she has to leave, she contacts the youth director, the assistant director or me to take her place. Having these cameras upstairs was part of the system started by the former director. I have other ideas on expanding the scope to the downstairs level as well based on procedures at the previous community centers where I worked. First, I'll address those concerns to Mr. Whitley. If he approves, I'll follow up at the next meeting of the board of directors."

She opened the door marked STAFF AND TEACHERS ONLY. He craned his neck and looked over her shoulder. "I don't see a copier in there."

"No, but I'd like more information, and the copy room is standing room only where others could hear our conversation. It's not designed for a serious discussion."

More of a glorified closet than a lounge, they could talk in here without anyone interrupting them. The smell of coffee permeated the room. She craved a cup right now. Officer Maxwell motioned, and she entered first. She arched an eyebrow and tapped her heel against the tile.

"What brought your investigation here for the second day in a row?"

The rain colliding with some force against the window accentuated the silence. His sharp glance didn't faze her. She stood her ground or, in this case, tiled floor. Living with a teenager, she could play the staring game all day.

Officer Maxwell broke the contact and settled in one of the two wingback chairs that provided enough comfort for someone to enjoy a relaxing read for a few minutes, but that was about it. "An underage juvenile tried to purchase cigarettes at a local convenience store. As he grabbed the ID and ran, he mentioned the community center."

She sat across from him. "But once again, there's no physical evidence the center is involved, is there?"

He shrugged and leaned forward. "I don't believe in coincidences."

"And I want to keep the integrity of the center intact. That's why I wanted to talk to you in private, so no one would overhear us. The last thing I want is for anyone to jump to conclusions or hesitate to use our services because they're concerned about any alleged activity that may or may not exist."

She wasn't sure whether her impassioned plea fell on ears that would care about propriety, but gossip had never been her friend. "I like to examine all the evidence," he said, "and right now, it's too early to make any determinations."

Satisfied with his answer, she nodded. "What do you want to know?"

"Returning to my question from downstairs, do instructors make their handouts somewhere other than the center?"

His presence seemed much larger in this small faculty room than yesterday when they toured the gardens outside. "For the most part, they've started attaching the files in emails to their students, who usually use their personal devices for notetaking. However, the teachers can use the copy machine and laminator for their classroom materials if they prefer to personally hand out hard copies."

His head jerked up. "Laminator? Can I see it?"

She rose, and they exited the lounge.

"This way, and then I'm sure you have somewhere else you need to be." *And soon.* His forceful impact touched her in ways she didn't want to feel.

She crossed the hallway, dotted with colorful pictures on the walls drawn by elementary school students, and he followed her lead. Entering the children's library and computer area, she waved to Olivia, the youth director, who stopped reading to a group of students and gave her a quizzical look. Brooke shrugged and mustered a confident smile. Officer Maxwell tipped his hat and said hello to the students, who left Olivia's side and gathered around him.

Brooke waited for him to finish answering questions. Then she escorted him to the miniscule back room adjoining Olivia's office. He reached around her, but she held up her hand and opened the door for him. "My treat this time."

He chuckled, and they entered the room, a tight squeeze for one, too cozy for her liking for the both of them. Her awareness of him spiked, including his sandalwood aftershave. The fluorescent lights hummed, as did the copier, which was one of the banes of her new existence along with the good officer. It occupied center stage next to a rectangular table with a caddy containing highlighters, pencils and other assorted supplies. He glanced back at the students already crowding around Olivia. "Can any of them slip away and venture in here?"

"Those kids are six years old, and there are always two adults watching them." Brooke shook her head and pointed to the window separating the rooms. "This copy area is off-limits to children, and Olivia is usually either out there or in her office planning youth events. She'd notice if someone, especially a teenager or a kid, was in here unsupervised."

"I never said I thought the person behind all this was a teenager, and you've admitted instructors can come in here, right?"

Her first week wasn't working out quite as planned, and her defenses went into overdrive. She strode to the side of the copier and yanked off the clipboard for his inspection. "Everyone who uses the room signs this, and the copier is password protected. I changed the password myself on Monday." She thrust the clipboard toward him and immediately regretted her lack of composure. Instead, she laid it on the table. "As I've mentioned a few times, this is my first week here. This weekend, I'll review the security procedures and run them by you to see if I've forgotten anything. A police officer with your experience should come up with some additional suggestions to my own."

"Experience, huh? That's one way to point out my advanced age of thirty-seven. Thanks." He jotted more notes. "Is this the room where you also keep the laminator?"

She crossed over to the cabinet and pulled out the compact device from its shelf. "As you can see, it's a standard laminator and not the same quality as the ones at the North Carolina Department of Motor Vehicles."

"The cabinets aren't locked, right?"

"None of the community centers I've worked at have ever had locks on every cabinet. Is that all?"

She'd worked her way up at different centers over the years while she studied for her degree. Why did this man rile her like this? He seemed naturally confident in his job, whereas she'd put a lot of effort into making sure her professionalism shone through.

"For now. You've been a big help." He donned his cap and adjusted the brim. "Thank you for answering my questions. If you find anything out of place, feel free to call me anytime."

That was the second time the good officer mentioned he'd be receptive to hearing from her. Did the offer apply to off-hours?

Would she mind more if it didn't?

CHAPTER THREE

OFFICER JONATHAN MAXWELL occupied too many of Brooke's thoughts as she found herself at the doorway of her aunt's salon, A New You, on this late Saturday afternoon. The cop's charming smile was already imprinted on her memory. He was a conundrum. He presented himself as laid-back, while his police mind seemed razor-sharp and anything but low-key.

Even more, she liked how he had walked beside her instead of forging ahead or trailing behind. And he listened as though she was more than simply someone with information to share. Was that just his work demeanor? Or was there an underlying connection that could develop between them? As much as she'd like to explore that further, it would be too dangerous to act on her impulse, given how she only had six months to prove herself. Any chance of the center being a beehive for something illegal might give Mr. Whitley grounds to start over with yet another fresh face, thereby ending her tenure before it even began.

What could she do differently here than at her previous jobs so this one would last? Taking an interest in the personal lives of her employees might be a good start. Standing on the outskirts and waiting for something to happen wouldn't accomplish anything either. If she wanted to be a part of Hollydale, she had to jump into life here.

She paused at the door to the salon, her plans for the night up in the air. She only knew she didn't want to be alone. Brooke hadn't met many people yet, and Colin was otherwise occupied with his friend Riley, whose parents had invited him on their last white water rafting excursion of the year. Maybe Aunt Mitzi would accept a dinner invitation as a thank-you. Since she wouldn't take rent money on top of providing meals, she was making it almost impossible for Brooke to search for a home of her own. In the best way possible, that is.

The bell on the door jingled, and a pleasant herbal scent greeted her. The steady hum of the hair dryers was a melody in itself. Last Christmas, Colin had presented her with a gift certificate to her favorite spa or salon with money he'd earned mowing lawns. It had been the best present ever, and her visit the day before her college graduation ceremony might have been the last time she'd indulged herself. The crowded salon told her she'd have to schedule far in advance for a pampering evening.

A girl whose eyes were rimmed with black eyeliner smiled from behind the reception desk and rose to her feet. "Hi, we're already booked for the rest of the day, but I'd love to schedule an appointment for you for another time."

"I'm just here to say hello to my aunt."

"Oh, you must be Brooke. I'm Ashleigh. I work here part-time when I'm not in school, and my dad's dating Mitzi." She settled back on the stool. "When you're ready to avail yourself to your aunt's amazing services, you can call directly or download the new app I designed."

Brooke touched her dark hair she'd thrown up into a messy bun this morning. She'd been aiming for sophisticated. Now she worried about whether she'd succeeded.

Mitzi ducked out from behind the frosted glass partition and gestured at her. "Brooke, honey, come on back and meet a dear friend of mine, Tina."

Brooke joined her. "I'll see you later if this is a bad time."

"You'll do no such thing." Aunt Mitzi bustled over to her workstation. "Surprises are the icing on the cupcake of life. I guess that means I'm the surprise filling inside." She laughed at herself and patted Tina's shoulder. "I crack myself up sometimes."

"That's why we all love you." Tina smiled and bit her lip as she stared at the bottles of nail polish on the shelves. "Deciding on a new color is a big decision since you said I can't go with my usual Pink Pearl."

"I talked Tina into a manicure before I trim her hair. She's going to look bee-you-ti-ful for her date with her husband, Drew, tonight at Dominic's. It's a romantic Italian restaurant that overlooks Lake Pine with a sensational view of the Great Smoky Mountains."

"We're celebrating my third year in remission."

"That's wonderful." Brooke walked over to the display. "May I suggest a fiery red or a passionate purple?"

"You're your aunt's niece all right." Tina pulled a bottle of each off the shelf and shrugged. "I can't decide."

"Go with your gut instinct, darlin'. That usually works for me. Why don't I shampoo Fabiana and talk to my niece while you mull it over?" Aunt Mitzi turned to Brooke. "I'm all yours for a couple of minutes, unless you're here for me to perform my magic on you."

Brooke spotted a customer she recognized and said hello.

Mitzi had collected her next client by the time Brooke caught up with her. While she stood a good six inches taller than her favorite aunt, Mitzi's exuberance made her seem larger-than-life.

Brooke noted the charming shampoo station, with a row of sparkling ebony sinks and fluffy towels, which took center stage.

Aunt Mitzi checked the water temperature against the inside of her wrist. "Fabiana, did I introduce my niece, Brooke?"

"Huh?" The spraying water masked any further response.

Brooke stayed away so she wouldn't get wet.

Aunt Mitzi shampooed Fabiana's thick curly hair, turned off the water and plucked the top towel from the stack. "She's the new community center director."

"You'll have to visit my home one evening and try my *ropa vieja*." Fabiana held the towel to her hair.

"Oh, Brooke, you haven't lived until you try Fabiana's flank steak with black beans and vegetables. Just thinking of it adds an inch to my waistline." Mitzi patted her ample hips and guided the other woman to a chair. "Fabiana, you're in great hands with my best stylist, Luanne, while I check on Tina."

Fabiana settled in Luanne's chair, and the

stylist with short pink hair raised the petite customer to a better height. Aunt Mitzi headed back to the manicure area, and Brooke followed. A yo-yo didn't move back and forth this much.

"Saturdays are always a whirlwind," Aunt Mitzi said. "To what do I owe this pleasure, honey?"

"I'd like to take you out to dinner tonight. My treat."

Aunt Mitzi came over and patted her arm. "Wish I'd known about that offer sooner. Owen's picking me up for a night on the town."

Brooke liked what she'd heard so far about this new man in her aunt's life. She only had misty memories of her aunt's first husband, who'd abandoned her many years ago. Somehow, Mitzi had rebuilt her life while Brooke's mother faded away before succumbing to chronic liver disease. Since Brooke arrived in Hollydale, she couldn't miss the glow on Aunt Mitzi's face whenever Owen's name came up, although she had yet to meet the elusive Owen Thompson.

Tina thrust a bottle of cherry red in Mitzi's direction. "This one. I'll be daring for once. You're rubbing off on me, so I'll brag on your boyfriend for a minute. He was a great help at the center today." She faced Brooke. "My son,

Caleb, worked for him before he accepted a job with the nature conservancy."

"Are you talking about Caleb Spindler? He was one of the people who interviewed me online during the director search committee."

"One and the same. I work for his wife, Lucie, as her bookkeeper." Tina watched as Mitzi buffed her nails. "I still find it hard to believe I'm a grandmother to twins."

After living in Houston, where she went weeks without running into anyone familiar, this small-town closeness, where everyone was related to someone, seemed a throwback to the days when she and her mother had lived in a tiny hamlet. Was moving here a mistake or the balm she needed?

"Well, I wish more of the men in town were like Caleb and less like…" Brooke halted, for she wasn't quite sure what she thought of Officer Maxwell, only that she was thinking of him way too much.

Aunt Mitzi kept her hand on Tina's while she faced Brooke and winked. "Less like who? Has some lucky guy caught your eye?"

"Romance. You can never ever go wrong with that. Hollydale has a particularly romantic gazebo in the town square." Tina's blush almost matched the color of her nail polish. She looked at Mitzi. "Drew proposed to me there. Where are you and Owen going tonight? I'm wondering if we'll bump into each other at Dominic's."

"He's taking me to the Timber River Bar and Grill, and I have my dancing shoes all picked out and ready to go." Aunt Mitzi kept a steady hand while applying the polish. Brooke should have left, but female friendship had been something sorely missing in her life. Aunt Mitzi brought out a blow dryer and aimed it at Tina's nails. "Brooke, honey, I'd love to see someone bring a little more happiness into your life, and you never answered me earlier. Is there someone for you in Hollydale? Has some mysterious man caught your eye?"

Brooke winced. Actually, she should have left while the getting was good. "It's more like this one guy keeps popping up every time I least expect it."

"Is he cute?" Aunt Mitzi raised her voice over the small blow dryer. "Take Owen, for instance. He's very cute, if I do say so myself. You can never go wrong with someone at your side. Makes life a little sweeter."

No sooner had she turned off the dryer than Tina nodded. "I've been married for over thirty years, and I'd still classify Drew as cute." She faced Aunt Mitzi. "I think I'll settle for getting my hair styled rather than cut today."

Aunt Mitzi guided Tina to her station, and Brooke started to slip away when her aunt met her gaze. "We may be a little nosy sometimes, but we care about each other."

Brooke pointed to the front door. "I won't wait up for you."

"The dinner invitation for *ropa vieja* is always open," Fabiana said from the next chair. "My son, Carlos, is visiting tonight from his outpost in Tennessee. Perhaps you'd like to join us."

She wasn't quite ready for anyone to play matchmaker with her love life. Instead, she'd use tonight to work on new ideas for the center. "Thanks, but I don't know what time Colin is due back from his white water rafting trip. I'd hate for my teenaged son to eat you out of your house."

"*Dios mio.* You're the mother of a teenager? You look so young." Fabiana waved her hand in front of her face. "Pay no attention to me. My gray streaks are on account of my husband's and Carlos's jobs as firefighters. If it weren't for them, I'd still have all dark hair like yours."

Brooke grinned and stepped toward the center of the salon, now eager to make her escape. "Nice to meet all of you. I hope to see everyone at the community center sometime."

"If only there were more activities for mothers and daughters. I'd love to do something there with Graciela." Fabiana moved, and Luanne nudged her shoulders.

"You've got to stop wiggling so much or I'll have to explain to my boss why one section of your hair is five inches shorter than the other." Luanne waved her scissors around, and Fabiana stilled.

Tina sighed as Aunt Mitzi combed out her hair. "I'd love a girls' night out. I love Drew, but sometimes a night away from our cute guys makes us appreciate them all the more. I'd especially like to have something to take home afterward. Something like a beaded necklace or a painting."

"Wait a minute." Brooke stepped back toward her aunt's station. "Aren't there any places in Hollydale that sponsor girls' nights out?"

Aunt Mitzi stopped combing and glanced back with a regretful shake of her head. "Not since Deana moved her art-glazing studio to Asheville."

"What if you could use the art space at the community center every other week and paint your masterpieces? Maybe one of you will be the next Georgia O'Keeffe." Brooke snapped her fingers. "Mimosas and Masterpieces! With nonalcoholic champagne, of course, because it's the community center."

Aunt Mitzi held the black comb an inch from Tina's hair and laughed. "Sign me up. When we meet at my house, I'll break out the real bubbly."

"Me, too." Everyone turned toward Brooke with expectant gazes.

Brooke shifted her weight. "I'll present the idea at the next staff meeting."

"And maybe you'll let me in on the identity of the cute guy." Aunt Mitzi's eyes sparkled as she brought out the flat iron. "You should ask him out to dinner tonight."

Except Officer Maxwell unnerved her too much. As it was, Mr. Whitley hadn't been pleased at her calling him two days in a row to update him on the situation. The next months would fly by in the blink of an eye.

And her last three dates had been disasters of the highest magnitude. They all fizzled like flat soda when she brought up work and Colin.

There was no doubt Aunt Mitzi would pursue the answer at home, but Brooke would evade her. She and Colin were settling in just fine. She didn't need anything else complicating her life.

CHAPTER FOUR

DURING HIS SHIFT that ended in the wee hours of the morning, Jonathan had been called to the Timber River Bar and Grill at the edge of town. Mark Sandell, who owned the popular watering hole with his grandfather, turned over a fake ID that a server had confiscated. Mark hadn't provided any new information, but at least Jonathan now had a third license in hand. This week he'd work on tracking down the teenager in the photo.

But first, family time. Jonathan slammed his car door with Vanessa and Izzy following suit, and the smell of cotton candy brought excitement pumping through his veins. Soon his daughters might be too old for visits to Ike's Pumpkin Farm, but he never would be. Fall was Jonathan's favorite season because of weekends like these. They'd started this Sunday with a late pancake brunch at the Holly Days Diner after he caught a few hours of sleep, and now afternoon was upon them. Ike's hayride was one of the season's highlights, and the spring in his step was just what he needed after an exhausting week of work.

"Dad." Vanessa pulled on his jacket sleeve. "Izzy wants a big fat pumpkin, and I want a long thin one, and you said we're only getting one."

Jonathan tried to push work out of his mind. Here he was complaining about working holidays and wanting that new detective position, and then he wasn't even present when he did spend quality time with his daughters. If he didn't watch it, he'd turn into his parents.

Unless he already had.

"We'll know the right one when we see it."

This was the perfect place for that. All around were pumpkins of various shapes, colors and sizes. Even Izzy, who was speeding toward her teen years, showed more enthusiasm than usual.

"Hey, Dad, there's a field of green pumpkins and those are all white. Ooh. I changed my mind." Vanessa jumped up and down and pointed to a patch near the back. "I want one with lots of warts. Those are cool."

She yanked his arm and dragged him that way, taking care to navigate around the crowds. He caught Izzy muttering something about him needing to buy tickets for the hayride, but she stayed on Vanessa's heels. By the fence, a woman with her back to him had the same posture and figure as Brooke. Unlike the new director, this woman's hair was loose and fell past her shoulders, a shiny curtain of dark brown that almost blended in with her burgundy belted coat.

"Daddy! This one!" Vanessa went over and thumped her hand on the biggest pumpkin, one that had a good weight and stood two feet tall. "Wouldn't it look great on our front porch?"

"Um." What was the word he was searching for? "No."

"Officer Maxwell, is that you? I almost didn't recognize you out of your uniform." The woman was now facing him. It was Brooke, and her cheeks reddened. "That came out wrong."

He smiled at the sudden unexpectedness of seeing her. "Just Jonathan. I insist."

"Well, Just Jonathan, who can resist when you put it like that? And who do you have with you?"

"This is my younger daughter, Vanessa." He threw his arm around her shoulder and then glanced around. He jerked his head for Izzy to come join them. "And this is Izzy."

She smiled and straightened to her full height. "Isabella. I insist."

"Isabella Grace. That's no way to speak to a friend of mine."

Izzy's eyebrow shot up, the exact same way Anne's had whenever he'd done something that annoyed her.

Brooke stepped forward. "It's a pleasure to meet you, Isabella." She pointed to a teenager who was texting. "Colin, meet some new friends of mine."

Colin looked up and shrugged. "Maybe later, Mom. Riley just arrived with her parents. Can I join them?"

Brooke chuckled and met Jonathan's gaze. "Seems our children are both surprising us." She nodded. "Do you need any money?"

Jonathan took a good look at Brooke's son. *Tall and lanky?* That sounded familiar. Colin shook his head and hurried away before Jonathan could make out more definable features, as Colin's hoodie with a baseball logo hid the teen's eyes from view.

"Let me guess." Brooke drew him out of his reverie. "Sixth grade for Vanessa and eighth for Isabella?"

Vanessa giggled. "I'm in fifth, and Izzy's in seventh cause she's older."

"I work at The Whitley Community Center, and there are some great programs for girls your age." Brooke had a way of talking with kids that Jonathan liked. She didn't talk down to them or use a high-pitched, singsong voice. "Next month we're launching Heartsgiving, a day camp during the week of Thanksgiving. I bet you'd both have a lot of fun."

The giggle monster apparently hadn't finished with Vanessa yet. "You came to my school and told us all about it. I'm already signed up."

Izzy scuffed the dirt with her sneaker. "I'm old enough to babysit both of us. But yeah, I'm coming, too."

Jonathan blinked at the changes in his sweet daughter. He wanted to take Brooke aside and apologize for Izzy's behavior. Instead, he glanced at the line for hayride tickets, which was longer now than when they'd arrived. "Have you ever been on one of Ike's hayrides?"

Brooke shook her head. "This is the first time I've been here. Ike promised some pumpkins for the center, and I wanted to get decorating ideas from a couple of the vendors."

"This is a beautiful fall day, too beautiful to only think about work. Whatever you do, don't miss out on the hayride." Before he knew it, they were all gathered at the back of the line. "This is my favorite part of the day."

Vanessa tugged at his shirt. "I thought the

caramel apples were your favorite." She rubbed her tummy and laughed. "Maybe that's mine."

"What about you, Isabella?" Brooke's hand moved as if to reach out to Izzy's arm, but she pulled it back. "What do you like?"

Izzy hesitated, a muscle flexing in her jaw, and Jonathan wondered what was coming over his daughter. She never acted like this around Lucie or Harriet or any other woman he knew. The silence continued for a moment before she scuffed the dirt again. "I guess I like picking out the baby pumpkins. Dad lets us make a display on our mantel." She sniffed the air, a little of that Izzy spirit coming back. "And funnel cakes."

The aroma of powdered sugar and oil caught in the breeze, and his stomach rumbled, brunch now a distant memory. He pulled out his wallet. "I can see the booth from here, and the line's not too long. Why don't you and Vanessa buy one to share and one for me? If they have one with apples on top, that's the one with my name written on it." He glanced at Brooke. "Care for one? My treat."

"Thanks for the offer, but I'm saving myself for a slice of pumpkin bread. Thanks anyway." Her eyes twinkled in bemusement. "Besides, I normally take a few bites of something sweet and Colin polishes off the rest. I wouldn't know what to do with a whole funnel cake to myself."

Izzy snatched the twenty out of his hand while Vanessa blew him a kiss. They rushed to the line, and Jonathan kept a lookout before he transferred most of his attention back to Brooke. From the looks of the line ahead, he and Brooke would know everything about each other before they reached the ticket seller.

That didn't bother him one bit.

"The wait is worth it, but if there's somewhere else you want to be…"

"Isabella would have preferred I stay back with the green pumpkins. All things considered, I'd say they're used to having you to themselves." Brooke stuck her hands in her coat pockets. "I gather you're a single parent, too?"

They moved ahead by two steps. "Didn't I talk about them before now? People have been known to run when they see me coming. Otherwise I tend to put them to sleep with the stories of the two of them or the myriad of pictures I have on my phone."

Brooke chuckled, and then her face took on a more serious expression. "Isabella is rather protective of you."

He smiled at the tactful way she phrased Izzy's behavior. "She has more memories of her mom, but Vanessa was only five when Anne died."

Sometimes it seemed most days passed in a blur, whereas the nights tended to drag without having someone who laughed at his corny jokes and kept the bed warm when he climbed in after a long shift. For the first couple of years, the grief over losing Anne left him tossing and turning. Now he was no longer sure whether he stayed awake some nights missing Anne or the warm haze of what they shared.

"Good memories from the sound of it?"

"The best. Anne was everything to me. The way you said that, though. Can you relate to what Izzy and Vanessa have been through?"

"My mother passed away a while back." Her lips pursed into a line until one side curled upward. "It's been just Colin and me since the beginning. Maybe that's a reason he's defensive of me, although you wouldn't guess that from a couple of minutes ago. I see the same in Isabella. She's looking out for you in the best way she knows how, and that means keeping her father close."

He laughed as they stepped onward to the ticket booth. "Is that a nice way of saying she's jealous?"

Before Brooke could answer, Vanessa and Izzy returned with two funnel cakes, along with extra plates and forks. "Ms. Novak, you can have some of mine." Vanessa cut off a piece of hers and shared it as they arrived at the front of the line.

"Can you hold this for me?" he asked. "I'm definitely not done with it." She nodded at his request, accepting his plate in her left hand while holding her plate in her right. He smiled his thanks. "Despite your protests, I know the funnel cake will be hard to resist, just like me, so I'd like for your first hayride to be my treat." He sensed hesitation in the set of her shoulders. "As a welcome to Hollydale."

She chuckled. "I'll grant you're persuasive with classic lines like that, so thank you. Can you purchase one for Colin? I'll pay you back."

He bought the tickets, stuffed the change in the tip jar and exchanged the tokens for his plate, knowing full well he wouldn't accept payment later. They walked over to the picnic tables. A group of four left as they arrived. Izzy and Vanessa flanked him, while Brooke sat on the other side by herself.

He whispered in Izzy's ear, "Why don't you move over to Brooke's side?"

Izzy stabbed a piece of her funnel cake with her fork, stony silence his answer.

Vanessa tapped his shoulder. "Daddy, do you mind if I sit with Miss Brooke?"

He wanted to hug her but nodded instead. They soon finished the snack and found themselves in the hayride line. He waved to several people and introduced them to Brooke while ignoring the daggers coming from Izzy's eyes.

Did he want Brooke's friendship? Or did he want more? Izzy wouldn't respond this way if she didn't sense something brewing between him and the attractive brunette. Still, it was too soon for anything romantic. He caught himself. Too soon since he'd met Brooke or too soon after Anne's death? Five years alone with only a few casual dates was a long time. Apparently, Izzy felt it wasn't long enough.

Brooke elicited a promise from the people behind them to come visit the improved community center. Then she craned her neck over Izzy's shoulder. "I texted Colin a couple of minutes ago that we bought him a ticket for the hayride and to meet us in line. He said they're on their way, but I don't see him."

Jonathan looked in the opposite direction and saw a young couple, hands locked together, heading their way. "He's about six feet, a gray hoodie and blue jeans, right?" Although that seemed to describe half the male teenagers in the general vicinity.

Brooke turned and waved. "Colin! Over here."

Brooke's son reminded him of something related to his case. Colin's gray hoodie with the logo of Jonathan's favorite baseball team. He stepped into their circle with a teenage girl. He reached up and brushed his sandy brown hair out of his eyes, which could have been described as hazel or blue or gray, depending on the light.

"Sorry we're late. It took longer than I thought to buy Riley a ticket." Colin turned to the people behind them. "Sorry, ma'am, but would you mind if Riley and I join my mom? It wouldn't be right to cut in line without your permission."

The woman smiled at Brooke. "You and your husband are raising a fine gentleman."

"He's not my brother, and that's not my mother." Izzy spoke up with more vehemence than he'd ever heard out of her before. He'd have to address this at home.

The line moved again, and they climbed the steps to the boarding platform. Izzy somehow maneuvered it so the three Maxwells were on one side while Brooke was wedged between Colin and Riley on the other side of the wagon.

He settled into the scratchy hay, a good amount cushioning his bottom. The fumes of the tractor's diesel motor made him cough and overwhelmed the lingering apple and sugar aroma of the funnel cakes. The putt-putt of the motor became a low hum. With a rumble and a small jolt, they were off around the scenic perimeter of Ike's Pumpkin Farm, with the Great Smokies a perfect backdrop.

Brooke turned toward Riley. "I'm sorry I didn't get to meet you and your parents before yesterday's white water rafting trip."

"If you'd like to meet them, ma'am, they're here. My mom picks out six or seven pumpkins and a couple of hay bales for the front lawn. I hope you don't mind that Colin's already offered to help her load them in my father's truck since my brother's at basketball camp this weekend?" Riley's soft voice barely reached their side of the wagon.

"Exterior decorating. That sounds like it might be a wonderful class for the community center. If your mother has any free time, I'd like to talk to her about that."

"Mom." Frustration tinged Colin's voice. "I know you love your job, but enjoy the hayride, okay?"

That was interesting. Jonathan wasn't the only person in the wagon who loved his occupation and thought about it even when he wasn't on duty. Colin reminded him of his younger self pleading with his parents to take some time off. Still, he couldn't shake the feeling he'd seen Colin before.

The wagon stopped while the tour guide spoke about the wildflower field surrounding them. Magenta, yellow and pink flowers extended to the tree line. The colors reminded Jonathan of the wall of vibrant fishing flies and lures at Mo's Gas and Bait Stop. He caught his breath. Mo had described a teenager who resembled Colin right down to the gray hoodie with a baseball logo.

And Colin had recently moved here, so he probably wouldn't be familiar to Mo yet.

He couldn't come right out and ask Colin in a public area if he'd visited Mo's bait shop with the intent of purchasing cigarettes as a minor using a fake ID, not without having a solid piece of evidence.

"Daddy." Vanessa pulled on his sleeve. "Are you thinking about work again?"

He glanced her way, but not before catching Brooke's bemusement. "Busted."

Izzy poked him in the ribs. "This is supposed to be our family time together."

Whether that was a poke at him or at Brooke, he wasn't quite sure. He was doing everything he could to find ways to spend more time with his daughters, including lobbying for that promotion, but Brooke? If he had his way, he'd love to get to know her even better. Of course, if Colin had presented a fake ID to the cashier, arresting her son would scuttle any chance of a relationship.

"Would you like me to take a picture of the three of you?" Brooke interrupted his thoughts almost as if she knew his mind had once again drifted to work.

He'd missed having someone who recognized that about him, even more so since police and detective work could lead him down dark paths. He knew all too well how everything could change in an instant. He pulled his cell phone from his jacket pocket and extended it to Brooke, her soft hand brushing his, a pleasant sensation warming his skin. "Thanks."

From the startled look on her face, she might also have felt that spark. She rubbed her hand and then snapped some shots. "Check them. If you don't like them, I'll take more."

The opportunity was too good to pass up. "I'll take one of you and Colin." He raised his phone and pressed the white circle, taking their picture.

Brooke laughed. "I hope it's a good one. Wait. Did you take our picture with your phone to get my number?"

His eyes widened, and a smile lifted the corners of his lips.

"Busted."

He could only hope he didn't say the same about Colin once he showed the photo of him to Mo. He wanted to be wrong about Colin being the underage teen who tried to buy cigarettes in the bait shop. That wasn't his only concern. He also crossed his fingers the gossip chain would never reveal to Brooke the conversation he'd be having with Mo later this week.

CHAPTER FIVE

BROOKE PROPPED OPEN the door of the men's locker room with the rolling cleaning cart and glanced around. When the custodian, Al Floyd, fell ill with a fast-acting stomach virus and left early on this dreary and rainy Tuesday, she stepped in and volunteered for the rest of his shift. A director sometimes had to do what she asked of her employees, and this was one of those times.

It meant a longer evening as she'd just locked the center doors five minutes ago at the stroke of six. Colin had replied to her text that he was occupied with homework and not to hurry home on his account. He'd even volunteered the information that he'd walked Daisy. Evidently, Riley had gone with him.

When had he grown up so fast? And when had he noticed girls, let alone started dating? It had been a bit of a shock to discover Riley wasn't just a buddy, but she only had herself to blame for that assumption.

It seemed she had something in common

with Isabella Maxwell. Both of them wanted to protect the men of their family from getting hurt.

She peeked at Al's daily routine checklist. *Dust all flat surfaces, replenish the soap and paper towels, clean the lockers.* Snapping on her gloves, she nodded her approval and dispensed with the first two items with ease. She then gauged the height of the lockers and shook her head. She'd need a step stool to tackle the highest of the six rows of square, compact lockers and work her way down. Within minutes, a quick trip to the storage closet yielded the necessary step stool, and she grabbed a couple of extra rags for good measure.

Returning, she opened all the lockers on the top row. Mustiness wafted through the room, and she fanned her hand under her nose. She'd address this with Al upon his return. Did he skip the top ones often or were they always a little musty since they probably weren't used as much? She wouldn't know. It wasn't as though she came in here often.

She opened her phone to her popular music app and nodded appreciatively as her favorite Kelly Clarkson song filled the air. In no time, the trash bag on the cart handle was nearly full of grimy paper towels, and most of the lockers were in much better shape. The room already smelled fresher as the industrial-strength cleaner worked its magic. Once she knocked out the last two lockers, she'd place an order at Mario's for an extra-large olive-and-green-pepper pizza for Colin and herself, since Aunt Mitzi was eating with Owen and Ashleigh.

Should she contact Owen and find out what his intentions were? She laughed. Did family members even do that anymore?

Her stomach growled. She'd better get a move on. In the next locker, her hand bumped into the back wall sooner than she expected, and her eyebrows furrowed. Something was wrong. She retrieved her phone and shone the light into the one beside it and then into another. Then she moved the step stool and flashed the beam into each locker on the top row. There was something different all right. The back wall of that troublesome one was a good five inches shallower than the others. She knocked on the one farthest on the right and worked her way over to the alarming space. A hollow sound was her reward.

Biting her lip, she tapped her phone and turned off the flashlight. Should she call Jonathan or investigate more? She shook her head. If he visited in his official capacity and that news spread around Hollydale like wildfire, Mr. Whitley might not be happy with the police visiting the center for the third time in not even so many weeks.

What would it hurt to check this out more? For all she knew, the lockers were built this way and she'd feel foolish reporting an architectural anomaly. That must be it. She was nervous, that was all. Laughing, she tapped the metal for a few seconds, and the thin sheet fell. She pulled out the panel and laid it atop the cart, taking care with her gloves so nothing would be smudged. Then she returned and peered into the locker with the flashlight from her phone. A small plastic sack rested there with something inside that looked like small cards, most likely IDs.

This discovery left her no choice, and she placed a call to her new friend's police number.

JONATHAN ARRIVED AT the community center, his adrenaline pumping. This might be the lead he needed to advance his investigation. If this panned out, there was a good chance he could convince Mike to allow him to spend some extra hours on the matter until the case was solved. As it was, his attention had been diverted to patrolling the outskirts of the city, pulling funeral detail for old Mr. Preston, who had died two months short of his hundredth birthday, and checking on a report of a suspicious smell, which had turned out to be a false alarm. Two high school seniors had been storing eggs for a Halloween prank when one of their siblings came upon the find and broke the first dozen, the fumes causing a noxious odor a neighbor had gotten a strong whiff of.

He hadn't even had time to follow up with Mo about Colin. Breaking the case on the false IDs would give him a leg up when he interviewed for the detective position, more so than busting up a kid's prank.

He'd take anything he could get to bolster his chances of receiving the promotion. Sure enough, when Mike had posted the job listing online, Everson's niece sent in her application. As far as Jonathan knew, and he wouldn't be a good detective if he didn't have his sources, he was the only other candidate to apply for the position.

However, the real bonus to his day was seeing Brooke again so soon after they ran into each other at Ike's Pumpkin Farm. He'd thought long and hard about saying something to Izzy regarding her behavior and decided against it. He wanted to give Izzy time to hopefully come to terms with the idea of him dating. For her sake, he didn't like her getting defensive every time he became interested in a woman, although it only took one right woman for interest to blossom into something deeper.

Until now, he hadn't given any careful consideration to dating again. Never had five years seemed so short and so long. Raising two daughters, moving away from Savannah and working full-time and then some kept him busy. Truth be told, except on the anniversary of Anne's death, he didn't mark the time in years. No need to do that. She was gone, and it didn't matter whether it was five weeks or five years. She'd never enter the room with a new handmade Christmas ornament, her eyes sparkling, or be standing there with his mug of coffee and a kiss when he ran back into the house, realizing he had forgotten something. Most of the time, however, he hadn't and just used that as a convenient excuse for one extra kiss. They knew and laughed afterward at his transparency.

It wasn't a matter of replacing Anne. That wasn't possible. However, he wasn't opposed to finding someone new. Someone who made five years seem like five minutes and five minutes seem like an eternity of happiness.

That didn't happen every day. Finding that once had been a treasure beyond compare. Was he selfish for wanting to find that again? Izzy thought so, if her attitude this past weekend was any indication. There was no way, though, he'd allow his twelve-year-old daughter to dictate his love life.

He spotted Brooke at the center's entrance. Today's gray pantsuit accented her attractiveness, and her hair was swept upward. He'd already memorized her features from her patrician neck to her amber-brown eyes. Cool and collected in a business setting while warm and approachable away from work, Brooke was a happy change from the life he'd settled into.

And something deep inside told him he'd be happy spending a long time finding out all facets of her. What made her laugh. Whether she cried at sappy movies. How she'd look after he kissed her.

Except he had to track down whether her son had purchased and used a fake ID to buy cigarettes. Not the best starting point for any sort of relationship.

Besides, he was here in uniform, although he was also a cop when he wasn't in uniform. He pushed aside his reaction to her.

As soon as she met his gaze, she waved. "Officer Maxwell."

They were back to official titles once more. "Ms. Novak."

"This way, please."

Something was different, and he took in the

latex gloves as they walked toward the men's locker room area. He sidestepped the cart holding the door open. After rounding the corner, he came upon a row with multiple lockers, all the same size. A wall divider separated the rest of the area. He peeked around the corner and found four navy shower curtains and bathroom stalls. He returned to find Brooke righting a step stool that had fallen on its side. Her hands trembled ever so slightly. He wanted to reach out and steady them, but this wasn't the right time. He pulled out his notepad and pencil. "Tell me what happened."

"Our custodian, Al Floyd, wasn't feeling well, so he left early."

He kept taking notes as she recounted her evening.

"Then I called you and waited."

"Appreciate it."

His gaze settled on a slight smudge of grime at the end of one of her sleeves.

She glanced at the spot, and her cheeks turned pink. "At the last center, I kept a change of clothes on site, but it's slipped my mind to do the same here." She gave a light chuckle. "I'll bring in casual clothes tomorrow in case of an emergency like this, but everything I own is machine washable. It's amazing what a good iron can do."

He dropped off his uniforms at the local dry cleaners. They gave him a discount and did a fine job.

"Can we go back to Mr. Floyd for a second?" The name didn't ring any bells even though Hollydale was small. And he tended to run into a lot of people since he did all the grocery shopping for his family and volunteered at the girls' schools. That, and his job, kept him preoccupied. "Do you know how long he's worked here or do you need to pull up his employment file?"

"Two years." She smiled and shrugged. "I make it a point to remember everything in each file. The heart of a successful community center is its staff."

Formidable, smart and perceptive. The more he got to know her, the more he sensed she was genuinely devoted to the center's future as well as the employees under her command. "Why did he leave early?"

"He clutched his stomach and ran out of here the second I sent him home."

Whether Mr. Floyd knew of the stash and had to leave before he could do anything about it was now Jonathan's top priority. The case had a new suspect, but why keep the fake IDs in the locker once a new director was hired?

If it was easy money, why not?

Snapping on his gloves, he climbed the step stool and shone his compact searchlight at the small satchel in the back. Carefully, he removed the sack and dusted it for fingerprints. Nothing. Opening it, he found ten generic IDs, half of which were finished laminated licenses with different names and addresses. A pile of blank North Carolina IDs rested at the bottom. He'd swing by the local DMV and find out if these had been stolen from the department or were clever rip-offs.

"Are those fake licenses?"

He'd almost forgotten Brooke was nearby, he was so preoccupied with new thoughts about the case.

He glanced around the room. Someone knew what they were doing when they picked this spot as a hiding place and possible exchange location. This was one of the few places in the center where there'd be no video footage since this also served as a changing area and restroom. "Who has access to this room?"

"Anyone using the facility, and Betty sees everyone coming and going." She accompanied him to the door, and he noted the reception desk and the women's locker room.

A visit to Mr. Floyd was in his immediate future. Jonathan began collecting and tagging the evidence. "Thanks, Brooke."

"Do you think one of my employees had something to do with this?" Fire came out of her eyes, and he appreciated the way she defended her crew, even though she'd only worked here a short time.

Whether that trust was justified remained to be seen.

"It's too early to say."

"You say that a lot. Sometimes, though, you have to believe the best in people, believe that a community can come together and make life better. People are basically good, don't you think?" Her gaze wandered over his uniform, and while he liked how she seemed to be checking him out, it was almost as though a light bulb clicked. "Or, maybe not."

He removed his hat and placed it on the cart. "Where does this go?"

"Thanks, I can put it away." She moved toward it, and they bumped into each other.

"I know, but I'd like to answer your question while we put it away together."

"Oh." Those expressive cheeks turned pink once more, and she swept her hand in front of the cart. "Be my guest. Hold on. The step stool doesn't belong in here."

He fetched it and tucked it into the cart. "Problem solved."

They walked in silence, and she stopped.

"I'm curious. Are you Officer Maxwell or just Jonathan?"

He also halted and adjusted the step stool, hanging too precariously to one side. "I'm always a little of both." He returned his hands to the cart and began pushing. "I take my uniform seriously, and sometimes I do see the worst in people. I understand where you're coming from, though. The desire to make life better for a community."

They had that in common. While he protected the residents of Hollydale, she enriched their lives with programs and events. They weren't so different in that respect.

She showed him the maintenance area and where to store the cart. "I'll return the step stool to the supply closet tomorrow. Do you really think Al could be involved? Wouldn't he have told me to skip the lockers or, better yet, moved the evidence once I began working here if he was behind this?"

"Both of those are valid points, and I'll keep them in mind when I interview him. I'd prefer if you don't give him a heads-up about this. Until I investigate this further, I'd appreciate it if you would keep this totally between us."

"Shouldn't I tell the staff?"

He shook his head and put his hat back on. "It's a small town. If word gets out, people will talk, and that could tip off the suspect. Promise?"

She hesitated, then nodded. "I promise. If you're done here, I need to lock up."

"Can you be here early tomorrow and let me return a different bag to the locker? Tonight, I'll dust these for prints but also stuff something in the bottom. And, I'll leave the one on top so it looks the same."

"Seven too early?"

"That's perfect."

He wanted to keep talking to her a little more, but he no longer had a valid reason. Besides, this was technically his own time, and he had to return to his daughters. Caleb and Lucie had invited them over to dinner, and he hadn't missed Izzy's glare when he excused himself early. By now, they were probably finished. Although Izzy and Vanessa loved to play with his cousin's menagerie of animals, there was only so long he could impose on his relatives for one night, not to mention one lifetime.

"I'll keep you updated if anything changes." Evidence in hand, he fell into step alongside her. "I'll walk you out."

"Thank you. I'd like that."

The problem was, he liked it too much.

CHAPTER SIX

JONATHAN STEPPED INTO Mike's office. This morning's visit to Mr. Floyd hadn't provided any sudden confessions or breakthroughs. Instead, the custodian admitted his sciatica had been acting up. He'd been slacking off on the lockers, only giving them a light cleaning every other week. Mr. Floyd begged him for a chance to talk to Brooke on his own and make it right. He needed the health insurance and the money from this job. From what Jonathan had seen of Brooke, she'd probably agree to give the custodian a second chance.

Mike studied some papers and placed them on his desk. "Come on in."

As much as Jonathan wanted to ask about the progress in the detective selection, he limited the conversation to the relevant evidence.

Mike tapped his pencil against the desk. "Have you had a chance to follow up with Mo yet?"

"I wanted to interview Mr. Floyd first."

"Right choice." The tapping became faster

and more insistent. "You're basically doing the work of two jobs with this hanging over you."

"This isn't hanging over me." Jonathan's palms itched at the characterization. "It's important to get to the bottom of it since the evidence points to this not being some ID-by-mail scheme."

Mike stuck the pencil back into its holder. "Review the evidence with me again." He adjusted his computer screen, and Jonathan shared the view. Mike scrolled through the different photos and images Jonathan had collected. "Did Eric have anything to add when you questioned him about where he bought the fake ID?"

Jonathan accessed the report on his phone. "He said he conducted most of the transaction over the phone. He erased the number, like the person asked, after he sent a photo and vital stats as well as payment. He doesn't remember the number, and he can't even remember his own area code." Jonathan pulled off imaginary lint from the stiff crease in his pants.

Mike reached for the sandwich at the edge of his desk and took a bite. "I'll get a warrant for his phone. We'll work on retrieving the deleted number."

"His lawyer, Penelope Romano, already turned it over, citing complete cooperation

from her client. I have enough expertise to retrieve the number, but I'm guessing the perp
must have used a burner cell. Do you want me
to pursue this line?"

"No." Mike swallowed and then sipped his
coffee. "Not a good use of resources if the
suspect used a burner. Not with an uptick in
criminal activity from the tourist season. So
far it's been relatively minor, shoplifting and
the like, but this is where that detective position will be a windfall."

"I went ahead and called Ms. Romano to
schedule another interview, this time to narrow
down the specifics of when and how he picked
up the license. She asked if Eric's continued
cooperation would influence his sentencing,
and I told her I'd check with the district attorney."

"Go ahead and contact Everson and see how
this pans out." Mike shook his head while his
gaze focused on one photo in particular. He
picked up his pencil and tapped the screen with
the eraser. "Someone knew what they were
doing when they selected the men's locker
room."

"That's what I told Brooke. I can't put a camera in there."

"Ask her if you can install one in the lobby
directed at the entrance." Mike clicked out of

the file and returned the screen to its normal position.

"Anyone coming and going would have a reason to carry a duffel bag." Jonathan rolled his neck as he considered more possibilities. "But the perpetrator will want privacy if he's doing something unusual in the locker room. According to Brooke, Betty monitors both dressing areas from her desk, and there's either a staff member or visitor in the rooms almost every minute of the day, which increases the chance he'd come either early in the morning or when the building was about to close."

"A camera's more objective. It doesn't need coffee, and it doesn't count down the minutes until its shift is over. Once the camera's installed, we can check for anyone entering who's not wearing workout clothes or anyone leaving immediately."

"I'll personally review the recorded footage from the new camera each night. Look for anything that seems suspicious. A facial expression might give something away if the person takes the time to search the bag there. Then they'd realize that the center or the police or whoever is onto them."

"I can't authorize overtime pay on this." Mike threw away his empty cup. "And I don't want you volunteering for overtime without compensation just to have an edge over Ms. Everson."

Jonathan leaned back until his head knocked against the wall. No matter how he looked at it, he'd never have the same pull over the search committee as Everson's niece. Jonathan was born in Chicago, unlike most of his mother's family, who'd been born in Hollydale. Aunt Tina and Uncle Drew had taken him in summers when his parents were so busy with work they'd been only too happy to let Jonathan fly south and stay in North Carolina. Although six years separated him and Caleb, that made his cousin feel more like a younger brother. His experience and conviction record from Savannah would make him a shoo-in for the same job elsewhere, but here in Hollydale, family connections probably gave Ms. Everson an advantage he'd have to overcome on merit alone.

An image of Eric's fender bender flashed in his mind. Both cars had minimal damage, but what if this happened again? If someone else in Hollydale used a fake ID and Jonathan didn't do everything he could to find the person responsible for issuing these phony driver's licenses, things could turn out differently next time. *Forget the detective position.* He still wanted the job so bad he could taste it, but he didn't want yet another family to go through that same pain he'd experienced when he came upon Anne's wreck if there was anything he could do to possibly prevent it.

"I'm not doing this because of that. Izzy and Vanessa have bedtimes. I can binge-watch any footage from the center then, on my own dime."

Jonathan rose to leave, and Mike's voice halted his progress. "Interviews are next week."

"Good to know."

"Everson and I will be two of the panelists conducting the interviews."

Jonathan turned around and faced Mike. "Shouldn't Everson recuse himself if he's related to one of the candidates?"

Mike kept his gaze planted on the paper. "I'd vouch for one of the candidates to the Pacific Ocean and back. The thing is, small-town politics play into everything about the job. When you're a detective in a town this size, you're going to know everyone you interview, and they'll most likely know you. Besides, the third person, and the one with the deciding word, will be the city manager, Aidan Murphy." He glanced up, his wide grin a change from the somber aspect from a second earlier. "It doesn't hurt he's my brother-in-law. However, Aidan's his own person and has a strong sense of what he believes. That's what makes him ideal for Nat."

The former soldier was indeed a perfect match for Natalie, Mike's sister, who was a free spirit, unlike her organized twin sister, Becks. The day Jonathan had spent at the Hollydale Park last year helping out with Natalie's parade float proved to everyone how perfect Aidan and Natalie were for each other. Finding that type of balance was rare. He'd found it once with Anne. With the holidays approaching and everything else on his plate, was the holiday season the right time to get involved?

Something told him Brooke wasn't the type who would only commit to something on a casual basis. When she went in, she went all in. He liked that about her.

"You either love me and my sense of humor, or you don't. The three of you should decide on merit alone." Jonathan wouldn't change for a panel, no matter how much he wanted the job.

Mike lowered the paper and scratched his chin. "I just thought of something. The fewer people who know about the stash and the camera, the higher the chance word doesn't get back to the suspect."

"I already anticipated that and elicited a promise from Brooke that she'll keep her discovery between her and the department." With

Mike and him thinking along the same lines, that justified his reaction all the more.

"Good anticipation, but I want to catch the person in the act of clearing out the locker. Did you mention the stash to Floyd when you interviewed him?"

Jonathan reviewed his notes. "Nope. I only asked him how often he cleaned the lockers. He had to know I was there for a reason, but I didn't mention the fake licenses."

"Good. I'd like to end this ring once and for all. Keep pursuing your leads."

Jonathan reached his desk as the full impact of Mike's words hit him like a cold shower. Brooke uncovered the fake IDs. So far, the perpetrator seemed like he conducted his business from afar, only using the center as a drop spot. Right now, it seemed like he found a cash cow, easy profit, without a high risk of discovery. What if that was taken from him? Would he turn violent if he realized the stash in the locker only looked the same on the top and the inside bulk was different, the extra inventory now in the evidence room? Without anything to lose, would he track down the person who turned him in and make them pay for their actions? A new sense of urgency chilled his veins. The sooner he found out who was behind it, the sooner Brooke would be safe from anyone who might not be happy with her throwing a wrench in his scheme and ferreting him out.

CHAPTER SEVEN

BROOKE UNLOCKED THE door and escorted the group of women into the art studio. Laughter rang out as Betty and Tina placed their purses on hooks, and Aunt Mitzi propped a cooler on the long table, where smocks and other supplies greeted the participants. Her aunt's black leggings and dark red tunic showed off the purple in her newly dyed bob. Either her aunt had cornered the market on youth serum or she aged backward. Ever since Owen entered Mitzi's life, she definitely acted more carefree and vibrant.

Time with these women was something she truly welcomed. This Wednesday evening, unlike other similar extended-hour nights at the center, wouldn't end when they left. Jonathan was dropping by later to discuss security procedures. Seeing Jonathan, whether it was in his capacity as an officer or as himself, was a nice way to end the day.

"Thanks, sweetie, for holding the door for me. This was getting heavy." Aunt Mitzi opened the top and pulled out two bottles, one green and one orange. "And before you say anything, this is nonalcoholic champagne, like I promised. We'll save the real stuff for meetings at Tina's house. She's the empty nester."

"It doesn't seem that way anymore, now that my son, Caleb, married Lucie, and he's adopting her twins, Mattie and Ethan," Tina said. "Our house is quite hectic when they come over."

"Graciela's moving into her own place next week. She says she's making enough money at the animal shelter to afford to live by herself. Don't tell her, but Roberto and I are throwing a private party to celebrate our empty nest." A standout with her dark curls flowing around her shoulders, Fabiana laid a tote bag next to Mitzi's cooler and started removing plastic goblets. "Do I need an extra one for the teacher?"

"I'm the teacher, so that makes five of us so far." Brooke picked up one of the smocks and placed her head through the opening before looping the long belt ties around her waist, bringing them to the front and twisting them into a bow. "I'm fully qualified in beginning sketching and art instruction."

An older woman with long curly gray hair and a flowing sunflower scarf with a matching bright yellow coat swept into the room. "Thank you for opening this center to us. I'm sure the art created in this room will grace the walls and lives of so many. Don't you love happy hours spent in pursuit of making the world more beautiful and edifying?"

This woman, rather on the chatty side, must be the sixth. Brooke handed her a purple smock. "I think you might like this one, and you are?"

"I'm Hyacinth Hennessy. This is simply a delightful way to wind down a long day of baking. When you get a chance, you must visit Sweet Shelby's Tea Room in the near future. Belinda and I are about to celebrate our first year of business together."

Tina came over and chose the orange smock. "More like celebrating not competing with each other over pies and the like for a whole year."

Brooke frowned. "Can someone fill me in?"

Mitzi smirked. "Belinda and Hyacinth put aside a long time rivalry as the town's best bakers to open the tea room."

"You know, Hyacinth, if you and Belinda ever sold tickets to your daily baking skirmishes, er, sessions at Sweet Shelby's Tea Room, you'd raise a bundle. Every resident of Hollydale would pay to see that," Fabiana said.

A fleeting wisp of hurt creased Hyacinth's brow before she perked up. "In one way, you're right, but Belinda and I understand baking pies is an art form. We take our pies seriously." She laughed and handed Fabiana the red apron. "I believe, dear Fabiana, if I'm remembering correctly, red is your favorite color. You look beautiful in anything, but red really suits you."

"Gracias." Fabiana murmured her thanks while donning the smock over her shirt.

"And for Miss Betty, this yellow one suits your sunny disposition," Hyacinth said.

"That's one way to phrase my sassiness." Her coworker was here as a visitor tonight, and Brooke welcomed the familiar face. "Joe might have phrased it another way, but when you've been married for fifty years, it's all about love, truth and a good jar opener for our favorite pickles."

Hyacinth turned to Mitzi and hovered near the plastic goblets. "Are we partaking of the beverages now or after we paint?"

Mitzi flipped the goblets facedown on the table. "Let's save our toast until later."

"Toast?" Brooke interrupted what was becoming a party rather than a class. She walked over to the easel with two canvases: one a blank slate and the other with the finished product. "Let's get started. This is an introductory art class. We're focusing on something simple. A tulip…"

Hyacinth clapped her hands. "What a gorgeous rendering of a *Tulipa gesneriana*." She then pressed her thumb and finger together and pulled them across her tight lips like a zipper. "You won't hear another peep from me."

Mitzi nudged her friend. "For at least two minutes."

This type of friendship and camaraderie was what Brooke had missed out on all these years. This ribbing with its backbone of support hadn't been a part of her life. She'd had no time, not with multiple jobs, online courses and a son.

"Okay, I'll pass out some materials, and then we'll get started." Brooke watched their interaction and handed out the necessary supplies. Socialization was as much a part of an evening like this as the class itself. Word of mouth would go a long way in boosting awareness of the new programs.

After a few more minutes of allowing them to catch up, she called them together, and each woman found a place behind one of the easels. Brooke made some introductory remarks about reproducing a painting rather than creating an original work of art.

"Then later, you can let me know if you

want to continue painting or if you'd like to try your hand at jewelry making or pottery or some other art form." She then launched into the basic instructions, detailing section by section, and then they dipped their brushes into the paint.

She had chosen this pattern for the painting as it would be next to impossible to mess up. Within minutes, chatter gave way to positive energy. The women let their creative juices flow. She glanced at the clock on the wall, her meeting with Jonathan never out of mind. In spite of everything, Brooke stifled a yawn, the long day catching up with her.

"Brooke, come look at mine and tell me what you think." Betty's excitement was invigorating, and Brooke couldn't wait to see what one of her favorite employees had drawn so far.

"I like it." Brooke gave her an encouraging smile. Then she showed her a different way of holding the brush, and Betty nodded appreciatively.

Brooke worked her way around the room, dropping murmurs of support to each woman until she reached Hyacinth. Then her jaw dropped. "That's not a tulip."

She didn't know whether to turn her head this way or that at the abstract shapes on Hyacinth's canvas. None of them resembled anything like a tulip.

"I know." Hyacinth patted Brooke's arm. Paint dotted the older woman's skin, drips smattering her arm where her smock didn't cover it. "Your tulip is a truly lovely representation of the flower, but art should be expressive and free-flowing. It can't be restrained. It has to be passionate."

Tilting her head, Brooke stopped and examined Hyacinth's canvas once more. While it wasn't the tulip everyone else was painting, it was quite good, bordering on remarkable. "Have you painted before?"

Tina stepped forward and hugged Hyacinth's shoulders. "Hyacinth is rather modest, but she's a wonder. Some of her paintings sold at the art gallery before it closed. Our Hyacinth is a gardener, baker and artist all rolled into one."

"When Craig was sick, I had to keep busy, or I knew I'd drive him insane with my hovering."

Aunt Mitzi leaned over to Brooke. "Craig was her husband," she whispered. "He was retired military and was one of the strongest men I've ever met. He died of cancer."

Fabiana tapped Brooke's shoulder. "Speaking of men, you never told us in the salon the name of the cute guy who caught your eye. If he didn't work out for you, my son, Carlos, is available. He's more than cute, and you'd give him an incentive to move back to town. He's the spitting image of my husband around the time I met Roberto. My husband is still one hot hunk of a firefighter."

"Carlos is definitely cute." Betty confirmed Fabiana's statement.

Brooke couldn't decide if she wanted the ground to open up for a minute to swallow her whole or if she liked the attention. Were they adopting her into their fold? That might not be so bad.

"But my Mason is cuter." Betty finished her sentence. "And also available."

That sinkhole would be a blessing in disguise. "Is everyone done with their masterpieces? During the week of Thanksgiving, The Whitley Community Center is going to have an open house to celebrate Heartsgiving. I'd love to display your artwork. It's all for a good cause. We're starting a new food bank at the center and delivering Thanksgiving meals to five families who need the help."

"I love it." Hyacinth clapped and slipped out of her purple apron. "Put Sweet Shelby's Tea Room down for five pies. Weather permitting, I hope part of your open house will be outside. My dogs, Artemis and Athena, so enjoy a good rousing visit with people."

Aunt Mitzi stepped forward. "Everyone should also look good. Count me in for five vouchers for free haircuts for the whole family." Aunt Mitzi jutted her chin downward. She strode to the cooler, grabbed the bottle of orange juice and unscrewed the cap. "This is a good beginning for the Mimosas. To being creative. May our endeavors inspire each other and all budding artists. You're women I'm proud to call my friends."

Brooke took a long look at the newly established Mimosas, who gathered around the table, accepting goblets from Aunt Mitzi. Even in this short time, Brooke could tell each was a formidable woman, capable of speaking her mind and holding her own. That was what Brooke strived to be someday. The long-ago whispers of those hometown denizens behind her back had left an indelible mark. *She'll never amount to anything, just like her mother.*

She gathered the paintbrushes and started cleaning them with soap and water.

"Hey, Brooke, come get your goblet for the toast," Aunt Mitzi called out across the room.

With a smile, she placed the brushes on a paper towel. Then she wiped her hands dry, walked over and accepted her drink.

"To the Mimosas." Aunt Mitzi held hers aloft as though raising the finest crystal. "To friendships that are as unique and individual as we are."

As soon as Brooke sipped her first taste of the light yet tart mimosa, her cell phone rang. Stepping aside to the hallway, she found it wasn't Colin but Jonathan. He apologized for running a few minutes behind.

"That's perfect. See you then." She slipped the phone into the pocket of her smock and rejoined the group.

"Ooh." Fabiana placed her goblet on the table and scooted over. "Was that Mysterious Cute Guy? I might just start saying MCG for short."

"It was probably her son, Colin." Aunt Mitzi raised an eyebrow before her face softened. "You know what, though? Brooke will tell us everything when she's ready. Maybe it was Colin, maybe it was MCG. I'll back off." Her face expanded into a grin as wide as the canvases. "For now."

JONATHAN ASSESSED THE exterior security features of the community center. Tomorrow, he'd present Brooke with a report of improvements for the outside and see how it compared with hers.

While the lighting was adequate, there should be a visible sign once a security company started monitoring the facility along with a few strategically placed video cameras. Tonight, though, was all about installing the interior surveillance equipment in the lobby. Brooke had consented to this newest measure once he'd outlined his conversation with the sheriff. An extra monitoring system trained on the outside of the men's locker room would hopefully identify any possible suspects.

As of ten thirty, there was only one other car in the lot. Even with Hollydale being a relatively safe area, he worried about an employee in the center this late at night without the new measures in place.

Or was it that the employee was Brooke?

Whistling a favorite tune, he popped the trunk of his squad car and retrieved the video surveillance equipment he'd brought for tonight's installation. He stopped and thought about the last time he whistled. How long had it been? A month or two? It couldn't have been years, could it?

Did this have something to do with Brooke? While he was attracted to her—and who wouldn't be, with her sense of compassion and go-getter attitude—he had a job to do. Her striking appearance captivated him in a way he wouldn't have thought possible. He grabbed the box of equipment, laid it on the asphalt and slammed the trunk.

Regardless of his attraction to Brooke, he still had to try to make a difference. Sitting back and losing control of a situation went against his nature, and he sensed that wasn't Brooke's personality either. Catching himself before he whistled again, he carried the box toward the building. It was one thing to be funny and charming in the walls of his home. It was another to act like anything less than a member of the force in the pursuit of his duty.

Conceited much, Jonathan? He laughed at how he assumed Brooke found him witty and likeable. Not to mention that he came off like a promotional brochure for the police academy.

A click sounded, and light flooded the area. His eyes adjusted to the brightness, and he spotted the motion-detection source. That was one positive he'd stress in his report. The electronic doors slid apart, and he entered with the box.

"Is anyone else here?" he asked as he approached her.

"No. You said not to tell anyone, so I encouraged Betty to leave with the other Mimosas." Brooke slid her gaze from side to side and frowned. "Why are you whispering?"

"I wasn't whis…" He placed the box on the

reception table. "I guess I was. You should make sure you leave the building with another person this late at night."

"I'm confused. I thought I wasn't supposed to tell anyone else about this new development. Besides, like I've told you before, Joe Ruddick, a feisty seventy-years-young, is usually the one who locks up every night. Is there a massive crime wave in Hollydale? I'd prefer to hear about it from you. Or is someone targeting the center?" She popped her hands on her hips, her normal blazer replaced by a ruffled cranberry blouse that brought out the highlights in her dark chestnut hair pulled up in a twist.

He glanced closely at her arms. "Is that paint?"

She looked down, then folded her arms so the splatters weren't as obvious. "Maybe."

"Were you painting walls or a canvas? Are you an artist?"

Brooke's different facets made her that much more intriguing. When this case was behind them, he hoped he'd be able to exchange his uniform for street clothes and ask her out.

Problem was, unlike what he'd intimated at the pumpkin farm, he was never just Officer Maxwell and never just Jonathan. He was always rolled into one mess of a man.

"I taught an art class tonight. My aunt found

a need in the community, and I filled it. There was a good turnout." Her eyes glowed in the dim interior. "Getting them out of here since you said this was urgent was another story. Why the secrecy and why the delay? I thought you were coming back early this morning. I've kept an eye on the locker room and so far no one has gone inside."

He removed the bag, which he'd carefully designed to have the appearance of the first one, along with similar heft and the same fake ID on top. "I interviewed Mr. Floyd, and then other police matters took precedence, but the sheriff and I came up with a plan that relies on that promise you made me. As of now, the perpetrator of this scheme doesn't seem to be any the wiser and still believes his cache is secure. It's safe to assume he doesn't know anyone's onto him." That was too true for Jonathan's liking. A couple of weeks into the investigation and Jonathan was no closer to discovering the criminal's identity than when he'd responded to Eric's accident. "There's an element of risk I hadn't considered when I swore you to secrecy. He might be upset when he finds out we're onto him."

"So, you're saying the center's guests could be in danger?"

Jonathan laid out the equipment needed for

the installation on Betty's desk. "Truthfully, I don't think so. His profile hasn't indicated any signs of being a threat to others."

"I see. You want to trap him in the process of returning for his cache. But why did you bring the evidence back with you?"

"This only looks similar from the side and the top. When he comes for it, he'll grab it or he'll examine it more closely while in the locker room and give himself away." Jonathan walked toward the men's locker room, bag in hand.

Brooke sidestepped him and blocked his path. "If there's a chance he could go haywire when he discovers that's not the same bag, I can't let you proceed with your plan. I won't put anyone at risk in this facility."

Jonathan didn't want her to figure out she was the one he was worried about. They hadn't known each other long, and the underlying pull he felt for her was unmistakable, but everything seemed to be going against them, and he hadn't even returned to Mo's Gas and Bait Stop yet.

For several seconds, they stood off in a heated exchange of gazes. He wanted to crack a joke or kiss her, but he settled for the truth instead. "Your safety matters." He was whispering as he couldn't trust his regular voice.

"If he's aggressive, the one he'll most likely take it out on is the person who found the bag."

"He'll think Joe or Al found it and called you. It's the men's locker room, remember? I don't want either of them in danger."

He melted at her concern for her employees. "We're getting ahead of ourselves. There's no sign he's a physical threat. The sheriff wouldn't have authorized this if he believed there was an increased chance of risk to people. By the way, thank you for getting the signed authorization to install the cameras back to me so quickly." He set the cache inside the locker and replaced the thin metal plate. She led him back to the lobby, where he checked the equipment. "I'll personally review the footage each night."

"Betty can…"

"You can't tell her. If he's local, he might be attuned to the gossip and change his tactics. I have to uncover whether this guy's from the area or is elsewhere and simply using this as a base of operations."

"Don't worry. I won't go back on my promise."

"The installation will take a while, and I'll need access to the electrical box."

She sank into the nearest chair. Her skin went ashen and, for the first time, he noticed a line of cute freckles on her nose. "If I go along with this and someone's hurt, that's on me. But if I don't go along with this, it could take you longer to find out who's behind this, and someone might get hurt."

That summed it up, and he fell into the chair next to her. "I can't promise you we'll catch him, but I'll personally promise you I'll give everything to this case."

She reached over for his hand and squeezed it, her warmth flowing through him. "I don't like either of those alternatives. I have a responsibility to keep every child and adult that crosses that threshold safe."

Child. His heart crashed against his rib cage. Two of the children signed up for Brooke's Heartsgiving program were none other than the people he loved the most. He took a few calming breaths. Assumptions wouldn't get him anywhere. Only cold hard facts would.

"Jumping to conclusions about how far he might go to protect what's been a good thing doesn't help anyone." The police officer in him agreed with this statement. The father in him? He couldn't separate the two as they were one and the same. "Police work is based on hard evidence. The stories I could tell could take hours, so I'll get this installed instead."

"Interesting stories?" In an instant, her enthusiasm rekindled that small flicker of hope that his emotions were waking up after five years of slumber.

Oh, he'd been laughing on the outside, but something inside him was hibernating, and this brunette with her positive energy, radiant and cool at the same time, sparked that flame.

"Some would keep you up all night." He'd seen the gritty side, the moments that would forever leave a scar on his soul.

"When I have a hard day, I go home and make myself a cup of something relaxing, either decaf coffee or herbal tea. Then I eat dinner with Colin and find a favorite movie or TV show that makes me laugh or turn on some soothing jazz music. Something positive to remind me there is always hope and that tomorrow may be a little easier."

She'd just described his perfect evening, what had kept him sane in the past five years. He glanced at her face, her eyes glistening. How he'd found her standoffish and unapproachable that first day, he didn't know. A rare detective instinct misfire.

She touched something that made him want to care about someone again. And he couldn't miss Brooke's tendency to see the good in people. The pumpkin patch proved she brought people together.

As much as he wanted to think that anyone

could have provided that wake-up call rather than the woman beside him, he couldn't. There was something mysterious and alluring about her that pulled him toward her.

This wasn't the time or the place to share his feelings, however. "I need one of your ladders."

She accompanied him to the maintenance room, and he selected a stepladder. She locked the door behind him, and she must have seen the way he stared at the knob. "Before you ask, I personally have started checking them all at night. Joe looked at me rather funny the day I checked every lock twice."

"It sounds like you keep Joe busy."

"He's been my go-to guy for all things mechanical, that's for sure. What's more, he and Betty crack me up with their repartee. Can you imagine being married for fifty years?"

He'd done just that the day he married Anne.

He toted the stepladder to the lobby and stopped to make a note of what she'd said. "It seems security was relatively lax under your predecessor."

"That's one of the reasons Mr. Hinshaw is no longer here." Ray wasn't at home either, when Jonathan had stopped by to interview him about his tenure at the center. Brooke motioned toward the bank of chairs. "Will you be okay for a minute if I call Colin? Even though he'll be sixteen next month, I want to make sure he's not getting in Aunt Mitzi's hair too much. Daisy, too."

"Daisy? Do you have another child lurking around I haven't met yet?"

She laughed and shook her head. "Daisy thinks of herself that way, but she's my labradoodle."

"Go ahead and call. I'll know more by the time you're done." He climbed the ladder and checked the equipment. The wiring was ancient, and he didn't feel up to the task. When she returned, he delivered the bad news. "The center's wiring is different from what I've seen in the past. I wasn't able to finish the installation, but I'll have someone come out and complete this tomorrow night, if that works for you."

She swiped at her cell phone. "I did have something with Colin, but he rescheduled that. He's studying for a test with Riley. I talked to her parents, and they're keeping an eye on them."

He gathered his tools and placed them back in the box. "How are you coping with a son old enough to date? I might ban Izzy from dating until she's thirty."

"Some days are easier than others. He knows he can talk to me about anything, and I trust him." She reached for the stepladder before he stopped her by picking it up first.

"I'll carry this. Not because you're not capable, but because I want to." He smiled and ushered her forward. "So, communication is the key with teenagers?"

She chuckled. "Food helps. He's usually open to talking more on a full stomach."

She inserted her key into the lock and flicked on the light. He lowered the stepladder onto its hook.

"Thanks for the advice." He stopped short of groaning. That was the best line he had? He'd been out of circulation too long.

"I'm glad I could be of assistance." Modulated and precise, her comeback couldn't be classified as romantic banter by any stretch of the imagination. She'd extended a branch all right. A friendship one.

Accepting that would be hard, but he valued Brooke. "You and Colin seem close. That's nice to see."

"He's been great despite all the moves and uncertainty in his life. This is the sixth place he's lived since he started school. Sometimes I wonder if I'm too sensitive about Colin, but that goes more to flashbacks of when I was a scared teenager, pregnant and alone. I lived in a small town, even smaller than Hollydale, and some people were…" Her face seemed tighter, almost pinched as if she was reliving bad memories.

"Were what?"

"Not as nice as you. Some people were rude, mean or judgmental. After Colin was born, I found a job in the next town. We moved, and a few women believed in me and gave me a chance." She waited until he passed back into the hallway before she extinguished the light and locked the door behind her.

"You were alone? Did your parents throw you out?"

"My father was never in the picture, same as Colin's. Enough about me, though." She twisted her hands and thinned her lips. Apparently, she didn't want to pursue this line of questioning. "What about you? Can you talk about Anne? That was your wife's name, right?"

Even with the low lighting of the corridor, he could tell her face was flushed. Pleased at her remembering that important detail about his life, he tried to put her at ease. "She died five years ago."

He waited for that familiar tug that accompanied him telling someone he was a widower, but none came.

"I'm sorry." A simple statement, and her softness was reassuring and genuine.

"Thanks." They reached the lobby, and he made a beeline toward the box of equipment.

"How did she die?"

"What time can you be here tomorrow night?"

Their voices overlapped, and he gestured for her to go first. "I can stay late again. Aunt Mitzi is more than capable of, well, anything. In fact, Colin and Daisy will be fine for a little bit longer tonight." She led him to the wall of chairs and settled in, curling her long legs underneath her. "If you don't mind telling me, I'd like to hear more about you. But are you still on duty?"

"I'm done with my shift. Returning the cache was something I wanted to do, needed to do."

"It's taken me a long time to be able to talk about how young I was when I had Colin." She rolled her eyes. "I see what you mean about the past. I haven't brought this up for ages, so I understand if you don't want to talk to me about Anne."

"It's not you." He didn't want her to think that. Talking to her was different. Maybe his family took their cues from his refusing to bring up her death around them, but somehow, she was different. "I've put up a wall on purpose."

Whenever Izzy and Vanessa had questions about that fateful afternoon, he hedged any details, preferring to pass on happier stories of their mother to them. They were young and didn't need their good memories erased by him recounting her final moments for them. Besides, Anne wouldn't have wanted them to dwell on her death.

"Then it might be good for you to talk about it with someone new."

"That's just it, though. We haven't known each other long." He shifted his weight on the hard, cold chair with a sliver of moonlight coming through the domed skylight.

"You have an air about you. Open, like you've been friends with someone for ages."

As much as he'd love to take credit for that, part of this openness was because of her. Communication with Brooke came without effort. He hadn't felt this way about a woman in years.

"She died in a car accident."

Her gaze remained on him as she shifted her legs under her. "It sounds like there's more to the story."

"It's not pretty." He should know. He'd run past the mangled metal, past the steam wisping out of the engine, to the door half ajar from the impact.

"I'm not powdered sugar."

He glanced at her, her amber-brown eyes expressive, almost pleading with him for the rest. Was there already a connection between them? He didn't know, but Frederick Whitley hired a gem when he chose her.

"I was a detective in Savannah when I noticed someone driving erratically on the interstate." He'd recalled this story so many times during police interviews after the fact that he'd started speaking in the same tone he used on the witness stand. Objective and neutral rather than as Anne's husband. Talking with Brooke, however, the emotion flowed through him once more. He no longer sounded like a robot but a grieving widower. "I called it in but, in that split second, the driver crossed the center line and crashed head-on into another car. Afterward, the driver admitted he'd fallen asleep at the wheel and that his license had been suspended for the same behavior."

Her eyes clouded with concern. "You witnessed your wife's accident?"

"Anne was on her way to pick Izzy and Vanessa up from school when the other driver hit her." He hesitated but continued, "I couldn't get there in time to stop the accident."

He jumped up, not wanting to look into her eyes. Pity and sympathy were always the two main reactions when someone found out he'd witnessed his wife's fatal car crash. That, and a reassuring pat on the arm or clap on the back. Months after the accident, he'd wanted someone to treat him like Jonathan, still alive, still breathing, still worthy of love.

That was one reason he moved away from Savannah. Too many memories haunted the dripping moss of Anne's favorite Southern live oak trees, the soft white sand of the beaches, their old house with the leaky main bathroom faucet he always promised to fix and never did.

He grabbed the box and strode to the entrance. The front door was locked, though, and he had to wait for Brooke to unlock it. "What about you, though?" Brooke asked. "Are you okay?"

He faced her. "I usually get an 'I'm sorry' followed by cooed murmurs of consolation. That is, if the person doesn't smile, nod and run for the hills."

"Understandable reactions, but I'm asking about you." She wiggled the keys and stepped on the sensor. The door slid open. "You can run for the hills, or you can talk. Your decision."

Why was this woman, this complicated, unexpected surprise, reaching those parts he'd closed off?

He set the box down and moved out of the way of the electronic eye.

"That first day? Signing the organ donation form was the moment it hit me Anne wasn't coming back." He took a deep breath and tried to slow his thoughts. "A couple of years ago, though, I received a letter from the heart recipient's mother, who wrote me the night of her daughter's wedding about what organ donation meant to her family."

"Was that one of the hard days or one of the better?"

"Both." He'd admitted more to her than he had to Caleb, his cousin and best friend. While he was on the subject of difficult admissions, he'd best be truthful about Izzy and Vanessa. He picked up the box and winced at what he had to get off his chest. "As a matter of fact, I'm thinking of withdrawing my daughters from your program."

A muscle in her jaw clenched. "They'll be here in broad daylight with trained staff all around them. I treat every child that comes through these doors like I treat Colin, and every adult the way I'd want to be treated." Her eyes reflected the honesty behind every word. "You want to know me, look around you. This center is important to me, and I'm dedicated to making it a haven for some, a fun place to hang out for others."

These weren't phony lines. This was her personality, a peek at the real Brooke, fiery and passionate underneath the cool facade.

He had to take a lesson from her playbook and become more reserved and cautious. He couldn't pursue anything with her. Not right now. Then there were all the what-ifs in his life he had to get under control. What if they hired the other candidate as detective? What if the perpetrator behind the fake IDs became violent?

What if he lowered his shield of corny jokes and one-liners and let her see the real Jonathan?

"I'll wait to make sure you leave safely. Good night." He fled to his squad car without giving her the chance to say another word.

He slammed the trunk door and groaned. What just happened? Had it been so long since he'd been attracted to anyone other than Anne he'd forgotten how to act around a woman as interesting and caring as Brooke? Had his heart shriveled to a size smaller than the Grinch's? At least the Grinch had a heart at the beginning.

He'd have to go back. He ran away, and he knew it. Casting doubt on her abilities when all she'd done was ask him about his feelings about Anne was low. She seemed to genuinely care when so many gave him a cursory "poor Jonathan." With a glance over his shoulder, he stood motionless as one by one the lights of the building went out.

Maybe he wasn't afraid something would happen to Izzy and Vanessa as much as he was afraid something else could happen to another person he cared about under his watch. Maybe he cared too much already, which was ridiculous considering they'd only met, and not under the best of circumstances at that.

All he had to do was get in the car and wait to make sure she drove off safely. That was the easy choice, the choice that would keep him from risking loss again. She exited the building, her purse in hand.

Eating crow wasn't as tasty as his favorite chocolate puff cereal, but even he knew he needed to make things right.

That was the easy part. The hard part would be doing everything within his control to keep from falling for her.

CHAPTER EIGHT

BROOKE LOCKED THE automatic door and double checked it for good measure, her heart rate slowly returning to its normal even keel. This night hadn't gone the way she'd hoped.

For a while, she sensed something different about Jonathan, a spark between them unlike any she'd experienced before. But tonight he cast doubt on her. Well, on her abilities, but those were one and the same. He didn't trust her with his children. If the people of this town didn't trust her with their time and lives, how could she make a difference for them?

"Brooke."

She jumped. She faced Jonathan, her hand over her chest, her heart thumping faster than ever. "You scared the living daylights out of me. I thought you were watching from your police car."

"Sorry about that. I guess I've worked on my stealth skills too long. Two daughters will do that to you."

The street lights overhead caught the twinkle in his hazel eyes, radiating security but still holding a wicked amount of charm, before his shoulders slumped. She couldn't tell whether he looked younger with the top button of his uniform shirt unbuttoned or older without the smile she already associated with him.

Once she calmed herself, Brooke pushed the strap of her tote bag, containing her tablet and other resources, to the top of her shoulder. Her composure had served her well these past few years. "You'll do fine as a parent of teenagers if you keep up your stealth."

"But I'd be remiss as a person if I left without apologizing. From what I've seen, you're a welcome addition to Hollydale. I'm sorry I doubted you."

She blinked, his apology throwing her for a loop. The lights were brighter than the dim interior of the center. That must be why her eyes were stinging. "Thank you. Have a good evening."

"I'll walk you to your car."

Her protest died on her lips, and she accepted his courtesy as merely that, a nice gesture from a police officer doing his duty. They fell in step beside one another, that comfortable kind of walking that always made the distance seem shorter than it was. And yet, what she felt for him went beyond comfort. This electricity was new, and she didn't trust it.

She pressed the keyless remote for her trusty compact from a couple of yards away, the ping-ping breaking the silence. When they reached the driver's side, she shuffled her feet, too conscious of him as a person, more than just the uniform he wore.

"If you're worried…"

They said the same words in unison.

She met his gaze and laughed. He held out his palm as an obvious gesture for her to go first, so she did. "If you're worried about your daughters' safety at the center for the week of Heartsgiving, drop by this weekend for our first annual Trunk or Treat. That should give you an idea of the center's energy as well as some of the new safety measures."

"If it's anything to do with Halloween, that sounds right up Vanessa's alley." He grinned, and this time the smile touched his eyes. "When and what is it?"

"On Saturday night, it's a fun event with a contest where people decorate the back of their SUVs or the trunk of their cars with a theme of their choice. Most will wear costumes to match and give out candy or treats to the other guests. They can take a break to look at the cars and collect candy for themselves. The center will award a prize for the best decorated trunk and the best costume. The cars will remain in a roped-off area so everyone can walk around safely. I'm also handing out tote bags and talking up our new activities." She glanced at the area that would be transformed into a Halloween funfest soon. "Guess we didn't advertise well enough if you didn't know about it."

"I've been busy. Now that I've heard about it, we'll try to drop in."

Once again, that smile was too endearing. She fumbled with the keyless fob before dropping it, the clang on the asphalt echoing in the still night. She bent down at the same time he did, and her head banged into his. "Ouch."

She grasped the fob, and they rose at the same time.

He stepped toward her. "Are you okay? If I've been told once, I've been told a thousand times I have a hard head."

He was close enough for her to smell soap and sweat and pine trees rolled into one. For a second, she stopped breathing and stared at his kissable lips. Was he going to kiss her?

His head neared hers, and she licked her lips. It had been a long time since she'd kissed a man. Online courses while working multiple jobs, dud dates and Colin were the tip of the iceberg about why she hadn't dated more in the recent past.

Then he stepped back, and she found her breath once more. He rubbed the edge of his uniform sleeve. "I just wanted to make sure you were safe leaving here by yourself at night. It's my duty as an officer."

The grin left his face, and her chest ached. He hadn't wanted to kiss her after all.

"Thank you, Officer Maxwell." His title was a good reminder of his presence at the facility tonight. If the fake ID mastermind was using the center as his drop-off location, she'd have a hard time explaining to Frederick Whitley why she chose to keep the police operation a secret from him, and a harder time keeping her job.

Another move wasn't in her future. Keeping this professional and businesslike was for the best. She'd made a promise to Officer Maxwell, and she'd honor her word.

He dipped his head and stepped back while she slid into the driver's seat and drove home. As she made her way to Aunt Mitzi's front door, the screech of a night owl cut through the air, the three subtle calls a reminder of the late hour. She unlocked the door, and Daisy jumped on her, a greeting of sorts. Her dog always provided a happy welcome at the end of the day.

Brooke reached over and turned off the porch light, and the living room was bathed in darkness. "Good girl." Daisy barked, and Brooke raised her finger to her lips. "Shh. I don't want you to wake up Aunt Mitzi."

Someone switched on a light, and Brooke adjusted her eyes to the brightness. Aunt Mitzi sat on the sofa, sipping from her glass of water, her gaze showing every expectation of receiving some juicy tidbit about Brooke's boring, nonexistent love life.

"Too late. I'm wondering if Mysterious Cute Guy has anything to do with why your cheeks are pink."

"Sorry. Nothing for the beauty salon tomorrow."

Hurt flashed in Aunt Mitzi's eyes. "Brooke Amber. Do you really think I only asked that so I could gossip about you?"

Her cheeks warmed. "Old habits."

Aunt Mitzi shifted on the couch, and Daisy left Brooke's side and leaped onto the cushion next to Mitzi.

Traitor dog. "See you tomorrow."

"Brooke, you know you're not alone anymore, right?"

Her throat constricted. It had been a long time since anyone had said anything like that to her. "For years, I've had to depend on myself."

"I'm sorry I didn't offer my spare room earlier. You could have finished your online degree anywhere."

Brooke shrugged but kept her distance. "I was supporting Colin."

"More like you needed to make sure no one stole from you again." Aunt Mitzi took another sip. "Yes, I know what my sister did to get rent money."

"If it had just been for the rent, I could have understood." Instead, her mother had blown Brooke's hard-earned dollars on a week of partying.

"I'm sorry. I should have interfered, but I was reeling from finding out about Dwayne's infidelity."

"We were both betrayed by people we loved." Another bond, but one she wouldn't characterize as good.

"I learned a long time ago it's easier to get through hard times with a friend. I don't know what I'd have done without Patsy Appleby."

"Your friends think the world of you."

Aunt Mitzi placed her glass on the end table and petted Daisy, who leaned into the touch. "It's taken a long time to build those friendships. Most good things don't happen overnight. Hyacinth sometimes comes off like a chatterbox, but she's fierce. Tina's tough, and Fabiana? If she's in your corner, watch out. She's feisty and loyal. And you know Betty after working with her for a couple of weeks."

The warmth from Brooke's cheeks spread to the rest of her. "I'm going to turn in."

"Don't be afraid to ask for help, Brooke. I'm here." She scratched behind Daisy's ear and winked. "Except when I'm out with Owen. I love you, you know."

"Sometimes it helps to hear the words." Brooke headed upstairs, her aunt's talk comforting and disconcerting at the same time. She'd almost forgotten what it was like to be able to depend on family. While Colin was an old soul, growing up fast, faster than she realized now that he was dating, she'd never hindered him with details about bills and tuition payments.

Aunt Mitzi, though, listened and cared. That wasn't something she was used to. Daisy bounded beside her, nudging Brooke's hand with her snout. Brooke obliged the cute gesture for attention, made all the more poignant by people who were starting to accept her. Needing someone wasn't what she often did, but maybe being in Hollydale was the place to start.

CHAPTER NINE

THE FIRST FROST of the season brought a bite to the air. Jonathan relished the coolness against his cheeks while appreciating the orange and maroon foliage of the maples along Creekside Road in front of Mo's Gas and Bait Stop. Officer Jillian Edwards exited the passenger side of Jonathan's squad car and joined him with six photographs under her arm.

"It's days like today when I miss Florida." She pretended to shiver.

"Nah, this is a beautiful morning." Especially compared to the lake-effect snow already falling in Chicago. It would be that much more beautiful if this photo lineup proved Colin's innocence. "Thanks for interviewing Mo for me."

Since he was the lead investigator on the case, rules prevented him from showing Mo the pictures. Jillian didn't know which picture was Colin's or the identities of any of the other five juveniles featured in the snapshots.

"Hold these for a minute, will you?" She

handed him the photos before taking off her hat and adjusting her medium-length dark hair held back in a ponytail. Once she replaced her hat, he returned the photos to her. "Any chance you'd consider switching shifts this weekend?"

All officers were required on duty with tourists flooding the town, and he had the night shift, which extended into the wee hours of the morning. "You're scheduled after me in the daytime, aren't you?"

"I could use the premium pay, though." Jillian frowned, slight wrinkles marring her young forehead.

"Can you find someone to stay with your mom at night? How's she doing?" Everyone in the department knew Jillian cared for her mother, who had early-onset dementia.

"Not good, and it's easier to get someone to watch her in the evening." He and Jillian approached the entrance. "The extra money if we traded shifts would come in handy. So I don't have to find a roommate when the time comes to put her in assisted living."

Jillian looked at him with some expectation. The members of the department had each other's backs. Mike led by example. If he switched with her, he'd miss Izzy's soccer game, but he'd have an opportunity to attend the Trunk or Treat with both his daughters. "Sure."

They entered the shop, and the stench of bait was particularly biting today.

"Two cops for the price of one! Good thing my customers don't expect that deal on night crawlers. I'd go broke quick." Mo laughed at his joke.

Jillian approached the counter, and Jonathan hovered behind, letting her do her work. "With your permission, I'll show you six photos, and you tell me if any match the person who came in with the false ID and tried to buy cigarettes."

"Sure thing." Mo scratched behind his ear. "No offense, Officer Edwards, but why are you the one showing me the pictures?"

"Officer Maxwell—" Jillian pointed in his direction "—is the lead investigator on the case. He selected the photos and marked each with a soft pen for identifying purposes, but I don't know any of the individuals or the identity of the suspect, so I won't give anything away."

"Makes sense." Mo nodded and reached for the photos. "It might be number three, but it might be four or five, too. Definitely not the first two or the last one."

Jonathan and Jillian thanked him for his time and proceeded back to the station in relative silence until they reached the conference room, where Mike waited. Jillian's walkie-talkie crackled with activity from Harriet. "Roger that. On my way. Over." She stood and headed for the door, halting with her hand on the knob. "Run our schedule switch by Mike, okay?"

She hustled away, and Mike turned an expectant eye toward Jonathan, who filled him in on the schedule change and the morning's events.

"So, Mo didn't identify a suspect." Mike's lips flattened to a straight line.

"And the DMV was no help. Unless the suspect comes to the center to retrieve the contents of the locker, I have no other leads."

A hunch the suspect wouldn't give up a good thing, though, wouldn't carry enough weight to prolong the investigation.

Mike shrugged as Jonathan's walkie-talkie crackled, too. Jonathan held up his device and listened to Harriet. He rolled his eyes. "I have to go round up Mr. Bricker's cow again. I swear I'm going to patch that fence myself one of these days."

"Drop by my office after Bessie's back home."

"Just glad Bessie's always at the next farm." Jonathan laughed and donned his hat. "Why does the urban cop get the farm calls?"

"You have a way with women and animals. Georgie, Rachel and Ginger are all I can handle." Mike chuckled, his face reflecting the happiness it always did when he talked about his wife, his daughter or his cat. His boss lifted his chin to indicate he was dismissed. "See you later."

Great. A Thursday afternoon of cattle roundup and no progress on the fake ID case. Jonathan left the conference room, the day's events not lost on him. Colin's face had graced photo number three. Mo might not have pinpointed the youth, but he hadn't cleared Colin either.

BROOKE COULDN'T HAVE planned a better fall day for the Trunk or Treat event. The blue skies held nary a wisp of a white cloud on this gorgeous Saturday, with the maple and hickory trees putting on a beautiful show. Families milled about the community center, talking and enjoying themselves. She already recognized some of the folks, while others visiting sought a fun activity to pass the time in Hollydale. Brooke was only too happy to oblige.

She adjusted her red headband, part of her Rosie the Riveter costume. She stood in front of a slow cooker, disguised as a bubbling cauldron. "Caramel apples. Absolutely free." Older kids and adults received whole apples while she distributed slices to the younger crowd. The sweet smell of the caramel was too tempting, and she'd sneaked a few Granny Smith slices in the past hour.

A little girl dressed as a butterfly smiled at Brooke. "I'd like some, please."

Brooke checked with her parents, who nodded their permission. Brooke dipped the ends of several slices in the cauldron and waited for the excess to drip away before handing the adorable girl a cardboard container with the treat. "For the butterfly, two slices, light on the caramel, heavy on the sweetness." She turned to the parents. "Would either of you like a sample?"

They shook their heads, but no one left her booth empty-handed. She gave them a tote bag featuring the center's new logo. Each contained a flyer of today's itinerary along with upcoming events, a sponsorship form and a water bottle. "There are some great dancing programs in the winter for preschoolers and early elementary students."

The family walked away, and Brooke waved at them as they left before counting the remaining bags. Less than ten remained. Foot traffic had been brisk all afternoon, although the trio of Maxwells hadn't been among those who'd stopped by her booth. Most of the Mimosas, though, had found time to come by, including Fabiana, who'd introduced her husband, and Hyacinth with her two boxers. While Aunt Mitzi had to work, she planned to help with the cleanup, along with Colin. Today was his big day as he was trying out for the Hollydale High basketball team. She crossed her fingers and then checked her phone in case she'd missed a text.

No news yet.

Olivia walked by, and Brooke hailed her. After chatting and exchanging updates, Olivia stayed at the booth while Brooke headed toward the building for more bags. Taking her time outside, Brooke strolled by the cars for a closer look and a breath of fresh air. The creativity astounded her. She wanted to linger at the Alice in Wonderland display but kept walking, intent once more on fetching the bags. Chuckling at the Mad Scientist with dry ice bubbling out of beakers with colored water, she bumped into a hard something. Apologizing, she turned and found green arms connected to an inflatable dinosaur costume, reaching out to steady her.

"Sorry I wasn't looking where I was going." *Some director she was.*

"Are you okay, Brooke?"

"Jonathan?" She glanced beside him, and Vanessa's giggles revealed the panda was his younger daughter. Isabella glared at her and crossed her bare arms, her soccer uniform performing double duty as a costume.

"You made it." Her voice sounded light, almost giddy.

His muscular arms holding her up were rather strong. It felt good to have someone to help support her for a minute. Then realization she was on duty made her jump back.

"That's J. rex today, thank you very much." He boomed a dinosaur roar.

Vanessa tapped Brooke's arm. "Who are you supposed to be?"

"I'm Rosie the Riveter." The blank expression on Vanessa's face compelled Brooke to explain. "She's a symbol of determination, of women coming together in a community and accomplishing anything they set their mind on doing. She became famous during the Second World War."

"Oh. That's neat." Vanessa expressed her approval before tapping her cheek like her father. "I can like that and pandas at the same time, right?"

"Absolutely. Someone with a heart as big as yours can find room in your heart for more than one thing. Liking one doesn't mean you have to stop liking the other." She glanced at Jonathan, and her cheeks heated. "I have to retrieve a box of tote bags. Have fun walking around."

"Do you need some help?" Jonathan removed his dinosaur head, his hair adorably rumpled.

"Dad, you promised." Isabella stomped her sneaker. "When you told us you switched shifts and couldn't make my soccer game, you said this would be a *family* outing."

Brooke shuffled her feet encased in brown boots as part of her Rosie costume. "I need to get back to work."

"Wait a second. Isabella, you owe Brooke an apology." Jonathan nudged his daughter's side. "She was just being nice."

"Sorry."

While not the sincerest utterance ever, Brooke accepted the gesture. "Thank you." She started to walk away. "Hold on." Jonathan waved his dinosaur arms and raised his voice. "Aunt Tina! Over here!"

Brooke couldn't help but laugh until Tina Spindler showed up on the scene, dressed as a park ranger. Tina and Jonathan were related?

"I should have known my favorite greatnieces couldn't stay away from me. By the way, great goal, Izzy!" Tina gave Isabella a high-five. She turned to Jonathan and then glanced at Brooke. "Oh, hello there."

"I didn't know Jonathan was your nephew."

The way Tina arched her eyebrow showed off the family resemblance Brooke hadn't noted before now. "Come to think of it," Tina said, mirth in her voice, "I should have thrown Jonathan's name out there with the rest of the potential possibilities. It might be the aunt in me, but he's every bit as good-looking as Mason Ruddick and can even hold a candle to Drew and Caleb."

"I don't know what you're talking about, Aunt Tina, but thanks for holding me in such high company." He planted his dinosaur hood back on his shoulders. "Brooke needs some help for a minute. Can you take Izzy and Vanessa around to the different cars? You'll be able to tell when I'm back. J. rex isn't hard to spot in a crowd."

Brooke groaned. "Maybe on the way to the storage room we'll discuss that nickname of yours. There has to be something better."

Jonathan stepped toward her. "Ooh. The storage room. That sounds interesting."

"Dad!" Both girls protested at once.

"I was joking. Brooke is working, and I'm helping her." He held up those short dinosaur arms. "Besides, I might take a detour to the men's locker room and use the facilities."

Brooke's ego deflated faster than popped bubble gum. Here she'd thought he wanted to be alone with her, and instead his real motive was to check to see if anyone had tampered with the locker.

"Then it's a good thing I have the key since I locked that room this morning." She reached into the side pocket of her denim pants, a far cry from the skinny jeans she preferred. "There are restrooms available at the main entrance, but the gym and the other areas are off-limits." She turned to Jonathan's daughters. "I'll have him outside and with you again in no time."

She rattled the keys and caught sight of Tina, whose face was the picture of smug. Something told her Tina had pieced together the identity of Mysterious Cute Guy, something Brooke wanted to keep to herself awhile longer.

JONATHAN OPENED THE side door for a large group exiting the center, his gaze never leaving Brooke, a red bandanna hiding her hair but helping her stand out even more. His heart had raced when he'd first caught sight of her. Whether she wore her customary work suit or her Halloween costume, her radiance came through.

"Where are the tote bags?"

"In the supply closet upstairs. It's taken me two weeks to figure out what Betty means by the supply closet versus the storage room, but didn't you want to check the men's locker room first?" She pointed that way, and he remembered he'd mentioned the room as an excuse to spend some time with her. Her gaze swept over him, and she blinked. "Sorry. That dinosaur costume is distracting."

Now that they were inside, he removed his inflatable T. rex head once more. "I forgot about it. In a town this size, people know what I do, and they ask all sorts of questions. Things like whether an alarm system or a big dog is a better deterrent to a burglar. I wanted some uninterrupted time with Izzy and Vanessa."

A guilty look came over her face. "I can handle the tote bags. It's not that big a deal, and they aren't that heavy."

He reached for her hand, pulling her to a stop. "I like spending time with friends." He interlaced his fingers with hers, noticing her soft skin. "It's important to be myself without labels."

She didn't let go.

They arrived at the men's locker room, and he released her with a little bit of reluctance and a lot of satisfaction. He stayed behind her while she selected the key. Her gasp startled him. "What's wrong?" Jonathan asked.

She moved aside, and his gaze went to the posted Closed sign. Then the problem confronted him like a splash of cold water. Long scratches marred the wood between the knob and the jamb.

"Do I need to report this? When I checked this morning, everything was still in place, and I thought the lock and the public event would keep someone from trying to access the lockers. I was wrong. I need to call off the rest of the event, don't I?" Worry cut through Brooke's words, and she glanced out the window. "Security first. I'll go make an announcement."

He reached for her arm and held her back. "Wait a minute." He glanced at the video camera above the reception desk, the red light flashing. "Let's see if anyone was able to pick the lock, and I'll call Sheriff Harrison. We'll see how he wants to proceed."

"Won't I be destroying any evidence if I unlock the door?"

Jonathan adjusted his costume and reached inside for the close-fitting green gloves that resembled claws and donned them. "The day isn't cold enough to wear these, but they should keep me from disturbing any fingerprints."

She handed him the keys, and he unlocked the door, waving her inside. He strode to the back and glanced at the showers and sinks. No damage or sign of any use. He met her at the lockers.

"According to the estimates this week, the cost of adding combination locks is rather steep. Although, I'm sure people will feel safer about leaving their valuables while exercising."

"Until the suspect comes back for the bag, I'm rather grateful you aren't adding them yet. Can you stand near the door for a minute and keep anyone who disregards the sign out of here?" Jonathan waited until Brooke stood guard.

He opened the specific locker and wiggled the false back away for a check. The bag was still in place. "It's here. He didn't gain access. I'll review the video footage personally tonight."

Brooke reached for the knob. "Can I run upstairs to get the tote bags while you call the sheriff? If you're concerned someone might disturb you, I'll lock the door, and when you knock, I'll let you out."

He cracked a smile. "Good thing I trust you. I'd hate to be in here all night, but can you make it quick? Otherwise, Izzy and Vanessa will think I deserted them."

"I'll be right back." A rosy bloom blossomed on her cheeks, and he liked seeing this side of her she kept hidden. "Pinky swear."

He called Mike, who concurred it would do the center more harm than good if they closed down the event over this incident. Jonathan would fill out the report later. He then knocked on the door, and Brooke answered, slightly out of breath, a box full of tote bags at her feet. She reached down, and he threw his dinosaur head atop the bags.

"Nope. Can't have you carrying all this around."

"But how will Isabella and Vanessa find you in the crowd without your head?"

"I'll find them."

She locked the door and double checked before they proceeded to the side exit. A friendly bark greeted them when they crossed the threshold. A shaggy ball of fur, all legs, bounded toward them with Colin hanging on to the leash. This time the teen matched his gray hoodie with a pair of black athletic shorts. Riley kept pace beside him, wearing a popular superhero costume. The dog closed the gap and jumped on Brooke.

"Daisy! Down!" Brooke spoke with authority, and Daisy sat, her tongue lolling, her long body quivering with excitement. "Hey, you."

Colin handed her the retractable leash. "Aunt Mitzi let me know she was running late, so I walked Daisy over. I texted Riley, and she met me here."

"Good thing, too!" Riley let out a small laugh and showed off her superhero costume, which was quite popular as Jonathan had seen at least three others wearing the same disguise. "He saved my skin a couple of minutes ago."

"Oh?"

Jonathan set the box on the sidewalk beside him and listened to Riley's story of colliding with an excited child whose soda spilled all over Riley's original pirate costume. "I wondered what was going on when he asked me to watch Daisy for a minute. I didn't expect him to lend me his costume. Isn't he the sweetest thing?"

Riley sidled up to Colin and hugged his arm. No sooner did Jonathan pick up the box than Izzy and Vanessa found him. Izzy sent a silent glare his way.

"Daddy." Vanessa pulled at his costume. "You have to see my favorite trunk. It's decorated to look like the solar system. They're giving out mini kaleidoscopes instead of candy. That's so neat, don't you think?"

Brooke handed the leash back to Colin and reached for the box. "I can take it from here."

She stepped toward him and took the box before Jonathan could object. Vanessa dragged him away, and Izzy smirked a little too smugly. Tonight, he and Izzy would sit down and have a long overdue talk about her behavior around Brooke.

It was time for him to start dating again.

And there was one woman who had caught his attention in an intriguing way. After he examined the video footage, he'd call Brooke. Pleased with his plan, he oohed and aahed with Vanessa at the inventive trunk.

The rest of the day was a blur until his daughters were in bed. He still hadn't had a chance to talk to Izzy, but tomorrow was Sunday. He had a standing date with Izzy and Vanessa at Holly Days Diner for a tall stack of pancakes with a side order of sausage. He'd bring up Izzy's attitude while Vanessa studied what was on offer in the jukebox. Licking his lips in anticipation, he settled at his office computer and pulled up the video footage from the center. He reached for a handful of buttered popcorn, his favorite snack, and made himself comfortable in his padded chair. He could be in for a long couple of hours. Opening his favorite music, he selected the alternative station to make the most of the time.

Before he knew it, he'd eaten the whole bowl

and not one person had shaken the doorknob of the men's locker room. A couple of men in gym shorts stopped and read the sign, turning away, their frustration evident. Jonathan yawned and wondered if it was too late to text Brooke when someone in a costume approached the door. The hairs on the back of his neck prickled, and he straightened his spine, the empty bowl clattering to the floor.

The person in question glanced around the empty reception area, and Jonathan paused the video, making notes about the time stamp. He ran to the kitchen and collected the tote bag Vanessa insisted on bringing home over Izzy's protests. Returning to the office, he located the paper with the itinerary of the day's events. According to the time stamp and the schedule, the suspect neared the door at two thirty, while Brooke was awarding prizes on the dais.

He resumed the video with the suspect rattling the door, only to find it was, indeed, locked. The suspect glanced around, pulled out a flat black wallet with a nick at the corner and tried the old credit card trick. When that didn't work, he stuck his wallet into his rear pocket and made his way over to the reception desk, coming back with a ruler. He scratched the door and then banged it with his fist. Jonathan enlarged the suspect's face, but the mask prevented any identification.

Nonetheless, Jonathan closed his eyes and groaned. He'd seen a similar, if not duplicate, costume today on Riley, whose words came back clear. That wasn't her costume.

She'd borrowed it from Colin.

CHAPTER TEN

MOST OF THE TIME, Jonathan loved living in Hollydale. Eleven months out of the year, there was nowhere else he'd rather live. Nothing was quite so gorgeous as the sight of the leaves showing their glorious fall foliage. Trouble was that the tourists agreed with him and flooded the town for six straight weeks. And now, it seemed as though every one of them had discovered the joys of his favorite Sunday breakfast joint. He shifted the buzzer the server handed him when they arrived two minutes ago from his right hand to his left, not sure he could wait outside in this line for at least a half hour for a cup of coffee.

"Are you certain you don't want me to call Caleb?" Izzy and Vanessa stopped staring at their tablets from the comfort of the bench overlooking the crowded parking lot and glanced his way. "You love his pancakes as much as the diner's."

Vanessa looked torn at his offer. "Caleb does make chocolate milk come out my nose."

She made that sound like a good thing. Izzy shot him a look of pure exasperation. "This is our family time. We're already going trick-or-treating with them this week since you have to work."

"Isa…" Before the last two syllables of her name stumbled out of his mouth, he caught sight of Brooke and Colin navigating through a crowd of people milling around the restaurant's entrance. The mother and son headed their way, a buzzer similar to Jonathan's in Brooke's hand.

If he thought the trees wore burgundy well, they had nothing on Brooke in her burgundy coat that accented her figure. His heartbeat accelerated at her smile, which showcased plump, pink, kissable lips. In such a short time, he'd found brief glimpses of her intriguing. He wanted those to become longer stretches of time.

As soon as he wrapped up this case and heard the outcome of who was getting the detective job, there were two things he needed to get under control. He'd make that priority one.

"Good morning, I thought I heard a familiar voice, and here you are. We've been waiting for about fifteen minutes on the other side. Aunt Mitzi told us about the diner's breakfast. When I saw the spinach-and-artichoke-egg-white omelet on the menu, I knew Colin and I had to brave the crowds." Brooke made a healthy dish sound like the most delicious offering.

He could get used to her positivity.

"It's not usually this crowded on a Sunday morning." Even without his normal cup of coffee, Jonathan enjoyed how Brooke changed the wait into something bearable.

Then he remembered the video footage from last night, and his smile faded. Tomorrow morning, at the conclusion of his shift, he had a meeting with Mike to discuss whether they had enough circumstantial evidence to request Brooke's and Colin's presence at the station.

And that would end any type of relationship with her before it began.

"I don't mind waiting outside. The fresh air is so invigorating. So far, I've talked to a couple of parents about Heartsgiving." Brooke beamed.

"I can take my mother out of her office, but I can't take the office out of my mother." Colin jammed his hands in the pockets of his hoodie before shrugging. "Then again, she loves what she does. There are worse things than that."

"Yeah, like having to work all the time." Izzy piped up, and Jonathan sent an arched eyebrow her way.

"But having a father who cares about you?"

Colin's tone was wistful. "You shouldn't complain about that."

"He's gone so much." Izzy rose from the bench and glanced at Colin with something almost akin to hero worship in her eyes.

Jonathan started to speak up, but Brooke's light touch on his arm held him back. Colin laughed and rubbed his stomach. "Well, believe me, it's nice to have food on the table. Sometimes Mom worked two jobs to pay for her tuition and everything else we needed, but she's always been there for me."

Maybe Brooke's son was conveying more to Izzy in this brief exchange than Jonathan could in twenty long conversations.

"Excuse me, Miss Novak? Oh, hi, Jonathan. Almost didn't see you and the girls. Morning." Jonathan waved at their usual server, Jolene, her blonde beehive as starched as her light pink uniform with a hot pink apron stretched across her waist. She turned toward Brooke. "We had a lot of couples ahead of you, so all the two-seaters were just occupied. We did have a big booth open up if there's anyone here you'd like to eat with. Thought I'd ask, seeing as you're local and all."

The shy smile that spread over Brooke seemed to take over her entire body. "Thank you—" she squinted at the white name tag "—Jolene. That's the nicest thing anyone could have said to me."

Vanessa pulled on his jacket. "Daddy, my tummy is hungry. Ask if we can be the people she eats with."

Brooke leaned down. "I'd like that very much."

Within minutes, they were hanging their coats on the hooks next to the booth, where Izzy claimed a seat on the cracked red pleather next to Colin. Jonathan didn't even want to think about Izzy developing crushes and noticing boys. Good thing Colin seemed to take her under his wing, as an older brother would.

Jonathan gritted his teeth. How could he think Colin Novak was a troubled kid one minute and a straight shooter the next? Jolene brought over a pot of coffee, and he sent a grateful smile her way when she turned over his cup and filled it to the top. "You're a godsend, Jolene." Then he turned to Brooke. "Thanks for inviting us to join you two."

"Daddy says his bloodstream is just liquid caffeine," Vanessa blurted out, and his face heated.

Colin laughed. "My mom's the same way. Aunt Mitzi made sure she had at least two cups of coffee before we came here."

Now, it was Brooke's turn to blush, a nice

complement to the rich burgundy silk top that brought out her coloring. "It's my biggest vice."

Jolene laid the pot on the table, whipped out her pad and took everyone's order. Then she grabbed the pot, to Jonathan's dismay, and hurried away. Jonathan faced Brooke. "How can you order an artichoke-spinach-egg-white omelet yet be a caffeinator like me?"

Colin raised his hand. "Mom's too modest. She limits herself to two cups of coffee on weekdays, but on weekends, she indulges herself with some drink that has more syllables than the molecular names in my high school chemistry class."

Brooke cupped her hot pink mug, taking time to inhale the aroma, her lips curling ever so slightly in appreciation. "I happen to function better after a cup of coffee. That's not a bad thing. Besides, you never complain about my stopping at The Busy Bean since I buy you something. You get out of riding the bus, and I spend time with you before work."

"Yeah, about that. Riley says I'm on her way if you trust her brother to drive me to school. He's captain of the basketball team." Colin thanked Jolene, who delivered juice and water with lemon wedges to him, Vanessa and Izzy.

Jonathan glanced at Brooke, who held the cup near her face, her expression almost mask-like. She placed the coffee on the table and nudged her son ever so lightly. "It was nice taking you to school every morning while it lasted. If you want Riley's brother to be your chauffeur, make sure you offer him gas money."

"Mom!" Colin reached for the little black box with sugar and artificial sweeteners. He selected three of the white packets, dumping the contents into his water before squeezing the lemon wedge and stirring the mixture. "Riley and her brother would be offended if I did that."

Hold on. The cigarette ID suspect had entered Mo's on a weekday morning. Had Brooke missed any days of taking Colin to school? If she vouched for Colin's whereabouts in the morning, he wasn't the person who tried to buy the cigarettes at Mo's. Jonathan plunked down his cup too hard, and all eyes stared at him. Not what he'd intended at all, but he'd make the most of the awkward situation.

"Have you gone fishing around here? Sully Creek is lovely this time of year."

Brooke chuckled and unfolded her napkin. "That came out of nowhere. I expected a question about whether I'm handing out candy or toothbrushes tomorrow night, but nothing about fishing."

Colin cleared his throat. "Um, Mom. I think Mr. Maxwell is asking you on a date, although fishing isn't exactly what I'd call your cup of coffee."

The collar of Jonathan's shirt tightened, and the cool air in the diner heated to the boiling point. How could he shift to asking Brooke out when he was interrogating her son?

A chuckle escaped from Vanessa, and then a full blown case of the giggles erupted out of his daughter. She laughed so hard their side of the booth shook from her wiggles. Jonathan glanced at Izzy, hoping she'd be able to talk some sense into her younger sister, when his two girls caught each other's eye.

"Dad and fishing?" Izzy scoffed before letting out a laugh. "I'd pay a month's allowance to see that."

"Just because I'd rather clean all the bathrooms in the house rather than go fishing isn't a reason for you two to have a giggle fest." *Great.* He went from asking Brooke out on a fishing excursion to talking about scrubbing out toilets. Some smooth operator he was.

He was right about one thing, though. Interrogating Colin was a fishing excursion, and he'd pulled up a muddy brown boot.

Jolene appeared with three plates of pancakes and delivered them to the kids. "What was in that coffee I gave you anyway?" She grinned. "Whatever it was, I wish more customers were having a good time like y'all. Be right back with your short stack and your omelet."

Jonathan stared at his cup, almost empty. "If you could swing by our table on your next refill tour, we'd appreciate it."

"Sure thing." Jolene bustled away after someone by the counter called her name.

Izzy and Vanessa began cutting their pancakes when Colin cleared his throat. "It'd be nice if we wait for the 'rents to get their food."

Izzy's face fell almost as quickly as her fork until Brooke shook her head. "Don't be silly. Go ahead and eat."

The three kids dug in, and Brooke looked at Jonathan, a laugh dancing on her lips. "So, you're not really a fan of fishing, huh?"

Jonathan shrugged and sipped the last of his coffee. "Nope, and that's practically a sin in these parts. Not sure why it came to mind." He reached over and stopped Vanessa from pouring a puddle of syrup as large as Sully Creek on her pancakes. "You might try having some pancakes with your syrup."

Vanessa rolled her eyes. "Are you sure Caleb can't give you more cooking lessons?

He makes the best pancakes and did a good job teaching you how to make homemade salsa."

Izzy laughed so hard she spit out a chunk of pancake. Jonathan scrunched his eyes shut for a second. Fishing, toilets and now mention of his poor culinary skills? This was no way to impress a lady, especially one as professional and sophisticated as Brooke. He peeked to find Jolene refilling his mug, and he nodded his thanks.

"Well, now you know my secrets. I prefer a clean house to fishing and every so often, I turn the girls loose from the dungeon and take them out to eat."

"Only some of your secrets?" Brooke sipped her coffee, and Jolene arrived with their food.

He learned Brooke took her time and savored each bite. Her delight in her food spread to his toes, and he felt lighter, happier. The kids finished long before the adults, and Vanessa pointed out the diner's jukebox to Colin. "It plays weird songs like 'Chantilly Lace' and 'Mister Sandman.'"

"Sounds cool. Let's go see it," said Colin.

Brooke fished a couple of dollar bills out of her purse, and Colin added them to his thin black wallet with a nicked corner. "I like fifties music. It's catchy," Brooke said.

The morning wouldn't be a total disaster if

he continued learning new insights about her. They both slid out of their respective sides of the booth, and the three kids headed to the rear of the diner, where the big jukebox held center stage.

"Thank Colin for me." Jonathan slid back and speared the last bite of sausage. There was nothing that said Sunday morning like sausage links with a dollop of syrup.

"For what?" Brooke halted her fork in mid-air before placing it back on her plate.

"The way he handled Izzy. I thought it might embarrass him if I thanked him."

"Colin is a good kid. One of his biggest flaws is sleeping through the alarm clock, so I drop him off on my way to work. He hasn't been tardy once and brought home his first perfect attendance certificate." Brooke swallowed one more bite and then pushed her plate away. "That is one delicious omelet."

In Savannah, he'd run into one case where a parent lied and provided a phony alibi for their teen, but Brooke didn't even realize she had just provided Colin with a genuine alibi. Without knowing it, she'd cleared him from any chance of being the teen who entered Mo's Gas and Bait Stop.

"Some mornings are a test for us, but they're on the bus when it comes." Jonathan was thankful for those five minutes and his second cup of coffee before he hustled to the station.

Brooke glanced around and leaned her body toward him. "Did you find anything on the tapes?"

He laid down his fork and kept his voice low. "I saw the person who tried to jimmy the door. Whoever it was wore a costume, so no help there."

"Was it an uncommon costume? Maybe you can track the person that way."

Jonathan shook his head. "I saw at least four people wearing the same disguise yesterday." He reached over and gripped her hand. "Don't worry, though. If he made this attempt, he doesn't know we found the stash. Since he didn't disrupt anything, that now becomes part of his profile. He's probably not a violent criminal."

"You think he'll try again?" Worry came over her pretty features.

Jonathan wanted to reassure her, but he stopped. "Yes."

But had she cleared Colin? Had the first ID been sold before or after their arrival in town? Could someone Colin's age have the resources or the know-how to pull this off? Doubtful. And why would he go through the trouble of breaking into the men's locker room when he could gain access with his mother's keys? Colin himself had mentioned changing out of his superhero costume in Brooke's office when the men's locker room was locked.

The fact that Colin was only fifteen and wouldn't have resources in the North Carolina Department of Motor Vehicles was enough comfort for Jonathan to finish his stack of pancakes.

Brooke removed her napkin from her lap and laid it over the remnants of her omelet. "I need to tell you something." Brooke kept her voice low, and he leaned toward her to hear over the din of the crowd. "I told Daisy about the camera."

Jonathan swiped his last bite of pancake through the syrup, popped it in his mouth and leaned forward again. "Daisy seems like a good secret bearer to me."

"Well…" Brooke glanced around as if making sure no one was listening. "Colin overheard me, but I made him promise not to tell anyone. He knows how important this job is to me."

The sounds of Fats Domino filled the restaurant as Colin rushed over and skidded to a stop in front of Brooke, holding his phone in the air. "I made the team, Mom!"

She jumped out of the booth and gave him a side hug. "I knew you could do it."

Colin blushed and extricated himself from Brooke. "Yesterday's tryouts were intense. I almost walked out early. That coach works his players, but he's fair and he's good. We were finished by two."

"I thought tryouts ended at three?" Brooke raised an eyebrow, but Izzy and Vanessa returned, cutting off any further conversation between mother and son.

If Colin had an unaccounted hour and if he knew about the recently installed camera, which was rather unobtrusive in a corner of the lobby, that would explain why he donned that costume. The locker room was the best hiding place for the IDs without being found at his home, and where he and his accomplice would both have easy access. And his flat black wallet with a nick at the corner resembled the one in the video footage. That was a long stretch, but it still provided enough reason to keep his distance.

His heart broke in an instant once before.

He wouldn't let that happen again.

CHAPTER ELEVEN

BROOKE WAS EXHAUSTED after Mr. Whitley's unexpected five-hour visit to the center on this Wednesday for a budget consultation. She rubbed the back of her neck and stretched. He had also grilled her about some minor decisions he'd given her the authority to make and the recent police activity.

Someone, either here or at the precinct, delivered precise details about Jonathan's visits. Dispelling Mr. Whitley's concerns while remaining true to her promise to Jonathan had taken every ounce of her energy. Nothing like being put between a rock and a hard place. What would happen when Mr. Whitley found out she hadn't been entirely truthful with him?

She plunked the paintbrush onto one of the Mimosas' art easels with more force than necessary. It fell to the floor, and she bent down and received a nice bump on her head for her trouble. A double ouch, as she wasn't sure Mr. Whitley would understand her motives for keeping Jonathan's mission a secret.

Tina rushed over, seemingly out of nowhere. "Is your head okay? That sounded awful."

Great. The first Mimosa on the scene this evening would have to be Jonathan's aunt. Since sharing breakfast with Jonathan and his daughters, she'd stayed busy with the center. Each night she'd checked the locker hiding spot before she left for home, and each night she breathed a sigh of relief the suspect hadn't returned for the rest of the IDs.

"Just a little clumsy. Long day." At least that was the truth. Withholding information from anyone was never her strong suit.

Tina's gaze swept over Brooke's outfit. "I wish I looked half as good as you after a long day. I remember, after my chemo treatments, I'd change into the softest outfits I owned since I didn't want anything rough touching my skin. Drew didn't mind, but I worried…" Tina halted and took a deep breath. "And then I knew. I had to battle the cancer, not the anxiety. He kept my morale up, saying how beautiful I was and that I'd get through it."

Brooke was taken aback at Tina's willingness to share such private details. She let the words sink in. "Thank you for sharing that with me. People in Hollydale are so close and it catches me off guard sometimes. That's incredibly hard, what you've been through.."

Tina smiled. "Thanks to my annual mammogram, the doctors caught it early. Wait until my next three-day walk. I'll ask you for a donation then. Trust me, men like Mysterious Cute Guy, if he's like my Drew, are the ones who'll support us through anything life throws our way."

Brooke nodded and glanced at her presentation table. *Darn it*. She'd prepared too well. Everything was ready, giving her no out from the romantic intrigue discussion. "Who said Mysterious Cute Guy was like Drew? For all anyone knows, he could be a scoundrel." One cute guy in her past had been a louse. So far, their son didn't take after him, for which Brooke thanked the stars above. "Or someone looking for a relationship with no strings attached."

Tina's eyes sparkled. "Aha. Mysterious Cute Guy does exist. And…"

Fabiana marched in, fanning her hand in front of her face. "Is it hot in here? It's hot in here. Brooke, can you turn on the air conditioning? If you don't, I'm going to sweat through my shirt."

She plucked her long-sleeve leopard-print silk shirt for good measure. Thankful for the interruption, Brooke walked over to the window and cracked it open. November in the Great Smoky Mountains provided quite a change from Houston, where she'd still be wearing short sleeves and the air conditioning would operate on full blast. Cool air seeped through the screen, and Brooke shivered. This weekend, she and Colin would have to invest in sweaters and gloves. "As soon as someone asks me to close the window, it goes down."

Fabiana perched herself on the sill. "That's fair."

Aunt Mitzi walked in with Betty alongside her, their arms intertwined. "Glad to do it. I'm just relieved Joe is feeling better."

Brooke's ears perked up, and she hurried over. "Is anything wrong with Joe?"

Betty extricated herself from Aunt Mitzi's hold and shrugged. "Nothing apart from old age. A touch of angina, that's all. I didn't want to leave him alone, so Mitzi arranged for Owen and Ashleigh to keep Joe company tonight. Isn't that the sweetest thing?" Betty turned toward Mitzi. "I know you keep turning down Owen's marriage proposals because he's younger, but if you continue doing that, someone else is going to snap him up."

Marriage proposals? This was the first she'd heard of this. "Aunt Mitzi? Has Owen proposed to you?"

Hyacinth entered the room and clapped her hands. "Oh, Mitzi! My heart overflows at the prospect of your upcoming nuptials. How exciting that you finally said yes to the wonderful park ranger. Have you thought about a wedding pie instead of a cake? Belinda could make one for the groom, and I can make a delicious flaky concoction for you. Lemon meringue? Strawberry chiffon? You name it, and it shall be done. Let me see the ring."

"Owen and I aren't engaged." Aunt Mitzi talked over the din of everyone offering their congratulations. Her aunt must have seen the fallen look on Brooke's face, and she shoved the bags in Tina's direction. "Here, Tina. Take the mimosa ingredients. I need to talk to Brooke for a minute."

In the hallway, Brooke swallowed the lump of emotion caught in her throat and composed herself. "Aunt Mitzi, we'll talk later. I'm supposed to be directing the class."

"That can wait. You look upset." Aunt Mitzi rubbed Brooke's arm.

Before Mitzi, it had been too long since someone displayed maternal instincts toward her. She'd been strong for Colin for some time, but her mother had taken leave not long after Brooke announced her pregnancy, saying thirty-three was too young to be a mother, let alone a grandmother. She'd only found Brooke and reconnected once her cirrhosis was too far gone for a transplant or treatment.

"This isn't about me. It's about you, and this isn't a good place to talk considering we're supposed to start in two minutes." Mr. Whitley had made it clear this afternoon she'd be looking for a job elsewhere if the police kept coming and going, making it even more imperative that Jonathan track down the person behind the fake IDs now.

Brooke tried to tug free, but Aunt Mitzi held tight to her. "Yes, Owen has proposed."

"Why didn't you tell me?" She stepped back.

"That explanation might take longer than the art lesson." Aunt Mitzi's laugh was anything but her usual belly buster.

"Don't make me put Hyacinth in charge." She offered a small smile.

This time Aunt Mitzi's laugh was more genuine. "You're catching on, sweetie pie." She sobered. "I love Owen, but I feel like I'd jinx our relationship if we got married. A certificate's not going to change the way I feel about him."

"Have you told him this?"

"Good heavens, no." Aunt Mitzi shuddered and then met Brooke's gaze. "I guess it runs in the family, same as you not telling me what's been bothering you all week. You didn't even crack a smile the other night when that cute little toddler came to our door dressed as a marshmallow for Halloween. And that was so precious."

Even Colin had slipped an extra piece of candy in the girl's bag. "Don't worry. It's nothing…"

Aunt Mitzi tapped her foot as though she wasn't buying Brooke's excuse. How could she confide in Aunt Mitzi without giving away the secret locker stash or the identity of Mysterious Cute Guy? Problem was, Tina had already figured out Jonathan was MCG. Still, Brooke valued her privacy. Guarded it, really. Since Tina had kept quiet, Brooke would do so as well.

"Maybe you're not the only person worried about the past jinxing a relationship." Brooke flinched, aware of how that might sound. "Not that I'm in one. You need to get past Dwayne, though, if you're going to move forward with Owen."

"You've given me something to think about. Perhaps I *am* letting my past stand in the way of my future." Aunt Mitzi linked her arm through Brooke's. "Let's lose ourselves in creating a masterpiece."

They walked back into the room, and Brooke did exactly as her aunt suggested. The hour flew by, and everyone enjoyed themselves while showing off their latest creations. Four women had duplicated Brooke's painting of stark tree branches with a simple blackbird. Once again, Hyacinth had gone out on her own limb and, once again, her painting astounded Brooke, who couldn't tell if the abstract bird was a joke or a masterpiece.

Hyacinth laughed and hugged Brooke. "It's okay if I perplex you a tad. That's a common reaction in these parts, but everybody loves me and accepts me the way I am, even if I am a bit chatty."

She let go, and Betty came over and wrapped her arm around Hyacinth's shoulders. "And these ladies found room for me after my best friend, Marie, died. They keep me young," Betty explained.

Fabiana came over and linked her arm in Betty's. "And *mis amigas* are my rock. Plus, the time away from Roberto helps us appreciate each other all the more when we are together."

She winked at Brooke, who smiled at the bond among these women. Tina did likewise before Aunt Mitzi wound one arm through Brooke's and the other through Tina's elbow. "The Mimosas. Where there's always room for one more."

"And, Brooke, just say the word and I'll make a friendly suggestion to Mason that he should give you a call." Betty sent Brooke her second wink in as many minutes. "Cute paramedics don't grow on trees, you know."

"The next time Carlos is in town, I promise to introduce the two of you," Fabiana cut in with her own plug.

If they kept this up, Brooke would rename this group the Matchmaking Mimosas.

Tina chuckled and extricated herself from the group first. "Why don't we give Brooke enough time to see what develops between her and MCG?"

Brooke's cheeks grew warm, and she was thankful she'd opened the windows earlier, the cool air providing a welcome balm.

"Where are the goblets? I'm thirsty." Fabiana wandered over to the side table.

After the drinks, they pitched in and cleaned up before they made their excuses to leave. Before Brooke knew it, she hauled the box with extra canvases and other supplies that Hyacinth donated to the storage room. She flicked on the light switch, found space on the top shelf and rolled the round step stool over. With a groan, she lifted the box and placed it on the empty shelf. Her feet came out from under her, and she flailed and reached for the middle rack. With a deep breath, she steadied herself.

A tote precariously close to the edge tumbled to the tile floor.

Brooke caught her breath and took care the rest of the way down. She avoided the mess littering the floor. The lid lay to one side with Christmas decorations scattered everywhere. Testing her ankle, she was relieved there were no twinges of pain, but she couldn't say the same about the broken ornaments. Who stored loose ornaments like this without packing them better? It was almost as though someone had thrown them in at the last minute. She'd talk to Al and Joe about how they stored holiday displays.

Something was off. She glanced at the middle shelf, where brand-new office supplies sat stacked in neat rows. Not a Christmas tote in sight.

Concern aside, she'd best clean this mess up. *Where was that broom?* She spotted it in the corner next to another shelving unit. Her gaze swept over the its contents. Holiday decorations occupied every inch, celebrating everything from Hanukkah to Arbor Day. Those containers were clear with labels, unlike the solid blue one on the floor.

The hairs on the back of her neck prickled, and she stopped short of touching anything. Instead, she searched the office supplies for a pack of rulers and extricated one. With dread, she knelt beside the mess and poked into the box until a professional laminator, different from the one in the center's copy room and with a state logo, caught her eye.

She whipped out her cell phone and made the call.

THE CHILLY WIND whirled around Jonathan, a harbinger of the holidays to come. The oaks and maples were finally shedding their leaves. The rounded shadows of the mountains, solid and permanent, something he almost took for granted since he passed them now without actually seeing them, rose in profile against the dark sky. Jonathan approached Brooke, who was waiting at the center's main doors.

"We've got to stop meeting like this." The grin in his voice faded when her solemn expression clawed at his heart.

He put an arm around her shoulders, comforting her. For now, friendship would have to suffice.

"Why here? Why this center?" she asked.

"It's okay. Anyone this vested in this scheme must be antsy. He'll be coming back for the materials any day now."

She shivered and squeezed her eyes shut tight as if she were fighting tears. Ever since he'd responded to the grocery store owner's call regarding the first fake ID and then found a second in Eric's possession after the fender bender, he'd wanted to catch the person responsible. Seeing this composed woman upset and trembling brought a renewed commitment to do just that. Too much equipment remained at the facility. Jonathan had to believe the person wouldn't leave it here forever.

Brooke opened her eyes once more. "That's what I'm afraid of." She led him past the too-familiar bank of chairs. "Do you have a minute? Or would taking time with me interfere with your shift?"

"I swapped with a fellow officer for last weekend's night shift, but I'm back to working my normal schedule." He glanced at the clock on the wall. For the umpteenth time this year, he was taking advantage of his next-door neighbor, who'd agreed to come over and sit with Izzy and Vanessa, both sound asleep in bed.

But as much as he needed to return home, he wouldn't rush this investigation or Brooke. The misery on her face twisted his heart, finally waking up again after hibernating for so long.

She sat in the closest chair, her hands shaking. "Go ahead to the storage area without me."

"Brooke. I'm off duty. I'll stay here until you can come, too."

"Who's watching Izzy and Vanessa?" She sniffled.

He rose and plucked a couple of tissues from the box on Betty's desk. He returned and handed them to her. "My next-door neighbor. As soon as she arrived for the girls, I rushed over."

He met her gaze, and the air crackled at his admission. Somehow, he knew that no matter what, if she called him, he'd do everything in his power to answer.

"Mr. Whitley found out about your official visits." She then swiped at her nose with the tissue. "Nothing like showing your worst colors to someone and then showing them a red nose, too."

"It worked for Rudolph and Clarice just fine."

This time her smile was genuine. "I enjoy watching Rudolph every December. I should have known you were a closet romantic."

He performed a slight bow from the chair. "If the shoe, or in this case duty boots, fits…"

She stood and massaged the back of her neck. He longed to knead out some of her tension for her. "I imagine your neighbor would like to return home. This can wait. I'll walk you to the storage room." He wasn't budging, not with something so obviously wrong with Brooke.

"I imagine you need to talk to someone." He pointed to the seats. Somehow, he wanted to make room in his heart for her. He'd gladly spend the next fifty years figuring out what made her tick. "Nothing says romantic like hard plastic chairs in the middle of a deserted lobby."

She glanced the other way before she sat two seats down from his. He arched an eyebrow, and she slid next to him. It was nice having her close. It felt right having someone beside him.

Not just anyone. Brooke.

"I signed a six-month contract, at which time he'll review my performance and whether the community seems more willing to accept the center. Someone told him you've been here several times in your official capacity. Now he's second-guessing his decision to hire me."

Brooke wouldn't stay somewhere unless she could be useful, needed. "Are you upset about the prospect of losing your job?" He hedged for a second and then continued, "Or are you worried someone's reporting your every step to Mr. Whitley?"

She clicked her tongue. "Give that man a

prize." She rolled her neck. "I know I've done nothing to deserve loyalty yet…"

"I sense a *but* in there."

"While he signs the paychecks, it would be nice if there wasn't a mole." She wrapped her arms around herself as if she was warding off a chill. "That's strong language, but I feel anyone who's reporting everything I do to him is someone I don't want on my staff. Am I being cautious or paranoid?"

Those big brown eyes looked at him, and he struggled to keep control. "I feel that same push and pull every day in my job, too." He considered the idea of loyalty in his life. Were the sheriff and the district attorney looking for the best candidate?

Or the most convenient?

Her truth might have struck too close to home.

In the meantime, there was a lead to investigate. "Let's examine your discovery."

She snapped her fingers. "First, I have to close the window in the art room."

He escorted her to the opposite wing of the building, where it was a good five degrees colder than the lobby. "Wasn't securing the windows part of the nighttime closing list?"

"It is. But I was distracted. Betty's Joe needed her, so I agreed to close the center tonight." She slammed the pane down with more force than necessary, the thump echoing in the room. He clicked the locks closed and checked one extra time. Here, an ounce of prevention would reassure the both of them.

Brooke stood there, her arms folded. "Feel better?"

"Much."

She walked over to the light switch. "Ready to go to the storage room?"

"Why was the window open in the first place?"

"One participant in tonight's art class was too warm. The rest of the class concurred." Brooke shrugged and flicked off the light. "I was in a hurry to put everything away, but the new security system would have alerted me before I left."

"Were you the teacher again tonight?" He glanced at her outfit, not a speck of paint in sight.

She flushed before she nodded. "Art's been my lifesaver over the years. Coffee and art supplies have been my two big indulgences, and I was fortunate in that some of my fellow employees at other community centers knew how much I love painting. Instead of throwing away quality tubes that had a smidgen of paint left, they gave them to me. I'm a big believer in recycling and upcycling."

She finished talking just as they reached the storage room.

"I poked around with a ruler in order not to disturb any fingerprints."

A blue plastic tote was upended on the cement floor. Bits and pieces of shattered Christmas ornaments were scattered everywhere. "Did you find it like this?"

"Um, that happened when I saved myself from falling."

Good grief. Brooke could have been seriously hurt tonight. "Were the ladies from the class around?"

"Only me, I'm afraid."

"What if you'd hurt yourself?" How long would it have been before help had arrived?

The fact that he cared so much hit him like that container crashing against the hard floor. Sometime in the past couple of weeks, he'd realized he was always looking forward to seeing her, his pulse racing a little faster every time he knew she was near.

He stepped toward her, and the scuff of his work boots reminded him he was here in his official capacity.

"I had my cell with me, and Aunt Mitzi and Colin would have come running if I hadn't arrived home tonight." Her nervous laugh gave too much away. She'd considered the same outcome. She met his gaze, and the laughter ended. Sparks flew, and he didn't know whether to snuff them out or let them start a roaring flame. "I'll be more careful," she said softly.

"Good. You have people who care about you, you know."

The electricity crackled between them. "Are you one of them?"

Stepping on the broken ornaments by accident, he startled them both with the noise. Another reminder he was here as a police officer. "That's part of my job."

She looked away, thereby ending their connection, the moment lost forever. "There's a laminator in the tote. I saw a state logo on it."

He removed a pair of latex gloves from his pocket. Sure enough, a laminator peeked through. Not just one purchased at a craft store or office supplies shop either. This was from the North Carolina Department of Motor Vehicles. This was a bigger operation than he and Mike contemplated. He kept that to himself. "Someone went through a great deal of trouble to hide this. When do you decorate for the holidays?"

"The center has plans for three major displays, one for Hanukkah, one for Christmas and one for Kwanzaa. As soon as the special Heartsgiving family presentations are over on the Wednesday before Thanksgiving, I'm staying late that night along with four other staff members to decorate."

"Who knows about that?"

"Everyone. Apparently, that's the tradition around here."

He pulled out the laminator and placed it to the side. "Is there a broom handy?"

"In that corner." She retrieved it and reached for a new trash bag, only to discover there were none. "There should be more bags upstairs. Wait here."

Brooke sprinted out of the storage closet, and he scratched his chin, the light stubble slightly itchy against his rough fingers. He was missing something, but he wasn't sure what. On his phone, he pulled up the picture of Eric's fake ID and remembered the smooth texture of the lamination as he held the license between his fingers. Enlarging the picture, he studied each corner until it hit him. The lower right corner was off as though slightly pinched. Come to think of it, that anomaly had led him to separate the two licenses at the time. Tomorrow he and Mike would use this laminator to see if the suspect had used this exact machine.

Brooke returned with a larger broom in one hand, a whisk broom with a clipped dustpan in the other, and a trash bag over her shoulder. "This should cover everything. I was thinking on my way back here why—"

"The supply closet is so far from the storage room?"

She handed him the whisk broom with the dustpan. "Make that three questions. And a fourth! I'm on a roll now. Do we need to keep anything from this heap of stuff?"

"There's nothing worth saving except the laminator. What were your questions? Maybe I can be of service." He took a mock bow. Anything to keep his mind on his job. There had only been one other time when he'd been so distracted, and adrenaline and shock had helped him stay focused.

She swept the red-and-green metal pieces into the dustpan, then rested her chin on the tip of the broom handle. "Is this an inside job? Could the person who's been talking to Mr. Whitley also be the one who's selling the IDs?"

He dumped the dustpan remnants into the trash bag. "Are those the two questions or additional ones?"

A broad smile was his reward. "That was the first question with a new one attached."

Something told him talking to her would

always be this easy, whether now or forty years from now. "I have the employee list." He didn't tell her he'd already checked out the backgrounds of the five full-time employees, along with her. Actually, he'd asked Jillian to follow through on Brooke. "I'm investigating that angle. We make a good team, you and me."

She blushed, and his heart swelled at her reaction. "Why would someone be keeping everything here?"

His thoughts exactly. When he pieced that together, he'd have enough of a profile to figure out who was behind this.

Unless Colin kept his equipment here for easy access in a place where Mitzi Mayfield wouldn't find it.

Yet Jonathan was doubtful a teenager could pull all of this off, especially one without stronger ties to the area.

"From what you said, your predecessor, Mr. Hinshaw, was rather lax on security, and this is peak tourist season." So far, every effort to contact Mr. Hinshaw had failed. "Every other business cracks down on security this time of year. That could have something to do with this location. What else did you think about?"

"Why is this case important to you?"

He dropped the trash bag and blinked.

"What do you mean? Every case is important to me."

"This one's different. I'd like to know why."

That breath he'd been holding escaped, and he picked up the bag, thankful nothing had fallen out. He met her gaze, and that spark between them ignited into something warm and colorful. "I told you about the accident that took Anne's life." He waited for her nod. The connection between them was real. He'd stake anything on that. "Anne's death was preventable. If I can spare anyone else the pain of having a loved one seriously injured in an accident, or worse, because of sheer recklessness, I'll do everything to make that happen."

"You can't control everything."

He was getting a touch too comfortable around the smart brunette who made him feel again.

"I can try." He lifted the laminator and checked the room. "Thanks for calling."

A simple sentence changed the atmosphere in a drop of the hat. A ten-degree drop in temperature would have caused less confusion on Brooke's face. He wanted a return to the gentle camaraderie of a few minutes ago, but focusing on the case and getting that promotion had to come first.

Brooke shrugged and held the door open

for him. "You do your job, and I'll be able to keep mine."

He walked her to her car, taking care with the evidence. She drove away without a backward glance. His radar had been out of commission longer than he'd realized if he'd mistaken professional courtesy for attraction. Her attitude toward him was a means to keep her job.

As he placed the laminator in the trunk of his police car, the wind swirled around him, and leaves whirled about the parking lot in a frenzy. Fall had arrived with a vengeance today. He thought his heart had come back as well.

This was the time of year when bears and other animals found a cozy spot for hibernating in the Great Smoky Mountains. Rather than a cozy spot, however, his heart found a cold spot to hunker down and sleep awhile longer.

CHAPTER TWELVE

KICKING OFF THE weekend with cookie decorating classes before the holiday season was in full swing had been a stroke of genius by Yolanda, the community center's assistant director. Brooke wiped down tables for the next class starting shortly, this one for older elementary school students.

The first class, targeted toward adults, had been packed. Even last-minute additions, Frederick and Agnes Whitley, tucked away a couple of keepsake boxes of the iced sugar cookies with satisfied expressions. Perhaps the primary benefactor of the center was coming around to her methods.

The aroma of the cookies tantalized Brooke. She noticed she had sprinkles sticking to almost every inch of her apron. Unlike the previous class, where the adults had whipped up their own dough, the teacher had brought prebaked cookies and would only highlight decorating tips for the younger incoming students, who were more likely to end up with the finished product in their mouths than in the containers to take home.

Kids spilled into the cooking room, each with a chaperone. A group of women, presumably moms, huddled in the corner, laughing and moaning about holiday shopping. The split seemed to be right down the middle with half saying they'd already completed their lists, and the other half lamenting that they hadn't even begun.

Paige, the owner of the Night Owl Bakery and today's instructor, clapped her hands, and all eyes turned toward her. A guilty tinge of relief fluttered through Brooke at the absence of Jonathan and Vanessa, who'd signed up for the class, although she also cringed at the memory of how the other night had ended.

That evening had started out well. He'd opened up to her and let her in on something raw and sensitive, and she believed they were making progress, heading toward something substantial, unlike anything she'd ever shared with Colin's father, who'd been all talk and no substance. Hayden had said pretty words before she'd told him she was pregnant. Then he had begged her to keep his identity as the father a secret. He hadn't wanted to lose his parents' approval. Or the tuition money they promised him to stop seeing her.

Jonathan, however, was a combination of talk and substance, but he'd withdrawn without any warning. Taking her cue from him, she'd also walked away. Sprinting was a better description of how she'd tucked her tail between her legs and hustled away. Together they snuffed out that romantic spark with a tsunami of cold water.

She pushed that regret aside, a roomful of guests at the center demanding her full attention, not a shadow of her complete self.

Jonathan's robust laugh heralded his arrival, and she stilled. He and Vanessa crossed the threshold, their smiles lighting up the room. "We're late, and we'd better catch up."

Vanessa looked anxiously around the room.

He met Brooke's gaze, and those hazel depths brought about a fluttery feeling in her stomach. Last time anyone impacted her like this was Colin's father, an episode she had no inclination to repeat ever again. Jonathan was a complication, same as Mr. Whitley.

Lucie Spindler and her twins patted the chairs next to them, and Jonathan sent a smile Brooke's way that spread the fluttery feeling through her even more.

The class got underway, and everyone chattered and applied Paige's clever icing tips to their cookies. Perhaps it was downright cowardly to make sure Paige helped Jonathan and Vanessa, but concentrating on helping others had always saved Brooke before, and it should work now. It was hard enough to be in the same room and remain professional. Besides, she couldn't lose her heart to the charming cop if he walled up his emotions almost every time they talked.

The class ended, and the registrants filed out of the room, boxes of cookies in hand. Lucie waved to Jonathan and placed her arm around Vanessa's shoulders with an air of protectiveness. "Thanks for lending us Vanessa for a couple of hours. She and her cousins are going to have so much fun decorating Fred and Ethel's shed for the holidays. Caleb will drop her off at your house around bedtime if that works for you."

"A whole evening to myself? Who am I to complain about that?" The jovial tone of Jonathan's voice didn't quite match his eyes.

Vanessa giggled and hugged her father. "Don't eat all my cookies."

"I'll save you one." Jonathan smiled warmly, making him seem ten years younger. "Or at least I'll try."

"Daddy!"

His smile widened when Vanessa broke away and joined the other three. Paige waved goodbye and left along with the crowd, the room cleaner now than it was before the class. Brooke spied a few stacked containers waiting and ready to go to the storage room.

Jonathan walked toward her, and his presence heightened all of her senses. Even her toes tingled. "Can I help?"

"Every time you show up here, you help. And every time, you find something related to your case. It won't take me but five minutes to put these away."

"Oops. Wait a minute." He took off his orange apron decorated with colorful pumpkins and turkeys and rolled it into a ball. "Where was I supposed to put this?"

"It's part of the fee. You get to keep it." She had to admit Jonathan looked cute in that cable-knit green sweater. He definitely qualified as MCG.

That was the problem. He was more than cute. Finding someone attractive was more than skin-deep in Brooke's book. Humility and humor changed him from everyday good-looking to downright handsome.

"Thanks. Vanessa will love my wearing this leading up to Thanksgiving, while Izzy will say something snippy, as she's now full-on into tween angst." He laid the box with his cookies on the nearest table and scratched his chin. "How did you handle that with Colin?"

She laughed and set the containers down. "Ask me that when he's thirty." Her cell rang with her son's ringtone, and she held up her finger. "Hold that thought. It's Colin, and he doesn't normally call me at work unless it's important."

She navigated her way to a corner of the room, turning away from Jonathan, a distraction at the best of times. Colin asked her permission to watch some training videos at the basketball team captain's house and chill out with popcorn. "I haven't walked Daisy yet, but can I go?" The yearning in Colin's voice practically leaped through the line.

"That's also Riley's house, isn't it?"

"She's visiting her aunt in Asheville."

"Hold on a minute." Brooke opened the app and confirmed with the team mom there would, in fact, be adults present. She transferred her attention back to her son. "Text me when to pick you up."

"Riley's brother can drop me off. Can I go over now? Without walking Daisy? Aunt Mitzi's not home and it's about to rain."

"I'll walk Daisy…" She hadn't finished her sentence when her phone beeped his disconnect. She glared at the device. "…this once."

She turned around, and Jonathan was no longer in the room. She guessed he wanted to get started on that evening to himself. Walking over to where the containers were, she froze. They were here a minute ago.

"You were wrong."

Startled, she jumped and crossed her arms over her chest. "Jonathan! I didn't see you. Where did you come from?"

"The storage room." He grinned and crossed to where he'd left his box of cookies and balled-up apron. "For the record, it only took one trip and three minutes to get there and back, not five."

"Then I thank you, and my labradoodle thanks you. As soon as I check with Joe and Betty, I'm off to walk Daisy."

"You know what makes walks in Hollydale perfect?"

She eyed him with some trepidation. "No rain, good shoes and a bouncy dog?"

He laughed and rattled the box of cookies. "Cooperative weather, a great trail and a knowledgeable guide." He opened the box and swayed it under her nose. "Who's willing to share his cookies."

This camaraderie with him was new and exciting, if not a little overwhelming as well. They'd tried to dial it back, but here they were, and she wanted to curl up with him by a fire and find out everything about him between kisses. However, Mr. Whitley had laid down the law in no uncertain terms, and she'd promised Colin he'd stay in Hollydale until he graduated. Brooke's mother had never delivered upon a promise. Brooke wouldn't go back on her word to Colin. She needed this job.

"Thanks, but I don't know how long I'll be here finishing up."

His grin faded, and he shrugged. She instantly missed those crinkles. "Things to do. Got it."

Brooke gritted her teeth so she wouldn't shout a different answer. He walked out the door without looking back.

JONATHAN HELD OPEN the door to The Busy Bean for a new patron, and he exited, the sounds of mellow jazz sailing out with him. Seeing all the happy couples made him want to escape with his decaf and head for home. Even Harriet, the station's dispatcher, and Bert, her husband, were cuddled next to the stage, the soft lights emphasizing their radiant glow.

He wanted that magic again. The problem was, he wanted it so much he might have gone too far, too fast with the first woman he'd reacted to in a long time, and projected feelings onto the situation. He had to remind himself again of what should be his priorities.

He turned onto Timber Road and stood in front of the gazebo, using the warmth of the disposable cup to ward off the chill of November in the Great Smokies. All around him, the signs of the season emerged. Holiday lights, festive wreaths and a menorah were just a few. Loneliness spread through him. He was finally at the point where he wanted a special someone to share a kiss with under the mistletoe or exchange a meaningful glance with at the Thanksgiving table.

That had to be the answer. He missed the thought of someone sharing his life. He wasn't attracted to Brooke, but the time of year. He wanted a caring partner by his side to make the hard days easier and the relaxing days even happier.

This was the second time he'd had the same discussion with himself, and this time, he'd take control of his feelings. He set off for home until a dog's bark and a woman's voice halted him in his tracks. He turned and found Daisy bounding toward him with Brooke trailing behind. The glint of the red lights overhead reflected off Brooke's dark hair, tied back in that familiar messy bun. And he knew.

He wasn't projecting false feelings any more

than he could deny the truth. Every time he saw her, his feet felt as though they hovered a good six inches off the ground, and his heart hammered outside of his chest. Good grief, he sounded like a lovestruck teenager rather than a father with two daughters.

Maybe meeting that special someone did that to a person, no matter their age.

Daisy reached him first. Her bottom wriggled, and her body quivered with excitement. The dog barely knew him, and yet she acted like he was her best friend.

"Jonathan." That lilt in her voice threw him off guard. She tilted her chin at the cup in his hands. "It seems a little late for coffee."

"It's decaf, and there's a jazz ensemble at The Busy Bean tonight. Since you like jazz, I'll buy you a cup."

She held up Daisy's leash. "Daisy loves Wynton Marsalis, but I don't think they'll buy that she's a jazz fan trapped in a dog's body."

He laughed. "Good point. Care if I stroll along?"

His heart raced as he waited for her answer. Fortunately, she didn't keep him in suspense for long as she delivered a slow, careful nod. "Unless I'm keeping you from the concert?"

"I'll go another Saturday night. Perhaps with someone whose dog is a jazz fan." With the glow of the streetlights bathing her, Brooke flushed pink.

Brooke shortened the retractable leash, and Daisy trotted like she owned the town. Several passersby nodded hello, and he greeted them in return.

"Am I taking you out of your way?" Brooke navigated around the damp orange and yellow leaves, a reminder of the early evening rainfall that stopped before he ventured downtown.

"Yes, but I'm enjoying the night air." And that wasn't all. He might as well admit it to her. "And your company. How are you liking Hollydale? It's a long way from Houston."

"It's a bit of an adjustment, but it's the best thing to happen to me in a long time." She kept Daisy in line. "You're lucky to have grown up here."

"I didn't." She faced him, and he elaborated. "My aunt and uncle are from this area. Every summer growing up, my parents couldn't wait to drop me off for three months. Caleb's more like a younger brother than a cousin, really. Then every September, I'd leave the Spindler family and return to my parents, who stayed busy with work. Their careers always came first."

Long ago, he'd sworn to himself he'd be different. Yet when Vanessa and Izzy grew up, would they say he also valued career over family?

"Your daughters must be thankful you spend quality time with them." Brooke twisted the leash around her hand. "I had the exact opposite experience growing up."

"How so?" Daisy picked up the pace again, and he matched Brooke's progress. She stayed silent, and he didn't rush her. "You don't have to share if you don't want to."

"That's not it." Her protest warmed him. "My mother never took anything seriously, never met a job she could keep for more than a couple of months."

"Then Colin must be thankful you're not like her. We might have had opposite experiences—" His voice cracked, and he took a good, long look at her. She'd met adversity headfirst and kept going, but both of them knew what happened when a child didn't feel loved. This was something he'd buried, and would have gladly kept below the surface, until he met her. "But they obviously had an impact on us."

"I guess I fear turning into my mother, and I leap into work headfirst. But I'm determined to live more in the moment." Daisy found the one puddle in their path and jumped in it. He laughed, and Brooke groaned. "Like my dog.

Now I know what I'll be doing when I get home."

"I bet you weren't the type of girl to jump in puddles."

It might be wrong to want this walk to go on forever, but he did. Sharing his past with her felt like he was at home.

She chuckled and shook her head. "Nope. I was always too busy, trying to make sure I had enough food and a place to live. I grew up way too fast. I'm learning to sit on the porch during a storm since there's something about the steady cadence of rain that makes me stop and take it easy for a while."

"Too busy for relaxation? But that's the flip side of work." Jonathan bowed by her side. "Allow me to introduce myself, m'lady. Sir Jonathan of Relaxing Afternoons at your service."

Her chuckle turned into a full laugh. "There are so many facets to your personality. I like that. Are you saying that you're good at taking it easy?"

"The very best." He held his head high and executed a move as if he held a pretend sword in his empty hand.

"I have a hard time relaxing. I prefer to get out there and make things happen." She stopped next to a mailbox. "This is my Aunt Mitzi's house."

Good things always ended too fast. He opened the gate for Brooke. "M'lady, I shall see you to your door."

"Daisy…"

"Can play in the yard for a few minutes. You're already giving her a bath, right? Why not spend a few minutes with me on the front porch? You can take your first lesson from the master of relaxation."

"The master, huh?"

"Among my other charming traits." She wasn't the only one who needed a few minutes of stress-free living.

Jonathan sat on the wooden rattan bench on Mitzi's covered porch while setting his disposable coffee cup on the cement. He watched Brooke unleash Daisy, who romped around the yard. "Looks like you're already halfway asleep."

Suddenly, he didn't feel much like relaxing, not with her so near. He stood and approached her. One long wisp of her dark walnut hair escaped her upswept hairstyle, and he tucked it behind her ear. She gave every evidence of cool sophistication, but she was so much more than mere appearances. Her caring heart was leaving its mark on him. She'd made Halloween more special for an entire community while taking his daughters under her wing.

"Brooke."

Without another word, she hooked her hand around his neck and pulled him close until no space separated them. Her lips were as soft as they looked, and she kissed him, the faint taste of sugar and vanilla combining with something delicious that was Brooke herself. The coldness of her cheeks seeped into his warmer skin, and the sound of ocean waves rushed into his ears. He wound his arm around her back, the softness of her fleece jacket registered along with the sheer softness of her.

His heart rate accelerated, reminding him he was alive and grateful to be here on the porch with her in his arms, kissing her, falling for her.

She broke away first, and color exploded into his world again, the black-and-white aspect wearing away after so long. Oranges, reds and yellows sang with life all around him. She licked her lips. "Coffee-flavored Jonathan. I could get used to that."

"I should have had two cups."

"I'm glad we found each other, but I'm not the person you think I am." She stepped back, then added even more distance.

"I think your aunt would have noticed if

you weren't the real Brooke Novak." He approached her and cupped her cheek with his hand, willing his warmness to melt her icy skin.

He couldn't let her stand out here, freezing. The night air cooled fast here in the mountains. He took off his coat and placed it over her thin fleece jacket.

She pulled away and tried to hand the coat back. "I don't need this."

Her face grew more guarded, yet he wouldn't take back his garment. "Yes, you do." His eyes narrowed. "You're not used to people doing nice things for you, are you?"

Brooke blinked and stared at him. "Of course I am. Colin gave me the sweetest college graduation gift, and Mitzi helps me all the time."

Jonathan shook his head and wrapped his coat around her shoulders. "When was the last time you let someone outside of your circle in?"

Her throat bobbed, and she licked her lips. As much as he wanted to kiss her again, he stood still. "My employees." She started ticking off fingers, and he shook his head again. "And I'm making friends with a bunch of women at the center. They've nicknamed themselves 'The Mimosas.'"

He reached over and pulled the coat in front

of her, her warmth and assurance already important to him. This connection was something he himself had to wrap his head around. "You aren't comfortable letting people in, are you?"

Her lips formed a thin line. "Sometimes the ones you care about the most are also the ones who can let you down the most."

He didn't know which was worse, though. Letting down someone you loved or having someone you loved let you down. Either way, living with the consequences of that could be devastating.

"Are you talking about your mother or someone else?"

"Both. You already know about me, but Colin's father…" She lowered her gaze to the porch floor. "He chose which commitments to honor and which were disposable without consulting anyone else. He wanted nothing to do with me after I told him I was pregnant. When Colin was born, I tried one more time, but he turned us away."

Jonathan stepped forward and wiped away the tear falling down her cheek. "That man lost out on the best thing to ever happen to him."

"You haven't known me long enough to see if that's true."

One look at her expressive face let him know

she believed that. "I know you better than you think I do." Somehow, unwrapping every layer of her would take years, and he wanted that type of time with her. "You're elegant and lovely with a heart of gold."

"Elegant?" She shook her head and rubbed her hands along her leggings. "Thanks, but everything I own is courtesy of others. I upcycle well."

"Brooke, there's nothing you can say that's going to stem this attraction." He stopped smiling, and his inner glow from their first kiss was fading fast. "I don't know if you've noticed, but I can't believe the men in Houston didn't realize your worth."

Daisy scratched at the door, and Brooke rushed over and let her inside. She returned his coat. "I'll give her a bath later."

Her voice quivered, and he pointed to the door. "Shouldn't you invite me in? We can give Daisy that bath together."

She shivered, and he wound his arms around her, amazed at how she could feel so right. He stood there until her trembling subsided.

"You say that like it would be the most pleasurable way to spend a Saturday night." Without her usual heels, her head rested on his shoulder. He could stand here forever, but there was a weight to what she said, one he couldn't let go by without addressing.

He broke away and stroked a finger along her soft cheek. "I don't say something unless it's genuine." Winning Brooke's trust would take time, but it would be worth the wait. "Even giving Daisy a bath with you would make for a memorable evening."

The blinding lights of an automobile pulling into the driveway caught his attention. Before he could respond, car doors opened and slammed shut with laughter breaking through the still night. Mitzi and Owen hustled onto the porch, holding hands. "We have the most exciting news." She held up their hands. "We're engaged!"

"She's making an honest man out of me at last!" Owen beamed.

Mitzi chuckled and tapped Owen's arm. "You're not fooling me. You're doing this for the free haircuts."

Owen shook his head while Brooke hugged her aunt. "I'm so happy for you."

"Champagne for all." Mitzi turned to Jonathan, beaming and flashing her ring. "You're invited to come inside, too."

"Oh, no." Brooke frowned. "I forgot. Daisy's in there, and she has muddy paws."

"Oh, darlin', a little mud never hurt anyone.

It's celebration time." Mitzi wound her arm through Brooke's and opened the door before glancing over her shoulder at Jonathan. "Join us?"

"Thanks. I'd be honored."

More laughter broke out as he joined Brooke's family.

CHAPTER THIRTEEN

LATER THAT NIGHT, Jonathan waved goodbye to Caleb and faced Vanessa, her muddy jeans a sign of how much fun she had at the Spindler house. "Looks like it's shower time and then bed for you, young lady."

While she was in the shower, Jonathan cleaned the kitchen, his lips still tingling from the memory of kissing Brooke. This evening with her reminded him of those sappy first-love shows Vanessa was discovering. That kiss ignited feelings in him he thought long gone but had instead been dormant, the same way there was so much more to Brooke below the surface.

Before Jonathan could get Brooke all to himself after a champagne toast to the happy couple, Caleb had texted to say that Vanessa wanted to come home.

He wiped strawberry jelly off the countertop just as Vanessa entered the kitchen with wet hair and wearing a nightgown with kittens. She'd been begging for a pet for a while.

Maybe it was time to think about a kitten. Anne had been planning a trip to the animal shelter before the accident happened. He aimed the dishcloth at the sink and released it with a swish. It fell into the basin.

"Perfect timing on your part. All the kitchen chores are done, and it's bedtime." Then he'd sink into his favorite chair and relax with a little television.

"Daddy, can you be happy and sad at the same time?" Vanessa clutched her stuffed kitten, Miss Whiskers, and hugged it close to her chest.

So much for relaxing. His daughter needed an answer, not that he was sure a simple yes or no would suffice. Her pensive expression gave away too much, yet he needed more information.

"Why do you ask, Nessie?"

She scuffled the floor with her slippers and shrugged. "Just wondering."

Jonathan led her to the sofa, and they settled in. Anne had taken forever at the furniture store selecting this model. With each of the three finalists, she sat and whipped out her book and read for fifteen minutes, testing the couch. Even the salespeople had given up and left them alone.

Vanessa snuggled against his side, Miss Whiskers still nestled in the crook of her arm.

"Yes, a person can be happy and sad at the same time." *Take tonight*. Earlier had been an exhilarating high with that spectacular kiss and Mitzi and Owen's announcement, and yet it was bittersweet as he couldn't shake the feeling the timing of everything was off. There was so much uncertainty swirling around him with the detective position up in the air, Izzy taking such a vehement stand against Brooke and this whole case hanging over him.

He wanted Brooke to trust him, and yet he wasn't sure he'd earned that yet.

"Why do you ask?"

Vanessa hesitated, and he let the silence draw out, wanting her to feel comfortable enough to talk to him about anything, not just now but always. "When Lucie laughed tonight, I was happy. Then I thought of Mommy, and I couldn't remember what her voice or laugh sounded like. I was sad."

His heart gripped his chest. It tightened, and he could barely breathe. There were days when Anne's voice seemed near, and others when it was so fleeting he also had trouble remembering the cadence of it, the lilt of her smile and the softness in her gaze. Whenever that happened, however, Izzy would grin or Vanessa would shout something, and Jonathan remembered.

He brought her closer, comforting his sensitive daughter, resembling Anne in appearance and him in temperament, and who used humor as a shield for her soft heart.

He stroked her damp hair, the orange scent of her shampoo comforting and familiar. "All you have to do is laugh, and that's what her laugh sounded like." He carefully untangled himself from her and went over to the bookcase. He returned with a photo album, and she scrambled over to give him room. "Your mommy made this. Part of her is in here, and part of her is in your heart and Izzy's heart." *And the heart of the transplant patient.*

Vanessa flipped the pages, and Jonathan watched the wonder on her face. Then he glanced at his engagement picture. His and Anne's faces glowed with the exuberance of young love. Was it wrong to want that kind of happiness a second time?

After all, he had everything he'd ever wanted, and it slipped away in an instant.

Lightning never struck twice in the same spot.

And yet, kissing Brooke tonight? Rarely was something as good as the sheer anticipation, and tonight's kiss had been even better. He hadn't expected anyone like Brooke coming into his life after Anne, but that didn't mean it couldn't be beautiful and exhilarating.

Vanessa's soft snuffles of sleep made him smile. Brooke had pointed out to Nessie that his daughter could like pandas and Rosie the Riveter at the same time. Liking one thing didn't mean forgetting another. All he had to do was believe that something special was coming his way. A little action to control the situation never hurt either.

BROOKE LEANED AGAINST Betty's reception desk near the sign-in sheet. "How is it past three already? I'm running over to The Busy Bean for a cup of coffee and one of their wraps since I forgot my lunch, but I'll be back in no time." Tonight was the start of the new GED program and Brooke was assisting the instructor with the first class, which had hit capacity in an instant. "Do you want anything?"

"No, but the Mimosas are planning a surprise get-together for Mitzi at the Timber River Bar and Grill tomorrow night. You're invited." Betty answered the phone and then hung up the handset. "Another hang-up. Something's going on this week with our system. You should contact the phone company."

"I'll put that on my list, and thanks for the

invite." She waved and headed for the entrance while a warm feeling spread through her at how they'd accepted her.

Acceptance was a double-edged sword. That meant trusting those around her and cementing the relationships in her grasp. Yesterday, Jonathan had offered her his jacket and a chance at so much more. She wanted to believe he was different from Colin's father. Last night's kiss was certainly different. There was an inner strength to Jonathan that Hayden never had.

And Jonathan? While it was clear his parents' demanding work ethic had a powerful impact on him, he'd blended his duty along with quality time with his daughters. Hayden had taken one look at infant Colin and slammed the door on them. For Jonathan, work and family were commitments he'd never shirk.

With a new jaunt in her step, she reached the electronic doors and bumped into Colin, his arrival a surprise with his backpack hanging over one shoulder. She frowned and tugged at her purse. "I thought you were at basketball practice."

"Hi to you, too, Mom. Coach had an emergency, so practice was canceled. I came straight here. Riley has volleyball practice for another hour, but she's invited me for dinner.

Then we'll review for our test tomorrow. Can I go?"

How much studying would her son get done? "Text Aunt Mitzi you won't be home tonight."

He reached around for his backpack before his face deepened to lobster-red. "Riley left her cell at home today, and I lent her mine after school so she could text her parents. I forgot to get it back. I'll call her from your office and then study there until it's time to walk to her house."

At least she was raising a gentleman.

"Okay, but text me when you get your phone back."

"Thanks, Mom. You're the best." He brushed a kiss against her cheek and sprinted for her office.

Brooke rolled her eyes and walked over to Betty. "Since Colin's confiscating my office, I'll order that wrap to go and bring it back to the faculty lounge."

"Hmm. I think you'll revisit that plan." Betty's eyes twinkled, and she smiled at Brooke. "Mysterious Cute Guy has arrived."

Brooke whipped around and found Jonathan headed her way. Unlike the casual jeans he'd worn at the pumpkin patch, he was rather dressed up today in a pair of black pants and a blue sweater, a nice change from seeing him in uniform.

She turned back to Betty. "How did you know Jonathan is Mysterious Cute Guy? I never told anyone."

Betty chuckled. "You didn't, but I now owe Hyacinth a mimosa at the Grill. She thought MCG was Jonathan, but I was holding out for my Mason. A grandma's prerogative, you know. Are you still going to The Busy Bean? They close early on Sundays, you know."

Brooke ignored the rumblings in her stomach. "Guess not."

Betty unlocked the bottom drawer and pulled out her purse. "How about a compromise? If you watch the front desk and talk to Jonathan, I'll run home for my slow cooker of turkey chili. Joe said he had to work late anyway, and you're more than welcome to have a bowl of chili for a late lunch. I'll be back in fifteen minutes, twenty tops."

"Sounds great."

Betty waved to Jonathan on her way out. "Be nice to our Brooke."

Our Brooke. That had such a sweet sound. Sure, the Mimosas were betting on her love life, but that meant they cared. Brooke walked around to Betty's side of the desk and locked her purse in the bottom drawer just to be safe.

"Jonathan." Her mouth went dry, and her palms started sweating something awful. "Betty stepped away for a minute. What brings you here today?"

He widened his lips into that slow grin of his, the one that melted her heart every time. "I didn't come to talk to Betty."

Something about that smile sent her instincts into overdrive. "Thank you for staying to celebrate Aunt Mitzi's engagement last night."

He chuckled. "Is that the only thing you're thanking me for? What about the kiss?"

"It was sweet." *Okay, better than sweet.* She settled into Betty's seat, much higher than her own office chair, a testament to Betty's shorter height. "And unexpected, just like your visit today. I like that color on you. It's nice."

She swallowed, kicking herself for using the bland word when that kiss was special and unique and close to perfect. Had he dropped everything to come to talk to her? He certainly dressed up for the visit, and he was the kind of guy who wore clothes well. Two attractive attributes, indeed.

"I chose it specially for my job interview."

She kept her jaw from dropping open. *An interview?* Here she thought he was as much a part of Hollydale as the Timber River, the Holly Days Diner, and this community center. She never dreamed he'd consider leaving behind something that seemed such an intrinsic part of him. "Did it go well? How far away did you have to drive?"

"Five minutes." That grin was back, and she could have sworn she now saw a slight swagger in his stance. He met her gaze. "You thought the interview was out of town."

She glanced at Betty's messy work area and started sorting stray paperclips and assorted papers. "I was concerned for Vanessa and Isabella. They seem happy here."

He reached over and tapped the bottom of her chin until she looked at him. "Were those the only Maxwells you were concerned about?"

Biting her lip, she considered whether she should put her heart on the line. Those hazel eyes almost convinced her she should follow her feelings instead of what her brain was telling her. "The kiss was the most special part of my stay in Hollydale so far." And that was saying something, since Aunt Mitzi's announcement was huge and terrific and amazing, and she'd actually been here for it.

"Would you like to have dinner with me at Ristorante Dominic's this weekend? They serve the best piccata and their pasta is homemade. There's candlelight and the nighttime view is spectacular." His throat bobbed, and he stood up straight. "After my interview, which was a disaster, I couldn't think of anyone else I wanted to see, anyone else who could make me feel better by my being in their presence."

That might have been the single most touching compliment anyone had ever paid her. The electricity crackled around them. "How did the women of Hollydale not snap you up before I moved here?"

"Women, huh?" That twinkle in his eyes returned, and he laughed. "That's kind of you."

"Why do you think your interview was a disaster?" She quit tidying the reception desk and focused on him.

He traced the edge of the sign-in sheet with his finger. "I'm not related to the district attorney."

"What's the interview for?"

"A detective position opening up in Hollydale."

"That sounds like it would involve more hours." Hadn't he said his parents were workaholics?

She ignored the goose bumps that had popped up along her skin. Good thing he couldn't see them beneath her blazer or he'd be quite insufferable.

In the cutest way possible.

Jonathan shook his head and picked up the clipboard. "If that were true, I'd have turned down the interview."

"Is this something you really want to do?" She tapped her finger on her cheek. "Weren't you a detective when..."

He nodded. "It's okay to bring up Anne. That is, unless that makes you uncomfortable."

"That's not a problem. I assumed you decided on the job shift when she passed."

"There was an opening in Hollydale, and I love it here."

"Do you miss being a detective?"

"Yep. I have a degree in criminal justice, and I love solving puzzles almost as much as I love my chocolaty cereal puffs in the morning." He cracked a smile, and then his face lit up.

She could tell this was something he was passionate about. "If you were this animated during the interview, I'm sure you'll get the job."

He placed the clipboard down again. "Actually, I wasn't. I sat there like a stuffed shirt, probably because I want this so much. I'd have a more consistent schedule. While I'd be called in for emergency situations, the hours are steadier, and it comes with holidays off."

"You're a police officer. You must have known working holidays came with the job."

Why did talking to him come so easily to her? In fact, there was something about Jonathan that made her want to snuggle with him in front of a warm fire. Somehow he made everything a little simpler, and there were so few people she'd felt comfortable with so relatively quickly. Usually it was better, safer, for her to hold back.

"I know that, but in Savannah, I was on the holiday rotation schedule."

She froze. Was she part of his quest to become a detective? Or was she more? Before she could go any further, she had to know she counted for something. That a commitment to her would be as important as his work and his daughters. For years, it had only been her and Colin. Making room for someone else in their lives was something scary and different. She had to know he'd value her and Colin and wasn't using her like Hayden had.

"Does this investigation factor into it?"

He shuffled his feet. "Yes, I need to solve this case to have an edge, but I already told you why this matter strikes a chord with me."

The thread of a connection seemed rather thin, and she needed time to digest this development. "Do me a favor. Check out the locker, and then we'll talk about the kiss." One she'd thoroughly enjoyed and something she wanted to repeat and often. She'd be lying to herself if she denied it was the last thing on her mind when she went to sleep and the first thing on her mind when she woke up. "I'll wait here. Remember, my future in Hollydale is at stake as well."

"I'll be right back."

He walked away, slowly at first. Then he glanced both ways as if checking for anyone else who might be in the vicinity. Always vigilant, always aware of his surroundings. There truly was no separating the police officer from the man himself. Was that something she understood and could accept?

She glanced down and saw the extension for her office phone lit up. Most likely, Colin had called his cell and was talking to Riley. Now was as good a time as any to remind them of Colin's curfew. She picked up the handset and paused when someone other than Riley spoke. "This worked out better than I planned."

She started to let them know she was on the line when Colin's voice came through her headset. "I don't know who you are, but you have the wrong number."

The other person laughed. "Oh, I have the right number. All I need is your cooperation and five minutes. I'll make sure it's worth your while. A simple exchange, and you'll never hear from me again. Name your price."

"You obviously have the wrong person."

"Don't hang up, Colin Novak. You have access to your mom's keys, right?"

The line went dead, and Brooke stared at the receiver in her hand. What had she just heard? Her heart raced, and she stopped short of stampeding into her office and demanding an explanation.

Except Colin sounded as clueless as she felt right now.

She'd told Jonathan she trusted Colin, yet did she? What was her son involved in? She couldn't wait for Yolanda or Olivia to monitor the front desk. If someone came in right now, they could wait two minutes. She ran to her office and opened the door, not bothering to knock.

"Colin?"

He glanced up, that fleeting glimpse of fear gone so fast she wondered if she'd imagined it. "I'm leaving for Riley's in half an hour. Just enough time to finish my chemistry homework."

"I picked up the phone. What was that call about?"

"You tell me. I picked up the handset to call

Riley as the phone rang. I said hello without thinking much about it. Someone wants something from me, but why?" He shut his textbook and walked over to her. "Are you in some kind of trouble, Mom? We can go to Aunt Mitzi."

Someone called Colin, yet he was worried about her. How could she have thought the worst of her son?

"Of course not." Should she tell Jonathan about this? And what exactly would she say? Neither she nor Colin knew the caller, and Colin hung up before the man identified himself.

But what if Colin needed protection? The call sounded ominous. "Did you recognize the voice? Did he say his name?"

"No and no." Colin folded his arms. "I want this to stay between us. For the first time, I'm fitting in. I'm not giving that call a second thought. If the basketball coach thought I was trouble, he'd kick me off the team. And Riley's parents? If they think I'm getting weird phone calls, they won't let me hang around Riley."

Brooke rubbed her eyes and glanced at the hall. "I have to return to the reception desk. Will you be okay?"

"Mom, I'll be sixteen next week. I can take care of myself." He grinned and shuffled his feet. "Well, mostly. I still like you and Aunt

Mitzi looking out for me. And let's be honest, I'll never be too old for Aunt Mitzi's fried green tomatoes."

His message came through clearly, and she went back to work. She hadn't even settled in Betty's chair when Jonathan made his way to the desk. That gorgeous smile of his warded off some of the chill coming over her, but it didn't completely do the trick.

"Hey, there." He approached the desk and leaned on his elbows. "Sometimes the best news is no news."

The stash was still in the locker, but that didn't surprise her, considering the caller was probably the one responsible for planting it there. "Good to know."

"Let's talk about something better. You." He met her gaze, those observant hazel eyes glinting in the rays flooding the atrium with light. "You're pretty wonderful."

The electronic doors opened, and in rushed a fortysomething female. "Excuse me. Is this the right place for the GED class?" A nervous tic twitched, and she stepped backward. "Maybe I shouldn't be here."

Brooke went to reassure the woman. "Of course you should be. We have a marvelous instructor, and I'll be helping tonight."

Jonathan nodded and smiled. "Trust Brooke.

It'll be the best decision you've made in a long time."

The knots in her stomach had nothing to do with hunger and everything to do with Jonathan. *Trust Brooke.* She should mention that phone call, but she stayed silent for her son's sake. She didn't want him to be the subject of stares and whispers if people thought he was running with the wrong crowd. One mistake could haunt a person for years, and picking up the phone wasn't even a mistake.

Thank goodness for this class. Now she had time to decide how to back away from what could have been the best thing to happen to her in years.

CHAPTER FOURTEEN

BROOKE STARED AT her smartphone from the comfort of Aunt Mitzi's living room. This was the third text message from Jonathan today. So far she hadn't replied to any of them, unsure of what to say. Any response might lead her to spill the beans about that phone call she'd overheard at the center, and that would be devastating for Colin. Until last night, no nightmares about those nasty gossips had haunted her sleep since the move. She'd spent a good part of the day yawning, even drinking an extra cup of coffee to dispel her drooping eyelids due to a restless night.

Secrets had destroyed her relationship with Colin's father, and she'd been the one to pay the price, keeping his identity to herself for his peace of mind. The difference this time, though, was Colin would pay the price if anyone believed he was part of this. He didn't ask for that phone call, so it was up to her to keep it to herself. Jonathan had opened his heart to her, and she'd chosen to protect her son.

How could they build a relationship with trust at its foundation if she kept the truth from him?

Until Hollydale, she wouldn't have given that type of omission a second thought. However, her lack of full disclosure to those she'd become so close to tore her apart, an invisible fissure causing heartache on a scale previously unimagined.

The other night, Jonathan had lent her his coat, shielding her from the mountain wind. Maybe she should in turn let him in and tell him of the phone call while keeping Colin out of the conversation.

But what if Jonathan was only using the center to achieve that promotion he so wanted? Would someone once again be saying the nice words she wanted to hear to get what he wanted rather than putting his heart on the line and making a true commitment?

She typed a text and then deleted it, wanting to reply but unsure what to say. She finally gave up and decided she'd talk to him the next time they met. A new town and a chance for a real relationship called for open communication. With that in mind, she turned her attention to her next problem. Getting Aunt Mitzi out of the house.

"You know, Brooke." Aunt Mitzi spoke

from behind, and Brooke turned to see her aunt standing there in her fluffy floor-length robe and a pink floral shower cap. "I think we should order takeout. It was a long day at the salon, and I need a night in. Too much excitement lately."

The other Mimosas would never let her live it down if she showed up at the Timber River Bar and Grill for Aunt Mitzi's engagement party without Aunt Mitzi. Brooke reached for any excuse that would make her aunt change her clothes and get them out of the house as soon as possible. Late was better than nothing, right?

"That's exactly the reason we should go out. We'd both fall asleep after two bites. Being with others will give us enough energy to enjoy the rest of the night, so afterward I can relax with a good book, and you can have a relaxing foot bath."

She'd have to work on her excuses before she confronted Jonathan in person with a reason for ending what had just started between them. That flimsy argument was truly pathetic. Aunt Mitzi started laughing. "I'm fooling with you. I just wanted to see your reaction, and it was priceless." She removed the robe and revealed a beige duster sweater over a white T-shirt with her familiar black leggings and a beautiful multicolor scarf to pull it all together. "I know about the impromptu surprise party, and I wouldn't miss it for anything, especially since my favorite niece is taking me. That plum dress brings out your coloring. You should wear bright colors more often."

A night out was what Brooke needed. It would offer a little perspective, hopefully, and a way to figure out her next step with Jonathan.

JONATHAN CARRIED THREE long-necked bottles to the table where Caleb and Owen waited for him. An evening with the guys at the Timber River Bar and Grill was what the doctor ordered, considering Brooke had never returned any of his texts today. Although he held out hope it was her schedule that had prevented her from doing so, he pushed thoughts of his favorite tall and willowy brunette aside. He delivered one beer to his cousin and the other to the newly engaged park ranger, whose announcement was the reason for tonight's outing. That, and one tasty cheeseburger.

"This round's on me. Thank your daughter for babysitting tonight." He raised his voice over the latest Keith Urban song and clinked his bottle against Owen's. "And congratulations on your engagement. Any date yet?"

Owen took a long swig. "Mitzi has her heart set on Valentine's Day."

"Lucie and I'll book a babysitter early, seeing as Ashleigh will be busy." Caleb smiled and clinked his beer bottle against Jonathan's. "And what's going on between Mitzi's niece and a certain bachelor police officer cousin of mine?"

Jonathan adjusted his collar. "Is it hot in here? I think it's warmer than when we arrived."

Caleb laughed. "No, but I haven't seen you this red since you were too cocky to wear suntan lotion when we spent a summer day on the Nantahala River." He turned to Owen. "It was not pretty."

"Thanks. Why don't you reveal all my secrets?" he joked.

"The night's still young." Caleb grinned and then shrugged. "All kidding aside, I couldn't wait until you arrived every summer break. It was like having a brother."

No sooner did Caleb stop talking than Brooke breezed into the bar, and the sight of her propelled him to the stars.

He wasn't sure yet whether this was a good thing, considering how she'd ignored his texts. He crashed back to earth.

Mitzi, and several ladies all expressing their

admiration of Mitzi's ring, arrived, and Owen rose from the table. "Excuse me. I'm going to say hello to my future bride."

Jonathan took another long swig of beer and devoted his attention to Caleb.

"How did the interview go?"

Oh, that. Jonathan played with the paper at the neck of the bottle. "Nothing to write home about."

Caleb placed his beer on his coaster and did the same for Owen's bottle. "Why so down?"

Jonathan relayed the relevant details. "Mike's probably in my corner, same as Everson's in his niece's corner. Aidan Murphy's impossible to read."

"He keeps his cards close to his vest, but he's a decent guy, fair, too."

The server delivered their orders, three perfectly cooked cheeseburgers with all the toppings along with a heaping helping of french fries. Caleb ordered another round of beers.

"Make mine nonalcoholic. Thanks." The server nodded at Jonathan's request and scooted away to the next table.

Jonathan reached for the ketchup at the same time as Caleb, withdrew his hand and motioned for his cousin to go first. Caleb uncapped the bottle. "I can pour and listen at the same time."

Jonathan slipped the bun atop the cheeseburger. "I can't see Aidan going against what's expected of him."

"Underneath that stiff exterior is someone who'll do what's right." Caleb passed him the ketchup bottle and then chewed on a fry with obvious contentment.

He had to get this weight off his shoulder and confide in someone. Caleb was the closest thing he had to a brother, and his weekly five-minute Zoom meeting with his parents wouldn't do the trick. Here went nothing. "I've been giving some thought to my future if Ms. Everson gets the job."

Caleb straightened in his chair. "You don't really think they'll pass you over, do you?"

Jonathan gnawed on his burger. If they hired the other candidate for the position, could he in good conscience work under Sheriff Harrison and Detective Everson? They'd all be on the same side of the law, but his pride over losing the job to someone fresh out of the academy who was related to the district attorney?

Would be shattered.

He placed his burger back on his plate and considered his options. His father-in-law had long advocated for Jonathan to accept a position with his cyber security firm. That was one possibility. Another also led him back to Savannah as well. His former lead detective and commanding officer had reached out to him after Mike asked for a reference. They'd shot the breeze before McEachern reminded Jonathan of an open position.

Izzy and Vanessa were settled here, and maybe he had even more reasons to stay. His gaze went to Mitzi's table and landed on Brooke. She was always a stunner, but her radiance bloomed tonight, and he didn't stem the attraction he felt. Brooke nodded at the group and came over to Jonathan's table.

"Hi, fellas." Brooke raised her voice enough to be heard over the crowd and Blake Shelton. "Tina said to say hello. If your food hadn't already arrived, we'd have invited you guys to join us."

His cheeseburger could wait. "Would you care to dance?"

"I'm here to celebrate my aunt's engagement, and you're eating." She glanced at her table, and then her gaze met his. She smiled. "Why, yes, thank you."

He entwined his hand in hers and led her to the dance floor. A slow song by Brad Paisley started, and he navigated them toward a spot where the lights weren't as bright. She moved closer, and he weaved his arm around her back until the sweet scent of sugar and vanilla overcame the smell of beer and barbecue. She nestled her cheek on his shoulder, and the silky strands of her hair brushed against his stubble. The feel of her in his arms sent time and space spinning in a whirl before everything silenced around them. He closed his eyes and savored this moment.

While the troubles in his life didn't fade away, they now seemed manageable. He and Brooke swayed in time to the rhythm of the guitar riff. This first dance brought his heart to full crescendo while her softness molded against his body in a way that made him believe new beginnings could happen for him. More importantly, new beginnings with Brooke.

There was nowhere else he wanted to be than on this dance floor.

A tap at his shoulder brought him out of the delicate trance. "The music stopped minutes ago," Aunt Tina whispered in his ear and left the dance floor.

He separated from Brooke, but one look at her and he knew.

He was falling in love with her.

CHAPTER FIFTEEN

JONATHAN ENTERED THE Timber River Bar and Grill for the first time in nearly a week and slipped off his sunglasses. He wasn't used to the bar in the broad daylight, the smell of yeast and hops not unpleasing.

Mark Sandell, the bar's part owner, raised the mug he was drying, a mere hour before the place opened at eleven for lunch. "Jonathan. You got my message. Sorry I didn't call until today. Except for the Super Bowl, this is one of our busiest times of the year."

Jonathan strode over to him. "I can't believe I left my jacket here." Especially as it was the last present Anne had given him.

Had it been a simple slip that he'd left it behind the night he admitted he was developing deep feelings for Brooke? Or had he been purposely putting distance between him and his memories of Anne? Life as a widower had been a series of firsts: that first morning without waking up beside her, the first Christmas when her smile didn't greet him, the first anniversary of her death. Other firsts, he hadn't expected: kissing someone else, slow dancing and that exhilaration through his veins from falling in love again.

All week he'd avoided Brooke, hoping he'd get past the guilt of letting go of his grief.

Brooke made him feel alive again. Eventually he'd have to face her and own up to his feelings.

Mark reached down and handed the jacket to Jonathan. "Here you go."

"Thanks." Jonathan waved and headed for the door. He stopped when he heard his name.

Turning, he found Mark's grandfather and the other co-owner motioning for him to return. Lew was a man of few words, so if he wanted Jonathan for something, it must be important.

Lew placed a driver's license on the scarred wooden bar top, halfway between Mark and Jonathan. "Found this in the men's room in the crack between the trash bag and can."

Jonathan extricated a pair of blue gloves, similar to Lew's, from his utility belt along with an evidence bag. Considering where Lew had found it, he didn't even bother to ask about video surveillance cameras. "May I?"

After the two men nodded, Jonathan snapped on the gloves and examined the license. A pinched side in the corner along with an address he didn't recognize clued him into another fake one. "Either of you ever heard of Lantana Valley Court?"

Both men shook their heads, their same hawklike noses showing off the striking resemblance. "No."

A quick check confirmed it was a phony address. Jonathan asked some general questions about the routine maintenance and cleaning schedule. Then Mark reached under the counter once more, this time pulling out a washrag and wiping down the surface. "Anything I should do about this? I don't want my liquor license pulled."

"Keep carding and be on the lookout for any licenses with a pinched edge in the lower right corner." Jonathan pulled out his business card from his pocket. "Call me if you run across any more like these."

Mark threw the rag back in the cleaning bucket with a flourish. "Will do."

Jonathan took his time walking to his car and reviewed the evidence he had in his hand. He didn't expect any prints. Ones that had been there would likely be smudges by now.

He returned to the station and found Mike on the phone. He started to leave the office, but Mike motioned for him to enter. The sheriff made a wrap-it-up gesture at the phone and rolled his eyes.

Taking off his hat, Jonathan made himself as comfortable as possible. The sheriff set the receiver back on the phone. "Ms. Everson is visiting Hollydale late next week. She passed her exam and is now interviewing at several precincts. As much as I wanted a decision before now, Stuart is insisting on an in-person interview with her this time. Since Aidan's going out of town on business tomorrow, we're working around that."

"Our favorite license case is back." Jonathan dropped the evidence bag on the desk. "Someone left it at the Timber River Bar and Grill."

Mike arched his left eyebrow and grabbed a pencil from the holder. "Left it there?"

"Lew found it between the liner and the can. Someone either threw it away, which probably means it didn't get the intended results, or lost it."

Mike nodded and snapped the pencil in half, the sharp sound piercing the air. How many pencils did Mike go through in a day anyway? Mike looked at him and laughed. "Sorry. Habit. Can Mark or Lew pinpoint how long the license was there?"

"Less than a day."

Mike threw away the pencil halves. "Have

you been canvassing other places downtown? Any more activity at the Corner Grocery?"

Jonathan pulled out his notepad. "I went back and checked with Mo and at the other gas station and convenient stores and the liquor stores in the twenty-mile radius. One owner admitted he'd seen something similar, but the person left with the license when he wouldn't sell to him."

"Good work. Do you think the person will come back to the Timber River Bar and Grill tonight? Look for the lost license?"

Jonathan thought about the layout of the restaurant. There was one table in the far back that had a view of the bathroom. "I'll talk to Mark. See if I can stakeout the bathroom tonight without being too conspicuous if I'm there for hours."

"Georgie and Rachel are busy tonight." Mike's face lit up at the mere mention of his wife and daughter. "I'll take over after seven."

"Sounds like a plan." Jonathan remembered the stash in the locker. "With your permission, I'd like to come up with a few more ideas about the community center. Ten licenses, which in total could net over a thousand dollars, at least, might be worth coming back for."

"Any more recent evidence that's a serious place of interest? What about the high school?"

Mike situated his computer screen between them and pulled up a map. "And it's not like Hollydale has a shortage of hiking trails for an out-of-the-way exchange."

"Eric confessed he picked up his ID in the men's locker room. The last time I looked, the fake cache is still there." *One new substantial lead.* That's all he'd need to break this case wide open. Why had the suspect given up on the bag in the locker? Why hadn't he gone back for it or the laminator? "Considering how the edge of the license is pinched, though, I'm convinced someone purchased this ID from the perp's first supply. Once that inventory gets low, the perp might try to retrieve his equipment and create new ones to sell."

Mike scrubbed his chin before reaching for his coffee mug. One sip of the brew brought a grimace. "Cold and thick as motor oil. I think I'll head over to The Busy Bean before Deb closes for the day." He glanced out his window. "I'll authorize whatever you come up with. Also follow up with the surrounding counties' Department of Motor Vehicles offices again. I'm not convinced this is a one-person scheme, and one of the offices must be missing the laminator by now. You can stay on this until Thanksgiving. After that, we have too many holiday events that need a watchful eye."

So he had a couple weeks to crack this case. That was better than nothing.

Plus, he had an excuse to see Brooke. After the official disclosures were out of the way, it was time to bite the bullet and ask if they should spend the holidays as a couple.

IN THE CLASSROOM on the upper level of the community center, Brooke uncapped the dry-erase marker and wrote a new first grade math problem on Emmie's whiteboard. "You can do this."

The little girl with the big glasses scrunched her face and reached for the marker. She carefully wrote out her answer and relaxed. "I think this is right."

Accepting the marker once more, Brooke placed a check mark next to Emmie's work. "I know it's right. See, you just need confidence in yourself."

Emmie beamed and accepted a happy face sticker, placing it on her shirt. "I did it!"

"Yes, you did." Brooke held out her hand and waited for Emmie to connect with a high-five. "It's time to end today's class."

"But I'll see you next week, right?" Emmie placed her hands on the sides of her wheelchair and rolled it away from the desk.

"I wouldn't miss spending time with my star

math student for anything." Even though this tutoring program was the youth director Olivia's idea, Brooke had agreed to volunteer for the first six weeks' worth of sessions. It was important to her to have a personal connection and taste of everything that was happening at the center.

Brooke nodded and then tapped her fingers against her chin as though pondering the weight of the universe. "Except maybe a turkey leg and pumpkin pie." When Emmie's eyes widened with shock, Brooke shook her head. "I'm just teasing. I'll see you once more before you get a week away from me."

Brooke kept her tone light, drawing a giggle out of the shy girl who'd made a lot of progress in their two tutoring sessions.

She stood and made her way to the front of the room, clapping for everyone's attention. More eyes than last week landed on her, and she smiled. "A special thank-you to our new volunteers." She winked at her son before turning her attention to Belinda, the town's award-winning pie queen, who now owned Sweet Shelby's Tea Room with Hyacinth. "And you were welcome with or without that delicious pie."

"So, that means no pie next week?" Humor laced Belinda's voice, but the kids still groaned.

"We-lll." Brooke drawled out the word. "Considering there's not even a leftover crumb, I don't think we'd turn away such kindness." Everyone laughed, and she jerked her thumb toward the exit. "I hear parents in the hallway. I hope to see everyone next week for one more session before Thanksgiving break."

Brooke opened the door, and Emmie's father, Jeremy, walked into the room. Emmie took the lead and left with him first. Then others filed out, leaving Brooke, Belinda and Colin behind.

"Don't mind me." Belinda marched toward her pie plate as if she were in formation. "I'm waiting for my husband to pick me up. He can rattle off statistics about the best times of day to fish or what the score of the game was five years ago, but he can never remember that I'm here, and instead, drives to Sweet Shelby's Tea Room on autopilot. I hate that my optometrist restricted my driving for six months." She reached in her purse, pulled out an eye patch and placed it over her left eye. "Stupid iritis."

"Next time, wear it. The kids won't be scared of a patch. If anything, they'll think you're a cool pirate tutor." Brooke hustled toward the side table and stacked the plates. "Colin, could you bring me the spray bottle from underneath the sink?"

Colin handed it to her before he faced the older woman. "That pie was delicious, ma'am. Thank you. If you need anything else, say the word."

A hearty laugh came from the direction of the doorway. A heavyset man in denim overalls paired with a burnt-orange plaid flannel shirt made his way into the room and picked up the oversize picnic basket as if it was a feather. "Belinda, I swear you have males of all ages falling at your feet for your pies."

"You must be Belinda's husband. I'm the new director of the center, Brooke Novak, and this is my son, Colin." Brooke held out her hand, and the man switched the basket to his other hand and shook hers.

"I'm Mo, and I've been Belinda's proud husband for the past forty-five years." He stared long and hard at Colin. "I've seen you somewhere before. Do you do a lot of fishing?"

"No, sir." Colin picked up the dirty towels. "I can't say as I have."

Belinda adjusted her patch. "Don't mind my husband. He lives and breathes all things fishing. That and sudoku."

Mo kept his gaze fixed on Colin, then removed his navy baseball cap and scratched his head. "I never forget a face. I know I've seen yours at my local bait shop and gas station."

"Sorry, sir, but I've never been there before. I'm sure I will be in the future, though. I'm getting my license this month."

Mo snapped his fingers. "I've seen your picture." He gulped and sought out Belinda. "Ready to go, honey? I grabbed a copy of the weekly newspaper before I left the convenience store. Just came in, hot off the presses. It's got the new sudoku and I want to get started after dinner."

Belinda laughed. "I swear that's why you won't retire and come work with me at the tea shop. You like getting the paper a day earlier than everyone else way too much."

Belinda and Mo hustled out with Mo still muttering about having seen Colin before. Brooke shook it off and faced Colin. "I hope you still have room for dinner after the pie."

Colin straightened to his full height and appeared sheepish. "I'm a teenager. I'm always hungry." Then a big grin came over him. "I can't wait any longer. Mo practically ruined the surprise." He went over to his backpack and brought out a newspaper. "The sports journalist of the paper delivered two copies to the coach. I was going to show you and Aunt Mitzi at dinner, but I'm the featured player of the week for the Hollydale Hornet basketball team."

Brooke side-hugged Colin. "Way to go."

She rifled through the pages looking for the article. She blinked back tears when she found it and his picture next to it. "I'm proud of you. So Hollydale suits you?"

"Hollydale suits me very well, thank you for asking."

Footsteps heralded a new arrival.

Brooke looked toward the door, and Jonathan's warm smile caught her off guard. Ever since their kiss and that slow dance at the bar, they hadn't found time to talk about what had happened. For the rest of that night, she'd found herself wedged between Aunt Mitzi and Fabiana, who kept the conversation lively.

Her heart raced at the instant attraction zinging between her and Jonathan. Something about the warmth he shared with his daughters and Hollydale defrosted the cool exterior she'd built around herself, a guard against the blows of the world. She'd also chipped away at that wall, first by getting her GED, followed by ten years of hard work for her college degree and keeping a roof over her head and Colin's. She was finally fulfilling her dreams.

Maybe it was time to move on from the scared girl she'd been so many years ago. Especially since this had the potential to become the most romantic relationship of her life. Slow dances and heady kisses with a relaxed guy didn't come along every day.

Colin claimed the newspaper from her and scurried to the door. "I'm heading home and showing this to Aunt Mitzi since this doesn't hit the stands until tomorrow. Don't worry, I've got Daisy covered tonight."

She murmured her goodbye, but her gaze stayed on Jonathan, tall with shoulders that filled out that navy uniform. Even better, he respected the uniform and the duties that came with it. There was something about a person who followed through with his commitments that was especially sexy to her.

The fact that he was a great dancer only sealed the deal. Dancing, kissing and laughing. Was there nothing this man couldn't do? Maybe that was one reason she found herself falling for him.

Forget falling. She already cared for this family man who had shared his concern about turning into his parents but was nothing like them. Devoted to his daughters, he spent quality time with them. Jonathan was a bit charming and a bit serious in a way that screamed trust.

And she did trust him. With her life and her heart.

If she let herself, she'd fall in love with him

in a heartbeat. Maybe she already had fallen in love with him.

She strode across the room and brushed her lips against his, the familiar mix of soap and sandalwood quite intoxicating. "Hello."

"Next time I'll stay away longer." He stepped aside and licked his lips. "Mmm. You taste like pie."

It was her turn to retreat. "Is that all you have to say?"

He closed the distance between them once more and silenced her with another kiss, this one deeper, sweeter, a moment that could spark a lifetime. Breaking away, she realized an invisible bond already existed between them. "I know what you've put on the line since you're still at the start of your six-month trial period. A public display with a police officer in uniform, no less. You're telling the world you're serious. The only thing is, you're not alone."

The magnitude of their potential sank in, and she leaned against her desk. "I think that dance pushed us past the point of no return in terms of letting the world know."

"You dance even better than you kiss. But business first, then pleasure."

So, she'd been a part of his thoughts as much as he'd been a part of hers. That hadn't been the only thing on her mind, not with Colin's phone call still between them. That ended now. Honesty and communication were integral parts of any relationship. "As an officer, how do you separate what's important from something trivial?"

"Brooke, what's going on between us isn't trivial. I know it's hard to believe that a catch like me wasn't snatched up." He grinned, but then his face became more serious. "All kidding aside, the hardest moment of my life came when I realized Anne was in that car. For a long time, I kicked myself. What if I'd seen the driver sooner? What if I'd arrived at the scene quicker? Maybe that was the reason I've held myself back. Maybe not. Maybe it has to do with the right person coming into my life, a person who has a tough exterior with the heart of a lion and a kind, compassionate soul. Someone I very much want to kiss again and again."

She'd seen his calm steadiness as a police officer and his caring wit as a dad, but this romantic side? Her heart melted, and love poured in.

Over the past couple of weeks, she'd fallen in love with everything about Jonathan Maxwell.

She'd best set him to rights about the secret call. "I wasn't talking about work."

His shoulders relaxed, and the biggest grin came over his face. "That's a relief. I'm glad we can be open with each other and talk about something other than work. I'm not going to lie. Before now, I was convinced I was becoming my parents. Workaholics for a good cause."

This wasn't going the way she had planned. Still, it would be even better. Getting everything into the open would make their next kiss all the sweeter. "This investigation—"

"Has taken a new turn. That's why I'm here."

Perhaps he'd already apprehended whoever had called Colin. That would save her the trouble of explaining why it had taken her so long to speak up. She settled into a chair and motioned for him to do the same. "What happened?"

He sat next to her. "Another license has come to light, so I'd like your permission to try a couple of new strategies. Tomorrow, I'm joining your gym so I'll have an excuse to be here undercover in the mornings. I'm also increasing patrols at night over the next few weeks, both here and at some local convenient stores. Have you heard back from the security companies? If they install outdoor cameras, I could then review the feed to maybe get a line on the suspect, if that's okay with you."

Her mouth went dry. After the police apprehended the suspect, she'd have to explain to Mr. Whitley why she hadn't confided in him. Her future hinged on the chief benefactor and chairperson of the board understanding the promise she'd made to Jonathan. "So you'll be here even more often?"

"Yep." He grinned.

"I'm interviewing one security company tomorrow." She rose and crossed to the door. "Can you show me the best position for outdoor cameras?"

They walked out to the parking lot, where only a few cars remained. Something gnawed at her, but she couldn't put her finger on it. It must be guilt.

"I'm thinking here and over there." He pointed to the most distant part of the lot, where her car occupied the last spot.

I grabbed a copy of the weekly newspaper... Just came in... I want to get started after dinner. Mo's words echoed in her mind, and she turned to Jonathan, folding her arms to ward off the chill that had nothing to do with the gray overcast evening and falling temperatures. "How did Mo see Colin's picture in the paper if he hadn't opened it yet?"

"What?" Jonathan shrugged and walked

over to her. "I thought we were discussing the best angles for the cameras."

Brooke blinked and tried to remember what Jonathan had told her about the case. "When you came here looking for the laminator, you talked about an underage teen who tried to buy cigarettes at a convenience store with a fake ID. Was it Mo's Gas and Bait Stop?"

He came over and laid his hand on her arm. "You're shivering. Why don't we go inside so you can get warm?"

"Don't change the subject." She repeated her question, and his protracted silence provided the answer. "Mo had seen Colin's picture."

Chills having nothing to do with cold weather and everything to do with Jonathan, or rather, Officer Maxwell, wracked her body. "Brooke…"

Only Jonathan had ever said her name with such intensity that caused her veins to hum. She couldn't catch her breath, and she wrenched her arm free from his grasp. "Without asking me or Colin if he'd ever been to Mo's Gas and Bait Stop, you showed the man a picture of my son, didn't you? Where did you even get his photo?"

Ike's Pumpkin Patch.

She backed away from Jonathan, not wanting to look at those warm hazel eyes that had, at one time, assessed her son and found him lacking a conscience. "It was the photo you took at the pumpkin patch, wasn't it? And the only reason you'd show it to Mo is if you believed Colin was a criminal."

"I have to protect the community."

"I have to protect my son."

A few minutes ago, she'd fought with herself about whether to tell Jonathan about a phone call Colin didn't instigate, one that could sound incriminating to someone who didn't believe Colin was a good kid. She wouldn't subject her son to the same glares and stares she'd endured when others judged her and found her wanting.

If Jonathan didn't believe in Colin, how could he believe in her, the woman who raised Colin? How could trust sustain a relationship when there was no trust? The one man who had seemed perfect for her was, in fact, not.

"I'd have done the same thing if I thought Izzy or Vanessa committed a crime." The catch in his voice left her little doubt he told the truth, but that didn't provide comfort.

It only provided her an excuse to stop the madness she experienced every time he entered the room, feelings that ended now before she got hurt. Except that it was too late. This hurt was raw and complete and consuming.

"That may be the case, but Colin is my responsibility, as is this community center. Have your person install the cameras tonight, and text me with updates."

The second she turned, Joe and Betty left the building, and she hurried over before they locked her out and her keys inside.

The cold nip in the air froze the tears to her cheeks. At least she didn't have to wipe them away.

CHAPTER SIXTEEN

BROOKE WAITED FOR Aunt Mitzi in front of Odalie's Closet and thrummed her fingers against her thigh. She only had forty-five minutes remaining of her lunch break to try on the contenders for the bridesmaids' dresses her aunt had chosen for her, Ashleigh and Lucie.

Her aunt ran up and hugged her. "I know, I know. You're in a hurry. Odalie's waiting for us, but Lucie had something come up, and Ashleigh's in school. That's okay, though, we'll have some time together until they arrive."

Aunt Mitzi shuttled her inside, where Odalie greeted them and then disappeared to retrieve three dresses for Brooke's inspection.

"You, Ashleigh and Lucie have such distinct personalities, it was difficult to narrow my choices. Then I said to heck with it. Y'all are different, and let's celebrate that." Aunt Mitzi went on, but Brooke only half listened.

Aunt Mitzi touched Brooke's arm and, without thinking, Brooke recited the last two sentences she'd heard. "See? I was paying attention."

"Honey, when are you going to admit you're plain miserable and kiss and make up with MCG?"

Mysterious Cute Guy. The cute guy part fitted Jonathan to a T. Mysterious? Not so much as everything about him was open and warm and funny and charming. Everything except his distrust of her son.

Brooke sighed and then reclined in the overstuffed chair in Odalie's bridal parlor area. "Betty broke it to me. The Mimosas know it's Jonathan."

"I already knew that." Mitzi waved her hand across her chest. "I wanted to hear you say it. What do you think? Is Jonathan cute? Is he the right person to be by your side?"

Brooke shifted under the uncomfortable gaze of her aunt. What if Brooke agreed? It wasn't like she was going to let herself get involved with someone who would think the worst of her and her family.

"Yes, he is, but anything between us was like caramel, warm and gooey at first but rotten for the teeth afterward."

"Whoa there, honey. Those are pretty powerful feelings." Aunt Mitzi leaned forward in her chair. "Whatever happened between you two, you need to talk to him. Does this have to do with your mamma, God rest her soul?"

"My mother has nothing to do with this, although he knows about her."

"Then what's the problem?" Mitzi shook her head. "I know it's your nature to guard your feelings, but it's okay to talk about them."

Brooke looked at her aunt, who'd always been more like a surrogate mom to Brooke. "I envy how you're always so free and receptive. It's hard for me to know who to trust. When I was pregnant, even my best friend's mother banned her from talking to me."

Mitzi squeezed Brooke's hand, her eyes full of love. "You'll always have me."

Brooke shifted in the chair. "We're here to celebrate your wedding, and that reminds me. I need to contact a Realtor and find a rental for Colin and me."

"Why don't you stay in my house? I'm moving to Owen's, and you and Colin can stay put."

"As long as we make it official and you let me pay you rent and utilities." That was one weight off her shoulders at least. "As far as Jonathan and me…"

"What about Jonathan? Is he different than what's on the surface?"

Unlike her, he was exactly who he was on the surface, a caring father, an observant officer, a smooth dancer. Every time she was around him, her heart beat a little faster, and she was a little happier. "He's up-front and honest."

"Sounds good to me. What's the problem?"

"It's not that simple."

Aunt Mitzi let out a chuckle. "Oh, darlin'. You might be more mysterious and guarded than Jonathan, but your face is saying plenty. Honest and cute guys don't come along every day."

"Okay, he's cute." More than cute. He smoldered, and his shoulders were as strong as his heart.

"Then why haven't you talked to him?"

"He doesn't trust me."

Their gazes met, and Brooke knew exactly from which side of the family she'd inherited her stubbornness. Odalie stepped into the room with a tray holding two glasses of bubbly. She glanced at Mitzi, then Brooke, then Mitzi again. "I'll leave the champagne on the table and let you two settle whatever's going on." She backed away and then smiled at Brooke. "The dresses aren't that awful, I promise."

Brooke took one look at her aunt, and they burst out laughing. Aunt Mitzi reached for a glass and sipped. "Half a glass is perfect so I don't go back to work and give all my clients mullets like that rival of mine Chantal does. Odalie's right, though. Lucie has good taste when it comes to these matters." Licking her lips, she placed the crystal goblet back on the tray. "Did he say he doesn't trust you?"

"Not in so many words." Brooke paused. The last thing she needed was for any suspicion to be cast on Colin.

As long as Mo didn't spread the news Colin had been part of a photo lineup, Colin could continue to hold his head high.

Aunt Mitzi handed her the other filled glass. "To finding people who accept you even when you think they'll never cross your path." She clinked her glass against Brooke's.

It would be impolite to refuse to drink to that beautiful toast, its meaning not lost on her. Here she blamed Hayden for not taking a chance on her and Colin and breaking his commitment to her while she blamed Jonathan for doing his job and honoring his many commitments. Maybe this was really about the fear of the unknown. But in reality, she knew all she needed to know about Jonathan. Brooke took the tiniest of sips, the tasty drink tickling her nose. "How did you know Owen was the right person for you?"

Aunt Mitzi laughed. "Oh, honey, it happened, and it was right. After Dwayne—"

she shook her head and sighed "—I thought it would be better if I made life a little better for everyone else in town. Made others sparkle. Then Owen walked into my salon, and magic happened."

She and her aunt were more alike than she'd realized. Same goals, same resistance, but different outcomes in love.

She loved Jonathan, and he'd hurt her. He might not have done so on purpose, yet it still was painful. However, if she accepted that he'd been following through with his commitment to his job, that would change everything.

"I'm glad it worked out for the both of you." And she was. Her aunt deserved the moon at her feet for what she did for others out of the pure kindness of her heart.

Odalie entered again and hung three dresses on the rack. "Lucie has an excellent eye for bridal fashion." The soft chimes of the doorbell signaled a new customer. She sent an apologetic glance their way. "Excuse me. My assistant is running late on her lunch break. I'll leave these here and come back to see if one of them catches your eye."

Odalie hurried out of the room, and Brooke rose and examined the dresses, all in varying shades of pink. She fingered the simplest one, an A-line with a curved neckline and a flared tea-length skirt. Aunt Mitzi joined her. "Is it official? Are you getting married on Valentine's Day?"

"It's my favorite holiday." Aunt Mitzi pulled the dress off the rack, held it up against Brooke and nodded. "This one will look right pretty on you. I think dusty pink for you, light pink for Lucie and the burgundy for Ashleigh. I can't wait for them to get here. Ha! Owen would get married tomorrow at the Hollydale municipal offices by a judge if it were up to him, but he knows Dwayne and I eloped when we were both too young to know better. So Owen and I are getting married with the works, everyone's invited, the gazebo for the ceremony, cold weather and all, with the reception to follow at the Whitley Pavilion. Sometimes it's better to move on from the past and get on with life, you know?"

"You might try being more blunt, Aunt Mitzi." Brooke laughed so her aunt would know she was keeping this light. "That's why I moved here. New town, new job, new possibilities."

"Honey, possibilities can become realities when we don't let ourselves stand in the way. You've been miserable. Talk to Jonathan."

Odalie rejoined them and beamed. "That one's my favorite of the three. It will look beautiful on all of you. Great choice. The fitting room is through that door. You can try it on so I can see if I need to make any alterations."

From the keen look in Aunt Mitzi's eye, Brooke understood that Odalie had merely interrupted the conversation, rather than ended it. "I can't talk to Jonathan tonight. I have to work late."

Brooke swept into the fitting room, happy to have had the last word.

"By the way." Aunt Mitzi raised her voice. "Did I forget to mention Tina invited me and Owen over for Thanksgiving? She said to bring you and Colin."

Brooke halted the removal of her coat with one arm stuck in the sleeve. Aunt Mitzi had conveniently held on to that detail until now. "I'll think about it."

"Jonathan and his daughters will be there."

Of course they would be. An old-fashioned Thanksgiving with people bursting out of the rooms, exactly the type of holiday she'd always dreamed of when she and Colin celebrated Thanksgiving alone in their apartment, each enjoying a drumstick and the other's company. If she wanted the possibility of a family holiday with all the trimmings to become a reality, she would have to spend the day with Jonathan.

Would that make him happy? Would that make her happy? Her life was in Hollydale, and it was time to ensure her heart could lodge here, too.

JONATHAN SLIPPED A ticket under the windshield of a red SUV parked downtown in a handicapped spot. He let go of the wiper only to find Aidan Murphy headed his way. Jonathan stood there, his nostrils flared. "This isn't your car, is it?"

Interview or no interview, if this was Aidan's car, he wouldn't take back this ticket.

"I own a teal car that belonged to my sister."

Jonathan exhaled, relieved the city manager hadn't parked in a handicapped space. "Good. I'd have hated to cite you. What do you need?"

"When's your next break?"

"Why?"

"I'd like to talk to you." Aidan held up his hands. "In full disclosure, I already spoke to Ms. Everson."

Jonathan winced at how Aidan might misread his attitude for sheer snark. The city manager might not have much to do with the direct dealings of the police department, but Aidan had a say in selecting the first detective.

Aidan motioned toward historic Hollydale City Hall. "My office is inside. It won't take long."

With a mere thirty minutes until he was supposed to pick up Izzy at the community center, Jonathan needed to arrange for someone else to take his daughter home. "I'll be right there."

Aidan nodded, and Jonathan texted his aunt with his request. Aunt Tina replied in the affirmative. With that settled, Jonathan joined Aidan, wary of whatever the city manager was going to lay on him. This might be his way of letting Jonathan down gently. Jonathan still wasn't sure what he'd do if he didn't get the job.

They walked inside city hall, and they stopped in front of a vending machine. Aidan plunked in a couple of dollar bills. "Natalie's sensitive to smells. I can't drink my favorite flavored water around her."

Anne had a similar reaction when she'd been pregnant with Vanessa. "Then I gather congratulations are in order. When's she due?"

Aidan kept his gaze on the machine, but Jonathan sensed a small smile at the corners of his lips. "In May."

Jonathan bobbed his head in support. "What do you want to know about me? My educational background? Conviction rate in Savannah? My greatest weakness?"

"I've studied your file and Emerson's. This is informal. I wanted to see both the candidates in action, and I've done just that." The bottle plopped down, and Aidan reached through the metal divider, pulling out the water. "Strawberry blackberry was exactly what I wanted. Anything strawberry-flavored is my weakness. Can I get you something?"

A line on his chances would be nice, but Jonathan kept that to himself. "I only drink coffee from vending machines as a last resort. I gave up metal-tasting coffee after college. Now a cup of Deb's special roasted blend is my weakness."

"Good choice. I'll let you get back to your duties."

That was all. It took him longer to shave in the morning. Admitting he'd missed something, though, while interviewing for the detective position wasn't an option. "Thanks. Have a good day."

Jonathan left the building and shook his head. Patience only could take him so far. He'd call his former superior in Savannah tonight after the girls went to bed and talk about those current postings. If they moved back, Anne's parents would spoil them rotten. Maybe they could use a little of that. They'd even gone so far as to offer more than once that he and the girls were welcome to live with them. And that he could get his old job back. It wouldn't be the end of the world for his daughters, although it might be for him.

IN THE WARM coziness of Jonathan's kitchen, Brooke double checked the recipe for pumpkin cake on her phone and made sure she and Isabella had gathered all the ingredients. Baking had never been her forte, but she needed something to pass the time with Isabella. When Tina had contacted her about being late to pick up Isabella, Brooke had insisted on bringing her home and saving her the trip.

No sooner had the call ended than she realized that meant she'd have to see Jonathan. It was always better to talk in person anyway.

"It's not fair." Isabella measured the flour and patted it too hard. A powdery poof rose into the air. "Vanessa gets to have fun with Aunt Tina and Uncle Drew while I won't get Aunt Tina to myself until the day after Thanksgiving and…"

Brooke coughed and finished her sentence. "And you're stuck here with one of your least favorite people?"

"Exactly." Isabella's eyes widened, and she

threw her hands over her mouth. "Please don't tell Dad I said that. He'll tack on another week to my grounding."

"Maybe it's time we do something about the underlying cause instead." Brooke measured baking soda and powder, adding them to the mix. "I'll take care of the spices if you want to crack the egg and whisk it before pouring it into the other ingredients."

Isabella brought the mixing bowl toward her and assembled the ingredients with a light hand. "I don't want another mother."

Brooke had a feeling that was what this had been about the entire time. Even though she wanted to tell the girl she had nothing to worry about on that front, mending fences was more important. "I don't blame you. You know, my aunt Mitzi is like a mother to me, but she's not my mom. We're okay being who we are with each other. It's more fun that way."

They finished mixing the batter, and Isabella shoved the pan in the oven. "Not that Dad will enjoy it much." Isabella huffed.

"Why do you say that?" Brooke wiped her hands with the kitchen towel before placing the bowls in the dishwasher.

Isabella removed the oven mitt and bit her lip. "He's been different this past week. He hasn't been as happy as he's been since we went to the pumpkin patch."

Knowing he was as miserable as Brooke wasn't a comfort at all. She turned her attention to the recipe. "Well, we still have more work to do. What's cake without frosting?"

"Yuck. I don't like cream cheese." Isabella stuck her tongue out.

"Cream cheese frosting is different. It's sweet."

Isabella looked like she remained unconvinced. "Can we only frost half the cake?"

Whipping the ingredients with a hand mixer, Brooke shrugged and spoke over the noise. "Why don't you try it first before you judge?" Satisfied at the mixture's consistency, she found a spoon and held it out for the young girl, who took two steps back. "Are you having fun?"

Isabella folded her arms and pursed her lips as if she wanted to deny it. "Yes."

"Then trust me. Live a little and try something new." She held out the spoon, and Isabella reached for it.

She sampled a tiny bit of the mixture before licking the spoon clean. "Maybe we can frost the whole cake."

The front door slammed, and Jonathan's

voice reached the kitchen. "Aunt Tina? Izzy? Vanessa?"

"In here, Daddy."

Brooke hid her smile at Isabella's obvious attempt to butter up her father. It was time for her to leave, and Brooke's smile faded. She went over to the breakfast nook and picked up her coat and purse.

Jonathan stopped at the threshold, a sight for sore eyes. "I thought I recognized your car."

"Your aunt didn't text you?" Brooke folded her coat over her arm. "She left something at work, and Vanessa went with her to Lucie's business. She'll bring Vanessa home later."

"I'd better finish my homework." Isabella stood on her tiptoes and planted a quick kiss on her father's cheek.

She left the room, and Jonathan glanced over his shoulder. "Wait. That's Vanessa in Izzy's body. Where did you put the real Izzy?"

"She said you've been a little grumpy this week." Aunt Mitzi had intimated that very same thing about her this afternoon, so it was best to go with her original plan of talking to him in person. She set down her purse and coat and handed him an oven mitt. "The cake should be ready in a couple of minutes. Once it cools, the frosting is on the counter."

"Cake? Frosting?" He crossed over to the

bowl of cream cheese frosting and hesitated. "I'd make a joke, but I'm not connecting the dots. You bring Izzy home and made a cake while you ignore texts from me and get upset with me about doing my job."

Maybe it was for the best that this ended before it began if this chasm would always exist between them. She'd best find out if they could at least be amicable toward each other.

She stilled and placed her coat and purse down again before finding two clean spoons. She handed him one. "Your aunt invited Colin and me to Thanksgiving at her place."

"If that's what's concerning you, Mike posted the official holiday schedule today." He glanced over his shoulder and clenched his fist around the spoon. "I report to the station at six in the morning on Thanksgiving. In terms of complete disclosure, you turn me upside down. I've been having guilt issues about you and me."

Brooke dipped her spoon into the frosting and then guided his hand to do the same. "Frosting's supposed to make everything better. From what I know about you already, so does talking."

He laid the spoon beside the bowl and folded his arms. "I'm running second in a two-person contest for the detective slot, I'm missing my daughters' holidays and I'm not sure being a police officer is worth it anymore."

The last part broke her heart. She stood in front of him, glad she chose today to wear her power heels as she was almost eye-level with him. The burning embers in his gaze were unmistakable. Whatever was going on between them hadn't petered out. "If I believed you really meant that, I'd already have left your house with the door hitting my behind."

"You can't have it both ways, Brooke. Either I'm dedicated to what I believe in or I'm not. When I make a promise, I'm all in."

Until Hollydale, she hadn't known what it was like to have someone all in for her. Hayden had talked about commitment but cowered at the first genuine test. All her life, she'd been the one looking out for others. First it was her mother, then Colin. That changed when she and Colin drove into town. Aunt Mitzi, the Mimosas and Jonathan. For the first time, she could let down her guard, relax a little. Knock that chip off her shoulder.

"Are you always so persuasive?" She wanted to put herself on the line the same way he was showing her his heart, but she craved certainty. "Because it's been a roller coaster of a ride for me over the past sixteen years. I've had to watch out for Colin since it's only been the two of us."

"I know, and I admire you for it. Maybe it's time you let someone else in." She hesitated, and he moved toward her. He reached out as if to touch her, but pulled back at the last minute. "It sounded like you were about to say something else. Something that sounded like *but*."

Her throat clogged, and she tried to speak. She prided herself on retaining her composure no matter what. That was her hallmark since Hayden slammed the door. Heck, it went even further back than that.

"When Colin was a toddler, I earned my GED. A few years later, I applied to colleges and felt like I had to decide my whole future there and then. I wanted to help others like myself, and so I chose community development for my major."

"It fits you." He brought her toward him and embraced her. His firm chest provided security and solidity, two things she had craved.

Off-the-charts chemistry was a bonus.

"I wanted Colin to be able to look me in the eye someday and be proud of what he saw." She stepped back and swiped her cheeks. The damp spot on his shoulder caught her attention, and she tried to wipe it away. "Sorry about that."

"I'm not. When you're in, you're all in."

Baring her soul to someone was what she wanted every day. Not with just anyone, though. She loved this funny, serious, wonderful police officer. She wanted him at her side. "For the first time, Hollydale is more than just a community that needs help. It's my town, too."

He cringed and took two steps away from her. "About that detective position."

"From what I've observed, you'd be perfect for it. You're smart and logical, always adhering to fairness and justice. I can't see you in any other profession other than law enforcement."

"Actually, I wanted to be a doctor from the time I could walk until I was about sixteen. You see, my cousin Caleb suffered from scoliosis, and I wanted to help him and others like him."

The oven buzzed, and she held up a finger. "Hold that thought." She removed the plump layers, and the sweet, spicy smell of pumpkin filled the kitchen. She set the cake on a trivet and then faced him. "What made you change your mind about becoming a doctor?"

"Caleb again. One summer day, kids were picking on him, and I put a stop to it. It was then I knew I wanted to be on the side of the underdog."

"What if Colin had been the person Mo had identified? Would you have been on his side?"

"Brooke." He breathed out. "If this is always going to be hanging between us…"

"No, it won't. I just need to know you'll have his back when he deserves to have it." She shook her head. "And mine."

"Having your back may be doing or saying the hard things sometimes. You're a parent, surely, you understand and accept that. Now that I know him, and you, I'd have his back even though I am and will always be fully committed to doing my duty. I know Izzy doesn't feel like I have her back right now. She didn't know I was outside the door when she bragged to Vanessa about getting away with cheating on a test. I made her tell her teacher. I've loved her forever. Still do, but she had to face the consequences of her actions."

And this was what separated him from Hayden, who made promises but turned his back on those same words as soon as his actions gave way to real consequences. With Jonathan, that would never come between them.

"You know, Isabella thought I was trying to be her mom. Guess she saw something between us before we did."

Without another word, she closed the distance to him and kissed him, pouring everything she'd held back for so long into the kiss, into them. His hands weaved themselves into her hair, and she craved his touch, not just now but always. The sugary taste of the frosting gave way to the taste of him. For years she'd convinced herself she'd be stronger alone. It wasn't a matter of giving herself up. Instead, it was sharing her load, her happiness, herself.

The kiss deepened before he wrenched away from her. "You need to know everything," Jonathan said.

She blinked, her eyes adjusting to the dim light of his kitchen instead of the brightness of the stars she'd seen when he kissed her. "Like what?"

And he wasn't the one who should be revealing everything. She should tell him about the phone call. First, though, she needed to listen.

"I might also have been putting distance between us this week."

She processed what he was saying. "But why?"

"I had everything in the palm of my hand, and then with a small swerve that turned into a collision, it was taken away."

Part of her understood. She'd been on track to graduate high school second in her class. Instead, two lines on a pregnancy test changed everything. She didn't regret Colin, though. "When I found out I was pregnant with Colin, my mother took off. I dropped out of school so I could work full-time. Sometimes things don't work out the way we planned, but we forge another path."

He exhaled, and it was as though the weight of the world was lifted from his shoulders. "I haven't told anyone else this." She'd be honored if she wasn't scared of what he was about to say. "I don't know what will happen if I don't get this job, and I might have to start down another road. The benefits of becoming detective here are a boon, as are the challenge of new cases and potentially saving or protecting more lives. However, if they hire the other candidate, Anne's parents live in Savannah, and I have connections there. I've been offered my choice of two different jobs. If I moved, I'd have more say over my future, something I can't do here with three people in charge of my fate."

She understood a thing or two about being unsure of the future, but it was time to concentrate on the here and now. "Did I tell you about the final two weeks of my previous job?"

He shook his head, looking almost as if he were relieved. "Not that I can recall."

Then she hadn't. His attention to detail was

meticulous. "I loved my boss. He was more of a mentor, really. He was close to retirement age and knew I was finishing my degree online. He recommended me for the director's position, but he suddenly died, and someone else with less seniority was promoted. When Aunt Mitzi told me about this opening, I was thrilled to leave that old job behind, but without a recommendation from my former boss, Mr. Whitley decided on a six-month trial period with other strings attached like keeping the center on the up-and-up. If I'd been promoted at my last center, I wouldn't have moved here."

He set his lips in a straight line, most unlike his usual smiling self. "Then you think I should move? Start over?"

"No, that's not what I meant. I understand pride." *A little too well.* Her stubbornness had kept her from asking Aunt Mitzi for help sooner, but it also propelled her to move every time a better offer came her way and always made Colin leave his friends behind. "Your heart is here in Hollydale. You're committed to the place and the people. That's something you can't take with you and not something you'll necessarily find everywhere."

"I want to explore what's between us, but it feels like I can't control anything here. Once this case is wrapped up, once I know about the detective position, once Izzy comes around…"

"But control in that sense is impossible to have." Brooke picked up her purse, shaking her head. She donned her coat and tied the belt. "You had no more control over those issues than I did over mine. You do have control over your choices. For instance, you can slather that frosting on thick or you can spread it thin."

She went over and brushed her lips across his, her purse not the only barrier between them. "The past has a hold over you, and it's in the way. Until you accept it and move on, we have no future." His eyes widened, and he reached out for her, but she slipped away.

"Brooke—"

"There's nothing more to say. I'm sorry."

CHAPTER SEVENTEEN

THE FINAL INTERVIEW for the detective position had taken longer than Jonathan had expected, considering it was the day before Thanksgiving. At least it was over and behind him. He circled the community center three times before a kind older lady pointed to her car, indicating she was leaving. He set aside his frustration at missing most of the center's Heartsgiving gathering, including his daughters' presentation, and was in awe of what Brooke had accomplished in the short time she'd been here.

Since their conversation, he'd done a lot of soul searching, mostly whenever he'd eaten a piece of that delicious cake. Brooke was right. Lack of control had manifested itself in guilt.

From the parking lot, orange and yellow balloons in a welcome arch greeted him along with music and the voices of the younger children staging what sounded like a funny play. He set his food donation of a jar of peanut butter in the full box near the front. Somehow he'd find Izzy and Vanessa in this maze of displays and people.

"Jonathan." He craned his neck and walked over to where his aunt Tina sat at a long table surrounded by her friends. She jumped up to greet him. "Just the person I wanted to see."

Uh-oh. That didn't sound promising. This was usually the tone she used when she needed Uncle Drew to move the furniture or paint the living room. "What do you need me to do? Take something to your car? Come to your house later and help set up extra seating for tomorrow? My brawn is at your service, dear aunt."

She laughed and motioned at the canvas in the middle of the table, one of three with price tags attached. "Not your brawn, but your pocketbook is requested here. How about you rescue your uncle Drew from having to purchase my artwork?"

How would Uncle Drew feel about unwrapping Aunt Tina's painting of tulips on Christmas? He'd find out next month. Reaching for his wallet in his back pocket, he asked, "How much?"

"It's for a good cause." Aunt Tina accepted his credit card and swiped. "There's a reason you're my favorite nephew."

"I'd like to say it's because of my good looks

and my devilishly witty humor, but it's really because I'm her only nephew." Winking at his aunt and sending a smile to the other ladies, Jonathan used the stylus and scribbled his name on the tablet.

"Oh, we all know who you are. You're…" Everyone cleared their throats, and Hyacinth glanced at their disapproving expressions, their eyes wide. They seemed to exchange some telepathic message, but he didn't know what it was. "I was going to say we know him as our favorite police officer. Really, give me some credit."

"Hello, Mrs. Hennessy." Jonathan pocketed his wallet. "I'm surprised you're not selling pies. That would have raked in the money."

Her cheeks turned as pink as her fuzzy angora sweater. She waved him off, her bracelets flashing in the brightness of the afternoon sun. "Now that Belinda and I create culinary magic together, I seek peace in other forms of beautification. It's so relaxing to feel the earth under my fingers and plant spring bulbs, knowing that soon little buds will issue forth…"

"She says that because her paintings were the first to sell," Fabiana interrupted, and pointed to the last two pieces of artwork. "My husband, Roberto, had to work today, but wouldn't these look lovely in your house?"

Before he could pull out his wallet, he caught sight of Brooke walking toward him. Overtime had stopped him from calling her, but a kick in the pants had been exactly what he'd needed. This woman was too good for him. Yet the air tasted sweeter when she was around, and the world seemed more hopeful when she graced him with one of her smiles.

He did have control over his choices, he realized. And it could make a difference. Instead of ignoring what was happening to Caleb in the schoolyard when he'd been limping because of his scoliosis, he'd stood up to those kids who were making fun of his cousin. Just like he couldn't control what had happened to Anne, but he'd made sure she received justice.

He smiled at Fabiana. "If they're still here when I come back, consider them sold."

When he walked toward Brooke, he heard one of his aunt's friends murmur something about MCG in the flesh. He was confused but kept moving in order to catch up with Brooke. "Have a minute?"

She clutched her clipboard to her chest. While her normal glow brightened the air, she didn't look too pleased to see him. "I'd prefer not to talk outside where someone might hear us. Follow me."

He rushed to keep up with her. "How are things going?"

Brooke arched a well-defined brow. "It depends."

"What if I said I was a world-class fool for not seeing what's right in front of me?"

"Are you saying it or *if* you say it? There's a big difference."

They reached the main doors, and they opened automatically. Inside, the quiet struck him, a contrast to the joyous sounds in the courtyard. Yolanda, the assistant director, glanced up from her book at the reception desk and nodded. "A few people have come inside. Only those using the facilities."

"I appreciate you volunteering for desk duty, Yolanda." Brooke smiled and jerked her finger toward her office. "Officer Maxwell and I need to discuss some protocol. Please interrupt if anyone needs us."

Having the desk staffed during public events was already one major improvement.

He scanned the area around the locker room door and didn't find any marks or scratches. Brooke unlocked her office. He hesitated and stared at her keys until she tucked them in her pocket. She entered, and he followed.

New management, new keys, new security precautions. Were those the heart of the matter?

He'd briefly interviewed Ray Hinshaw once, but he was still unavailable.

"I checked the lockers this morning before everything got underway. The stash was still there, and nothing was disturbed." Her voice sounded troubled, and he understood why.

The longer it took to have a new lead, the longer it would take to resolve this case. Had the suspect given up so easily? If this was a moneymaking operation, why stop?

So far, his following up on the laminator with the state logo had also resulted in zero new leads.

"Okay, well. We'll just have to be patient. We're doing everything we can at the moment." He grinned. "You seemed pretty sure I wouldn't be able to resist seeing you today, huh?"

"No, just pretty sure you wouldn't forget to pick up your daughters is more like it." Her wry sense of humor suited him.

Heck, he liked everything about her. Keeping him in line wasn't a task for the faint of heart. "Once I find them, I'm not letting you go."

"That would be hard to do since I'm working. I'll walk you to their table." She tapped the clipboard. "They're with Olivia."

She led him to the side entrance, and the sun

shone bright over the reds and oranges of the mountaintops. Only a few puffy white clouds accented the blue of the sky. This was the type of day to share with someone special, and there was no better person than Brooke. He had no control over the weather either, but he did have control over how he approached their relationship. "I thought about what you said—"

Before he could elaborate, Vanessa ran toward him.

"Daddy!"

An avalanche of arms encircled him, and he embraced his daughter. She released him, and he notched his knuckle in the dimple in her cheek. "How was the third day of Heartsgiving?"

"The best yet. Come see what I made for you. You're gonna love it." Vanessa pulled him toward the table until Izzy rushed toward them.

"Dad can't see it." Izzy sent her sister a laser beam of a glare. She then faced him with her angelic expression intact, something he'd seen less of in the past couple of months. "After all, it's just boring stuff. Nothing important. Nothing you haven't seen before."

Izzy sent a silent plea to Brooke with her eyes. While it didn't take a police detective to figure out Izzy and Vanessa were hiding something from him, likely a Christmas surprise, his keen sense of observation told him somehow Izzy had accepted Brooke.

Brooke hugged her clipboard to her chest and winked at Izzy. "Jonathan, no advance sneak peeks for you." It was as if she fit right in with his girls. "These two were a big help today."

Vanessa pulled on her windbreaker. "At first I thought my hand would fall off cause I put mayonnaise on so many sandwiches, but Olivia and Brooke said I was a really good assistant and gave me an I Helped sticker. See?" Vanessa showed off her sticker on her jacket.

"And Izzy created a shortcut for the sandwich line that saved us time."

He turned to Izzy, who shrugged off Brooke's compliment. "It was something new, and it was sort of fun." She scuffed the toe of her sneaker on the sidewalk. "Brooke's right. If you give something a chance, you might like it."

Izzy complimented Brooke? The woman was a miracle worker in disguise. His parents might have been workaholics, but they taught him to appreciate what was right in front of him. And what was in front of him was one remarkable woman, and a patient one, since she'd won over Izzy, same as she'd won over Izzy's father. He reached for her free hand, the one not holding the clipboard. "That's a wise observation."

Brooke didn't let go of his hand. That was a good sign. "I like to think everyone won today."

"Brooke." She met his gaze, and the crackle in the air had nothing to do with the crispness of late fall and everything to do with his reaction every time he saw her. "Thanks for the kick in the sweatpants."

She smiled. "You're welcome. It's a perk of knowing me."

"Do those perks include kisses?"

He stepped closer, and he didn't care how many people were around. Izzy and Vanessa also needed to know this relationship had the potential to be something special. She nodded, and the smell of vanilla filled his senses.

With her soft lips kissing his, he'd found where he belonged. The clipboard clattered on the sidewalk, and she broke the quick embrace.

"Um, I'm still on duty."

"Would you and Colin like to join us tonight for dinner?" he asked, hopeful the good feelings would continue.

She bent down to pick up her clipboard and then straightened with an apologetic grin. "I told Joe I'd help him with cleanup and storage. Then the staff is decorating for the holidays."

"We have a tradition of Chinese takeout the night before Thanksgiving. Want us to order something for you and return with dinner and help?" he offered.

Brooke looked at Izzy, who nodded and asked, "Do you like steamed dumplings? I love them, but Dad and Vanessa always insist on egg rolls." Izzy tried to sound nonchalant, but her tone gave too much away.

"I've never had them, but I'll try anything once. That's a way to find new favorites. Sounds like it might be fun to make a party out of this." She tapped her fingers on the clipboard and hummed. "If you don't mind signing a waiver of liability."

He brushed her lips with a kiss, the sheer electricity of it filling him with a contentment he hadn't felt in forever. "Brooke?"

She looked up, seemingly startled but happy. And then he knew as plain as the sun in the sky. He wanted to make her happy every day. "Yes?"

"I'll sign the waiver and be back to help along with dinner and the girls. I'll check with Aunt Tina to see if she can pick them up after that, so they don't get in the way."

All around him, families were getting into the spirit of Thanksgiving with some parents oohing over kids' crafts and others enjoying the beautiful cool day laden with the anticipation of tomorrow's feast. Now he looked forward to something as well.

What was a little heavy lifting and decorating when he had the promise of dinner and kisses as a reward?

CHAPTER EIGHTEEN

"I'M GOING TO eat the couch in a minute, Mom," Colin whispered in Brooke's ear. "I'm starving."

"How can you be hungry when you've been eating for the past hour? If Isabella and Vanessa can wait for Jonathan without complaining, so can you. It's Thanksgiving, after all."

Brooke raised her first glass of pinot noir to her lips and sipped. She was enjoying the comfort of Tina and Drew's basement, her new favorite indoor spot in Hollydale with full-to-bursting bookshelves and couches with plump, inviting pillows. The couple had set up a make-shift bar in the corner to serve their guests their favorite drinks.

In the next room, the couple had set up long folding tables with puzzles and board games alongside a billiard table. They'd postponed the meal until after Jonathan's shift ended at three since he'd started at six in the morning.

"I'll work on the puzzle to keep my mind off

food. He'd better arrive soon." Colin stepped toward the adjoining room.

She made her way upstairs to chat with Tina's other guests. Aunt Mitzi held on to Owen's arm and waved as most of the Mimosas held court around her. Fabiana and Betty were in a rather heated discussion about the merits of firefighters and paramedics, but from the looks on their faces, they were just bragging about their loved ones. Brooke stopped and said hello before heading over to the appetizers, snagging the last deviled egg.

"The beneficence of friends gathering is quite unique, don't you think?" Hyacinth placed a lattice pie on the table. "I attempted a new combination of flavors while baking two more traditional pies for those who aren't as adventuresome. This one is a raspberry, lemon and basil treat that tastes divine. You wouldn't think those flavors would mesh so well, but they do. A little like you and your MCG, Officer Maxwell."

Brooke had given up the ghost of that secret a while back. "I'm not sure he's *my* Officer Maxwell."

Hyacinth's lilting laugh told her otherwise.

"I'm more convinced the Matchmaking Mimosas believe that." Brooke took a bite of the deviled egg.

"If everything goes well, I think we'll start calling our group just that. The Matchmaking Mimosas. There's a ring to it, don't you think? Besides, there's something about the two of you that's refreshing. You're cool and collected, and he's…"

The older woman hesitated, and Brooke filled in the gap for her. "Funny? Charming? Sexy?"

A sly smile threw Brooke for a loop. "I just wanted to hear what you think about him. That says everything, you know."

Hyacinth walked away with a wry grin while Brooke popped the last bite of egg in her mouth and chewed, keeping her wineglass steady. The smell of the turkey and the fixings heightened the anticipation of the feast ahead, and that wasn't all she was looking forward to. Tonight she'd level with Jonathan. She'd tell him about Colin's phone call and go to work tomorrow with a clear conscience. Not that there was much to tell, but she'd let him be the judge. If he still wanted to be with her after she came clean about that phone call, she'd start a relationship with him on a clean page, full steam ahead.

She entered the kitchen, where she offered her services, but Tina shooed her away. Instead, Brooke found herself in the dining room, where a long table was decorated with an elaborate velvet runner, tapered orange and brown candles, and a variety of pumpkins in different sizes. Its elegance was offset by the multicolored notecards taped to the wall. Brooke stepped over and read the different messages of gratitude that today's guests had written. *"Three years of remission from breast cancer." "Eyesight." "MAY BABIES!"* She picked up a marker and index card and jotted down the words *"New Beginnings."* Then she taped it alongside the others.

Shouts from the living room indicated Jonathan had arrived. For some reason, she felt rooted to the spot. She'd faced hard challenges before—for instance, whenever tuition came due and she was a couple of dollars short, making a jar of peanut butter last a week so she could pay for school and the rent. Not that loving Jonathan was a challenge. It wasn't. If anything, his humor and love of commitment made it too easy.

She was making it harder on herself. Anything to keep those defenses up.

The sound of someone clearing his throat snagged her attention. There he stood in the archway, a handsome sight in his uniform. "How did you convince Aunt Tina to move dinnertime? She always starts at one like clockwork."

"Sometimes other people's sacrifices make a couple of extra hours seem insignificant. I considered running to the center and getting a jump on tomorrow's paperwork, but Tina had so many fun activities going on. Website updates and scheduling can wait until tomorrow. Someone's having either a good or bad influence on my work ethic."

Barely a second later, he was by her side, reading the cards on the wall. "Let me guess, you're 'New Beginnings'?"

"If I hadn't been brief and to the point, your aunt's wall would look like my final term paper."

He smiled and reached for her hand as his uncle brought in a ceramic platter of turkey and other people poured into the dining room behind him.

"Finally, we eat!" His uncle set the turkey on the table, and the pitter-patter of feet brought even more people into the room.

Jonathan squeezed her hand, and she knew the day was just beginning.

JONATHAN PATTED HIS full stomach and stood next to Vanessa, smoothing her fine blond hair. She pointed to a section of the jigsaw puzzle and beamed with pride. "I did this part all by myself."

"And a fine job you did." He plucked a piece from the side of the table and inserted it where it belonged. "And I did that part."

His gaze met Brooke's, and she motioned toward the other room. He found her sorting through a pile of coats and plucking out her burgundy one. "I have to go home and walk Daisy, whose kidneys are probably ready to explode."

"By any chance, would that walk tonight take you past my house on Timber Mill Way?" Jonathan went over and helped her with her coat. "I bought a box of dog treats, and I don't have a dog. It'd be a real shame for the box to go to waste."

She laughed and zipped up the front. "That could be arranged."

"You see, there's someone special who believes in new beginnings..." He leaned over and was about to kiss her when his phone rang, and he sighed. "Hold that thought."

"You were the one speaking."

"Exactly." He reached for his phone. "Maxwell."

Harriet identified herself, and he stiffened, bracing for whatever was about to come. "I know you just finished your shift, but you've been the one covering what's been going on at The Whitley Community Center. A passerby called and reported suspicious activity. Officer Edwards responded. There are broken windows, and she's securing the crime scene."

Jonathan glanced Brooke's way and found her laughing with Colin, who was eating yet another plate of pie, his third. "Has Edwards entered the premises?"

By this time, Izzy and Vanessa had left their perch at the puzzle table. Izzy's face said she knew what was coming next. Harriet kept talking, and he murmured answers and ended the call.

"You have to go back to work, don't you?" Izzy's shoulders slumped, and her bottom lip jutted out.

Vanessa wound her arm around Izzy's waist. "It's okay. Daddy keeps people safe. It's his heart's work."

Brooke stepped behind the two of them and placed a protective arm around both. She rubbed their shoulders and then released them. "They can come home with me if they want. What do you say, girls, to a Christmas movie and popcorn?" She glanced toward her son. "After we take Daisy for a walk."

Jonathan hesitated, wanting to capture the image of her in this moment, her eyes protecting his girls as if they were her own. Which, if he let her into his life, they would be. Brooke would never settle for anything less than giving her all, either to him or his daughters. Ruining her Thanksgiving with his news wasn't how he wanted to end her day.

"Actually, the girls are going to stay here with their aunt and uncle…"

"If it's because of me, Dad, you don't have to worry." Izzy tugged on his hand. "Brooke's nice."

Izzy's offered endorsement of Brooke wasn't lost on him.

"They can even spend the night, this time, since the center opens later tomorrow."

He didn't want to tell her about the break-in with their kids and the others watching, even though it would be on the lips of everyone in town by tomorrow morning, but he had no choice. He pulled her away and grasped her hands. "Brooke, there's been a burglary at the center. I have to go."

She reached inside her coat pocket and pulled out her keys, jingling them for a millisecond. "I'm coming with you."

CHAPTER NINETEEN

THE TEN-MINUTE DRIVE from Tina's house to the center tested Brooke's last nerve. She gripped the edge of the cloth seat of Jonathan's squad car and worried. How long had the culprit or culprits pillaged before someone noticed and alerted the police? She wished whoever was behind the fake IDs had never heard of Hollydale's community center.

As Jonathan's car rolled to a stop in front of the building, her gaze flew to where the security lights reflected off the broken panes of her office window. Her throat constricted at the vandal's brazenness. Thanks to this criminal activity, residents might hesitate before venturing to the center and participating. Or parents might no longer entrust her with their children. Not to mention taking into account the extent of the damage or stolen items.

Jonathan had assured her that the fake IDs represented a crime involving an element of detachment, while this one reeked of malicious intent. Was it possible this had nothing to do with Jonathan's investigation?

Brooke frowned as Jonathan turned off the ignition. "Stay here until I give you the all-clear."

She waited until he was out of sight before the tears fell. She prided herself on her ability to stay stoic, yet she didn't try to stop crying. Reaching into her purse, she pulled out tissues and wiped her face. The tissue came away with black smears, the remnants of her so-called waterproof mascara. She pulled herself together as tonight would be one heartache after another. Keeping occupied was the only way she'd get through this. She grabbed her phone and started a to-do list. First up was notifying the staff, then drafting a mass email to parents about the cancellation of tomorrow's afternoon activities. Was it too late to text Joe for a recommendation of the best window repair company in the area?

In the morning, she'd begin an inventory to establish the cost of any damage or stolen items. Electronics, office equipment and petty cash were easy pickings. And she'd contact the insurance company about a claim and reporting details.

Sleep tonight might be a luxury.

Especially given how she'd have to contact

Frederick Whitley. She didn't want to consider his reaction yet.

Next week she'd interview more security firms. Meanwhile, she had to find out the extent of the criminal activity and regroup. Thank goodness they hadn't replaced the desktop computers yet.

Her gaze went to Jonathan, now in view, talking to another officer, their faces resolute. Jonathan nodded and then headed her way. He opened her car door. "Officer Edwards has secured the premises. We'd like you to come in and assess the scene."

She exited the car, and the chill stung her cheeks, the stiff breeze picking up, a portent of a cold gray day around the bend. She shivered, unsure whether the weather or the situation was the cause, and looped her burgundy scarf around her neck one extra time. A full moon rose over the mountaintops, stark yet beautiful. She wished she could enjoy it and bask in the glow of the remaining hours of Thanksgiving, but any chance of that ended when Jonathan confided this bombshell.

She accepted his hand and straightened her spine. Thieves or no thieves, she wasn't about to let anyone stand in the way of this center giving back to the community. This type of crime had happened at one previous center during her tenure, that one in downtown Phoenix, and the other community center had thrived as everyone had come together.

She steeled herself for what she'd find. At the other center, thieves had spray-painted on the walls, destroyed whiteboards and stolen equipment for apparently nothing more than the thrill. The center had been closed for almost a week.

"You're in for a shock."

Slowly but surely, her spirits rose. She'd rally everyone around and open The Whitley Community Center for the holiday season as soon as was allowed. There was nothing holding her back from making Hollydale proud of Mr. Whitley for hiring her. "Okay, let's do this."

The main doors slid open, and she braced herself. She blinked hard, then closed her eyes and reopened them. No chairs were upturned, nothing untoward painted on the walls. She rushed over to Betty's desk. Everything appeared untouched.

"Is it safe for me to check my office and the storage room?"

He nodded and went with her to her office first. She opened the door and found some overturned chairs near the window. Being careful of the shards of glass littering the floor, she examined the area.

"It seems obvious that the intruder must have come in through your window." Jonathan's strong voice sounded from behind, but rather than taking comfort in his arms, she hugged herself and let out a shaky breath.

She tried not to let her emotions come to the surface. Maybe she would when she pulled the duvet over her head later, but for now, she could do this.

She checked her desk. Everything from her laptop to her favorite coffee mug was where she'd left it. She opened the drawers. Nothing, including her electronic devices and an envelope of petty cash, seemed disturbed.

"So far, there's nothing to report as far as stolen items." Her voice came out with a wobble she hadn't heard since her mother had tried to reconnect with her.

Jonathan came over and grasped her shoulders. "I'll do everything I can to find out who did this. The sheriff has assembled a good team."

She nodded and lifted her chin, the mere comfort of him a rock in this maelstrom of emotion. That was part of Jonathan. He could be a boulder when she needed strength and a soaring eagle when she needed his lighthearted humor. She'd done that for herself well in the past, and now it was time to let someone else in. She met his gaze, and the electricity between them sizzled despite everything going on at the center.

"Have you visited the men's locker room?"

"That's why I wanted you with me."

"Haven't you checked the locker yet?" Incredulity laced her voice.

He let go of her shoulders. "Officer Edwards and I did a cursory search to make sure no one still occupied the premises. Then I came to get you."

She knew what he was thinking. That even though they hadn't known each other long, somehow, from the minute they'd connected, they understood they would never be quite the same. Without a word, they hurried out of her office to see if his gamble had panned out. For that was what it had been. A gamble to draw out the suspect. They crossed the lobby and went directly to the men's locker room.

He opened the locker, and she stared, already sure of what he would find.

"Empty."

He used his walkie-talkie and communicated the news to Officer Edwards, who replied she'd meet them after she finished taking casts of the footprints in the dirt. Within minutes she'd joined them.

"Officer Edwards and I need to confer for

a minute. I'll meet you in the lobby and then check out the supply and storage closets."

She nodded. "I'll be at Betty's desk."

Once there, she exhaled the nervous tension. Jonathan joined her, and they went downstairs to the supply closet. She unlocked the room, and they found the blue tote in place. He lifted the lid and shrugged. "The laminator is still here. The alarm must have frightened him off."

"He must have wanted the licenses more."

She noticed his face turn pale under the bright fluorescent light.

"Were you serious earlier when you said you'd considered working at the center today?"

His husky voice matched the intensity in his eyes. He pulled her close.

"If you'd have been here, you could have been hurt."

He caressed her cheek, and she leaned into him. "I want to kiss you, but this isn't the time or place. After I'm done at the station, though, I'm stopping at your house."

She nodded. Being in his arms made her feel secure and cared for. She believed she was worth a real commitment and not just empty promises with no substance behind them. Even so, the first time she spoke of her feelings for him wouldn't be in the storage room, but some-where special.

His eyes showed a moment of conflict before his lips met hers, and his apparent relief at her safety melted into her, proving the depth of his emotions matched hers. He broke contact, and his gaze smoldered with a new intensity. "Brooke…"

His walkie-talkie crackled. There was an underlying urgency to Officer Edwards's plea to meet her in the lobby. He and Brooke hurried from the room.

They quickly discovered that her boss had arrived.

"Mr. Whitley?" Surprise registered in her words, and he glanced her way, his long drawn face foreboding in its disapproval.

"During my family's Thanksgiving dinner in Asheville, I received word from Horace Mackelroy about a burglary. He's a friend. I raced over here to find broken windows and squad cars. What *is* going on, Ms. Novak?"

"Mr. Whitley, I only just found out what happened." She recounted the details so far, and finished by stating that nothing of value had been taken.

"Ms. Novak, I'd like to see you outside."

She drew in a deep breath and exhaled slowly. The automatic doors parted, and she followed in his tracks. Security lights activated, brightness filled the entryway. She absorbed the brunt of the stiff wind without moving a muscle. He stopped, and she kept a reasonable distance from him, bracing herself.

"Were you going to wait until tomorrow, or even later, to inform me of this?"

She bristled at the implication that she was being deliberate about her secrecy. She loved her job and valued this opportunity, but she wouldn't let him question her professionalism. "I only found out about this at the Thanksgiving gathering I was attending. I accompanied Officer Maxwell here so I could find out the extent of the damage. In particular, I was concerned about the computer lab and other belongings that could be easily stolen and sold."

"The officer said nothing of value was taken, with *value* being negotiable. Was something stolen?"

Of all the questions to ask, he'd have to ask that one. *I promise I won't tell anyone.*

She'd made a promise to Jonathan about the locker, and her word was her bond. She wouldn't lie, but by telling the truth, she might be signing her resignation letter. Her shoulders tightened. "Yes, I am aware of something that went missing."

Only the soft hoot of a great horned owl broke through the long silence. "I'm waiting, Ms. Novak."

Mr. Whitley tapped his foot on the sidewalk, and she stopped from crossing her arms and rubbing her coat sleeves for extra warmth.

My job or the investigation? Her boss's stony eyes glinted at her. "I'll try to find out if I'm at liberty to tell you, but I need the police department's express authorization."

His frown reflected his clear displeasure. "I'll be here tomorrow afternoon at one to talk about your contract. If you choose to disclose what is missing from the center where I contribute a lion's share of the yearly budget before then, text me. Good evening."

No doubt he would consult with his attorney to find out what options he had for releasing her early from her contract.

Jonathan had said he wanted to stop by on his way home tonight from the police station, but what commitment could she offer or accept if Mr. Whitley fired her tomorrow? Once again, she'd be facing small-town residents as the poor darling who had a bright future but couldn't convert that promise into something permanent and real. No, that was the old Brooke talking, but still...

Depending on tomorrow, she might have to search for yet another bright new beginning. She should never have made promises to Colin and Aunt Mitzi about not moving again.

Would she be qualified for the few jobs available in Hollydale? She might have to apply in Asheville, saddling her with a long commute, which would leave little time for a fledgling relationship.

She'd wait for Jonathan to say whether he could stand beside her if she had to start all over again. She loved him enough to ask and enough to respect his decision.

BROOKE WAS TOO QUIET. He pulled into Mitzi's driveway and sneaked a glance at her in the passenger seat. Ever since Brooke talked to Frederick Whitley, she looked as though a strong wind would knock her over. He longed to hold her close until they both had enough stamina to face what lay ahead. Together.

Her hand went to the car door. From here, he'd head straight to the police station, since his daughters were spending the night at Aunt Tina's. His aunt was already excited about hitting the sales with Izzy tomorrow while Vanessa would assist Uncle Drew with decorating the house.

Even though he'd be pulling an all-nighter reviewing video footage and writing reports at his desk, Jonathan couldn't let this moment fade without telling Brooke how he felt. Life could disappear in an instant. Love in any form was too precious not to seize it.

Love. He loved the way Brooke tackled every project, the big ones and the small ones, wanting to spread happiness to some person's life. He loved the way she smelled the aroma of fresh coffee, holding the cup to her nose and taking a big sniff, then curling up one side of her mouth. He loved how she made him feel, energized, treasured and human.

Somehow this beautiful woman brought depth to everything around her.

On this day for giving thanks, he'd be remiss if he didn't tell her half of what he felt inside.

"Brooke, I..."

She turned toward him, anguish written on her features. "I have a meeting with Mr. Whitley tomorrow afternoon. There's a good chance he's—"

"I love you."

He blurted out the words and winced. Of all the places in the world to tell a woman he loved her. A squad car didn't scream romance.

And he wanted to be the man who shared that and more with her. Because in this world, connecting with someone was worth any price. Even the agony of putting himself out there without jokes, without his shield, without any promise of control.

"I…" She shook her head. "I—"

"You don't have to say anything." He leaned over until his forehead touched hers. She didn't flinch, nor did she move away. All good signs. "This has been a hard day."

"But there's a lot I should say. That I have to say." Brooke sighed but held steady.

"There are times when you don't have to say anything. You just cherish the moment."

She leaned in and kissed him then, a sweet kiss of longing, of promise, of new beginnings. He clung to the feeling. He'd never expected love to strike twice.

He brought her into his arms, not wanting to let her go. Now or ever. "You were right earlier. This is the day for new beginnings."

She crooked her head against his shoulder, and how she was nestled against him felt as though she were made for that spot and that spot alone. "Maybe so. Frederick Whitley can let me go and I'll need another fresh start."

This was the woman who won Izzy over. She could win over anyone, even someone as hard as Whitley. If not…

"There are other jobs in Hollydale."

She leveled a look in his direction. "I seem to recall discussing pride with a certain some-one."

His career path still wasn't resolved with

the decision coming on Monday, but he'd stay in town regardless of the outcome. "A beautiful woman pointed out I have control over my choices, and my choice is to lay it all on the line. We'll make it through this in Hollydale together." She closed her eyes, and he rubbed her cheek with his index finger, her smoothness a balm against his calloused skin. "With any other person, I'd feel compelled to come up with a corny joke that would ruin the moment. With you, the only compulsion I have is to be myself."

She opened her eyes, those beautiful brown eyes dynamic and haunting. "That may be the most romantic thing anyone's ever said to me."

"I'm glad I said it." He offered a smile. "For so long, I vowed I wouldn't let my job take over my life. I didn't want to be like my parents that way."

"You're nothing like your parents." Her protests warmed his heart.

"If I don't get the detective's position, I've made up my mind. The Maxwells are staying put." He saw hope in her eyes. "I'm Izzy and Vanessa's father, and I'd love for you and Colin to be part of my family."

Her breath hitched, and a fine puff of exhaled air dissipated in the car. It seemed to be growing colder by the second. "There's so much I need to tell you."

With some reluctance, he let go of her. "You need to rest, especially so you can talk to Whitley with a clear head. No sense in assuming something will happen when it hasn't. Neither of us can control the outcome. A wise woman taught me that."

He pulled away, but their connection still held. From now on, the mere smell of vanilla would make him stop and look for her.

"The issue with Colin..."

"Can wait until your situation and mine are settled. I'm sorry I doubted him, but not sorry I did my job." Not for the first time, he noticed the dark circles under her eyes. "Get some sleep so you can convince Whitley you're the best thing that's happened to the Hollydale community center." He smiled more. "Which you are."

A soft sigh escaped her lips, and she nodded. "Everything will come out tomorrow."

"Including every leftover turkey recipe known to humankind. Turkey tetrazzini, turkey noodle soup and, my personal favorite, turkey pancakes." He couldn't resist a little humor.

"With gravy syrup. Sounds delicious."

A knock on her window caught them both

by surprise, judging from her expression. He lowered the window, and a bark heralded Daisy and Colin, the boy's wide grin the mirror image of Brooke's. "It's not every day you find your mom in a car with steamed windows."

Colin laughed, leading Daisy to the sidewalk. Brooke rolled her eyes before she hopped out of the car. She shut the door and then peeked through the window. "Are you free for lunch?"

"My shift ends at three."

She removed her keys from her purse, then dropped them and bent to pick them up. "I'll text you to let you know what time I'm available. Wish me luck that I won't be permanently free for lunch."

She walked away, and he watched her unlock the front door. *Keys.* He blinked and considered everything he knew about the case. When she arrived at the center, she had the locks changed. At the Halloween event at the center, someone scratched the locker room door, a sign the culprit hadn't had a key. Somehow, this case hinged on keys.

He reversed the car, more eager than ever to review the camera footage and discuss his new lead with the sheriff before requesting search warrants. A theory formed, and he knew exactly what to look for in that footage tonight.

CHAPTER TWENTY

JONATHAN TAPPED HIS finger on the steering wheel of his squad car and waited for the sheriff, who would arrive any minute with the search warrant. A quiet, ordinary neighborhood with ranch houses marked this residential street where Ray Hinshaw lived.

While he'd given some thought to Ray, the former director was gone from the center before the trouble began. The one formal interview with Ray had taken place over the phone, but he'd sounded distracted, so Jonathan had kept it brief. Every time Jonathan had followed up, it seemed Ray was unreachable, but this morning had changed everything when Jonathan saw him coming out of The Busy Bean.

And the more he'd thought about it, the more the clues pointed to Hinshaw. Why the exchanges took place at the center. Why the suspect felt comfortable hiding the stash in the lockers where Mr. Floyd seldom cleaned. Why keys kept recurring in his dreams along with a certain brunette.

The sheriff slowed down as he passed him

and held up his thumb. Mike parked his squad car in Hinshaw's driveway, effectively blocking the exit of any cars from the garage.

That was Jonathan's cue to join Mike. Together they'd search Hinshaw's house and determine if they found any and enough evidence to take him to the station for further questioning. Mike gripped the warrants, and they progressed to the front door.

The hedges needed a good trimming, their spiky boughs sticking every which way. A rotted jack-o'-lantern sat next to the door, flies buzzing around the hollow orb. In the corners of the grimy windows, dew sparkled on strands of several spiderwebs. It looked like Hinshaw might have been telling the truth about being away from his house for a long period of time. Mike sent a careful nod in Jonathan's direction, and adrenaline coursed through his body. In this line of work, they had to be prepared for anything.

Mike did the honors of knocking. "Ray Hinshaw? Are you in there? It's the police."

Seconds seemed like hours while they waited. Jonathan heard footsteps on the other side of the door, and he kept his hand from approaching his weapon.

The front door creaked open to reveal a man in his late fifties with bloodshot eyes and unkempt hair. Scruff lined his prominent jaw. "Good morning, Sheriff Harrison, Officer Maxwell." Ray opened the door the rest of the way, tying the belt of his black robe. He yawned and waved them inside. "I didn't expect you to visit to pay your condolences."

Mike glanced at Jonathan and then back at Ray. "Condolences?"

"I've been out of town for a month. Dad took sick and sadly died last week. My flight landed after midnight and I didn't arrive home until three this morning. I went to The Busy Bean for a bag of my favorite coffee beans earlier, then came home and sacked out again."

Jonathan blinked back his surprise. Once they confirmed Ray was on that flight, he'd have an unbreakable alibi for the community center burglary.

Mike stood there, a flicker of shock apparent on his face. "I'm sorry for your loss, but this is an official visit, Mr. Hinshaw."

"What's with the Mr. Hinshaw business? Call me Ray. I've known your parents, Carl and Diane, for years, Mike." He rubbed his eyes and yawned again. "Come on in. Mind you, I haven't had my first cup of coffee yet."

Mike stayed on the stoop. "Officer Maxwell and I have a couple of questions about the community center."

"I guess now's as good a time to talk as any. Besides, I'll be moving to Cincinnati soon. Just came back to get the house ready to sell." They entered, and Ray motioned them toward the kitchen. The room was a little small, but had plenty of space for the three of them. Ray located a coffee grinder and the bag of coffee beans. "With all the weekend trips to Cincinnati, I let my job performance at the center suffer. After I was fired, I stayed with my father until he passed away."

Jonathan sighed and rubbed the back of his neck, the pain of apparently being wrong about Ray's involvement made his collar that much more uncomfortable. Then the hollowness in Ray's eyes tore through him. "I'm also sorry for your loss."

"Any distraction right about now works for me." Ray inserted the filter into the machine and leveled the grounds. "Best to get the questions out of the way."

Jonathan reached for his notepad, determined to see this case through. A minor delay wouldn't hurt either, considering the dressing down he was going to take from Mike back at the station. "I have a few questions about security procedures when you worked at the center and who all had access to your keys."

"Does this have anything to do with the

vague text I had from Yolanda last night about a break-in?"

"Yolanda, the assistant director?"

"Yeah, we dated for a while, but it went nowhere."

Jonathan stopped taking notes and stared at Ray as the pieces fell into place. Yolanda wasn't a mole, per se, but liked to pass along information.

"I texted her on Monday to ask if she knew of anyone looking for a house before I put this one on the market."

That most likely solved the mystery of who informed Whitley about what was going on at the center. Jonathan would stake his fading reputation as a detective on the scenario that Yolanda had believed Ray would return to Hollydale and maybe even try to reclaim his job now that he'd no longer be flying back and forth to Ohio. Presumably she hadn't known about the permanent move.

"So, you haven't even been in town for the past month." Jonathan stuck his stub of a pencil back in his pocket.

"No, although right about now, I sure wish I had been." Ray bent over and picked up a pizza box off the floor. More takeout containers covered almost every inch of counter space. The older man ran a hand through his messy hair and shook his head. He opened the dishwasher and piled in plates. With the rattle of every dish landing in the racks, Jonathan heard the death rattle of the detective position, so close and yet so far. It, along with any chance of solving this case today, seemed a lifetime away.

"Pardon the mess. My youngest son, Peyton, was supposed to take care of the house. I didn't expect him to trash the place."

Peyton had never been one of Jonathan's favorite people in Hollydale, not since he'd been the leader of the group antagonizing Caleb all those years ago. Still, this situation was rather embarrassing, and he kept his opinion of Peyton to himself.

Mike placed his notepad back in his pocket. "We'll come back another time."

"Are you sure? I don't mind talking now." Ray opened cabinets until he found a clean mug and poured a cup of coffee, stirring in powdered creamer. "I thought his new girlfriend would be a good influence on Peyton, what with having a steady job and all."

"A girlfriend?" Jonathan's ears perked up. "Do you know where she works?"

"In Asheville, at the Department of Motor Vehicles."

Goose bumps dotted Jonathan's arms, and his gaze went to Mike, who retrieved the warrant from his front pocket. "Ray, we have reason to believe your son and his girlfriend might be selling fake IDs and using the community center as a front. I have a warrant to search your house for evidence."

"Go ahead." Ray set his cup down so hard, coffee sloshed out the top. "Nothing will surprise me today."

The search commenced. Ray stood back, shaking his head and muttering under his breath. It wasn't long before Jonathan and Mike uncovered a cache of burner phones and other evidence hidden in a mattress, more than enough to justify them tracking down Peyton for questioning.

Although Jonathan's gut instinct told him he had most of the story. Peyton used the center with an insider's knowledge of its security measures. When Brooke changed the locks, he no longer had access to his father's keys. When desperation struck, he apparently resorted to burglary.

"Do you have someone you can call for support?" Mike asked.

Ray nodded, his lips in a straight line. Noises came from the living room, and Jonathan and Mike hurried that way, with Ray following them.

"What's going on?" A burly man in his midthirties stood at the front door.

Ray blurted, "Peyton, tell the police you had nothing to do with whatever happened at the center."

Peyton pursed his lips. Then he turned and ran. Jonathan hurried to the door as a white Ford Focus barreled down the street. Tires squealed as Peyton ran the stop sign. Jonathan rattled off the license plate number to Mike.

"Right house, wrong Hinshaw," Mike said while grabbing his two-way radio.

Mike informed Dispatch and issued an all-points bulletin for Peyton and the Ford Focus, stopping short of issuing a pursuit order. "The crime doesn't warrant a chase, not with traffic on the uptick today."

As hard as it was to let Peyton get away for now, Jonathan conceded Mike's point. They secured the evidence in the trunk of the sheriff's squad car.

Mike checked in with Harriet and placed his walkie-talkie back on his utility belt. "No report yet about Peyton or the Ford Focus. Nothing from the traffic helicopters or highway patrols. We alerted the Asheville police to pick up the girlfriend. Now we wait for him to surface. I'll meet you back at the station."

Their walkie-talkies crackled, and Harriet came over the line. "Accident at the corner of Creek Vista and Dalesford Road."

That was only a couple of blocks away. "I'll handle that if you process the evidence." Mike nodded, and Jonathan flipped on his flashing lights and siren.

Traffic pulled to the side of the road as Jonathan made his way to the wreck.

First on the scene, Jonathan surveyed the damage. The front end of a white Ford Focus resembled an accordion with smoke coming out of the engine. A check at the rear bumper confirmed this was Hinshaw's vehicle. From the looks of it, the gray SUV absorbed the brunt of the impact with the driver's side taking the hardest hit.

An ambulance siren cut through the air, and Jonathan checked on the occupants of the SUV. Approaching the window, he made out the driver's face, and the wind rushed out of him. He wanted to run to his aunt Tina, but he froze for a split second until years of training kicked in. He sprinted over in time to hear his aunt cry out, "Are you okay?"

Thank goodness. If Aunt Tina was conscious and coherent, the car's airbags had done their job.

"Izzy? Izzy?" his aunt called.

His blood chilled. *Izzy?*

His little girl was in the back seat of the smashed-up SUV.

CHAPTER TWENTY-ONE

BROOKE STOOD OUTDOORS and examined the space where her office window used to ward off the late fall chill.

"I have the replacement window in stock and should have the job completed by late this afternoon." The older portly man, who came highly recommended from Joe and Betty, slid the measuring tape back in place. "It's a standard size."

"Thanks, Travis. I appreciate this."

Brooke had already contacted the insurance carrier, and the policy did, indeed, cover vandalism. Considering this was the only repair, the center would recover quickly and resume normal operations tomorrow.

If only she could say the same about her tenure as director.

Speaking of her job, its future depended on Mr. Whitley, who marched her way, straightening his red power tie. "Ms. Novak," he said and raised an eyebrow, with a quick nod to Travis. "Since your office is unusable at the present time, I'm sure we can find another area to conduct our business."

"Travis, you have my cell if you run into any issues." She smiled at the man and then turned her full attention to Mr. Whitley. "I canceled all classes and activities today. We can use the upstairs faculty lounge."

He charged into the building, and she followed, pulling at the hem of her favorite suit jacket. Last night's insomnia had led to some soul-searching moments and some extensive internet browsing. Instead of fretting the entire night, she'd researched every job in a fifty-mile radius, determined to make her relationship with Jonathan work. The more she considered it in the wee hours of the morning, the more she realized the commute to Asheville wasn't that long.

Stiffening her spine, she wouldn't give up yet, and she wouldn't let Mr. Whitley intimidate her.

She intended to fight for her job and convince Mr. Whitley of her merits. Rather than immediate dismissal, she'd instead try to talk him into a contract extension. Standing up for herself was as important as standing up for the community.

Brooke left the lounge door open, and they

chose seats at a round oak table, facing each other. Her phone buzzed, but she ignored it.

"A burglary on Thanksgiving?"

He didn't waste time in mincing words. "That I didn't commit and had no control over."

"You said the investigation was narrowing in on something of value. What was it?" His craggy face betrayed no empathy, only interest.

Jonathan hadn't released her from her promise not to talk about the case with anyone else, even her superior. "Sir, there are two active investigations going on, and I still need to check with the police to find out if I can talk about one of them with you." Her phone vibrated again, and she stayed still.

"Two investigations? I only know about the one." He pushed up his black horn-rimmed glasses. "You realize who this community center is named for and who hired you, don't you?"

If he fired her, she could kiss any chance of a reference goodbye. Her phone buzzed yet again and again. "Sir, someone keeps trying to text me. It might be Officer Maxwell with an update."

Over Whitley's protest, she read multiple texts, all saying the same thing. Her jaw slackened, and her fingers went numb. *Tina and Isabella? In a car accident?* Jonathan would be shattered. She had to get to the hospital. "Excuse me." She stood, still gripping the phone tightly. "I have to go."

Whitley mirrored her action. "We're not finished."

"With all due respect, two people I've grown close to in a short time were in a car wreck."

She had been through rough times before; however, she'd faced them alone. If she lost her job now, she'd have Mitzi by her side. And the Mimosas. And Jonathan.

Friendship was also a two-way street. She had to stand by them and show her support.

Not to mention the man who'd claimed her heart.

She ran out the door without looking back.

THE HOSPITAL WAITING room was already packed when she arrived. Hyacinth knitted. Fabiana's fingers flew across her smartphone. Vanessa held on to Lucie's hand, no distance between them on the bench, both of their faces ashen and somber. Vanessa's gaze met Brooke's, and the young girl ran to her.

"Brooke, I'm scared." Vanessa threw her arms around Brooke's midsection and cried. "Daddy's back there with Izzy. They won't let me see my sister."

Lucie rose and joined them, smoothing Vanessa's hair. "We've only briefly met, but I'm Tina's daughter-in-law, Lucie Spindler. My husband and Jonathan are cousins. There's been no news about Izzy yet. Last I heard from Caleb, his mother's having a CT scan."

Brooke broke free of Vanessa's grasp and knelt, wiping the girl's tears away. "Isabella's made of strong stuff. She's sweet and stubborn, and I'm sure she's going to be fine."

Lucie pointed toward the bench, and the three of them settled in. Vanessa cuddled with Brooke, and love poured out of her for this girl who'd endured so much, losing her mother in a car accident and now waiting for word on the fate of her sister.

Lucie reached into her purse and pulled out a travel-sized pack of tissue. She plucked out several before handing the rest to Brooke. "From what I've gathered, Tina and Izzy were returning from Asheville after some Christmas shopping."

Vanessa's wide eyes stared at Brooke, and she let out a whimper. "I was having fun with Uncle Drew, and I wasn't with my sister."

Another sob came out of the girl, and Brooke waited patiently until Vanessa could look her straight in the eye.

"Someone broke the law, and did a dangerous thing. That's why the accident happened.

You couldn't have controlled what happened, but you can be there for Isabella when she's released."

"Really?" Vanessa sniffed.

"Really." Jonathan's firm voice echoed, and everyone in the room stilled.

Isabella stood next to him, her arm in a bright purple cast. Dark circles rimmed her eyes, but she smiled as Vanessa launched herself toward them. Jonathan stepped in front of her and gave his daughter a hug. "You need to be careful with Izzy. She has a broken arm, but she'll be fine. I just heard Aunt Tina has a mild concussion, and the doctors expect to discharge her in a little while."

Murmurs of relief went around the crowd. Brooke smiled at Isabella, then at him. "I came as soon as I heard."

Forgetting decorum and everything else, she threw herself into his arms and stayed there, wishing she could do so forever. He held her close and whispered, "Your presence is everything. You're the calm in my storm."

He let her go, but held on to her hand, connecting her to him, when the reality of this morning crashed down on her. She walked out on her boss, basically severing any chance she had of saving her job. What could she offer

Jonathan if she couldn't serve this community in a positive way?

Her heart.

Was that enough? One look at his eyes gave her the answer. She'd find another job; she'd never find another Jonathan.

"Let's get Isabella home," she said.

"You can call me Izzy."

Brooke's heart melted like butter while everyone crowded around, careful not to jostle Izzy.

As he tried to wrap up the latest phone call, Jonathan surveyed his living room. The girls had left their scarves and coats scattered about, but he didn't care. Izzy would be okay, and that was what mattered. He pressed the End Call dot on the phone's screen and retrieved the blanket Izzy had asked for.

He settled her on the easy chair with her electronic tablet and a gentle hug.

"That's the third person who's called to check on you since we've been home, and that doesn't count all the texts that are coming in fast. Another soccer teammate says hello and get well soon. Anything else for my pumpkin?"

She giggled, and he treasured the sound. "Daddy, you haven't called me that in ages."

Vanessa came into the living room with her special stuffed kitten, Miss Whiskers, and laid her in the crook of Izzy's arm. "She's going to guard you the rest of the day. She told me so."

Izzy's smile was a little loopy, thanks to the pain medication, but no less real. "Thanks, Nessie."

"Girls, about the hospital…" This might not be the perfect time to bring up the subject of Brooke, but it was the right time.

"You don't have to go back to work today, do you?" Izzy's eyes, already cloudy, darkened, and her fingers dug into Miss Whiskers's fake fur.

He ran his fingers through his short hair, still damp from the quick shower he'd taken. "No, I don't, although Sheriff Harrison will visit later." He held up his hand to stem any protests. "As a social call to make sure you're okay. He's bringing Georgie and Rachel with him."

Mike's daughter, Rachel, was in Izzy's class at school, and they were good friends. Mike's family was one of the few visits Jonathan okayed for today. Mike had already filled him in on everything while he'd been waiting for the doctor to set Izzy's cast.

Peyton had waived his rights and confessed to selling fake IDs. He and his girlfriend, his contact with the Asheville branch of the Department of Motor Vehicles, acted together, and he'd taken advantage of his father to use the center as a selling venue. That was just the start. They'd also stolen office supplies and petty cash, anything to support his out-of-control spending habit. The department would wrap up the case, with Mike handling everything.

A month ago, he would have regretted turning the conclusion of the case over to Mike, but that wasn't his attitude now. He could trust that Mike would follow up and make sure there were no loose ends. Hinshaw had known what he was doing, and Jonathan had no control over his decision to flee. He could hold his head high, just as Brooke had held her head high yesterday when she and Whitley had talked at the center.

Brooke. He wondered what was keeping her since she should have been here already. He smoothed Izzy's hair before he glanced at his phone.

Izzy yawned and nestled into the chair. "I think I'll take a little nap."

"Brooke will be here when you wake up."

"I like Brooke. She'll never be Mommy. She'll just be herself, and we'll have fun together." Izzy laid her cheek against the cushion and closed her eyes.

Vanessa pulled at his sweatshirt. "Brooke makes me happy."

Brooke made him very happy, too. "I'm glad, because you and Izzy are going to be seeing a lot more of her and Colin."

Vanessa's eyes lit up. "And Daisy?"

He laughed and embraced his daughter. Being here for the little moments. That was what Brooke said mattered as much, if not more, than the holidays and the other special occasions he'd miss when he worked. He was still in the dark about who would receive the offer for detective, but he was at peace with whatever happened.

He'd never expected to fall for anyone again, but there was something about Brooke that he, a police officer, couldn't piece together. The first time he'd held Izzy in his arms, and then again with Vanessa, an instant bond formed, ones that changed him forever. When Brooke walked into the reception area of the center, and their eyes clicked, something similar happened. The amazing bond between them grew stronger every time he laid eyes on her.

That type of bond was worth acknowledging he had no control over whatever their future would bring. Now to tell her all that and find out if she felt the same way. That was the hard part.

BROOKE BOUNDED UP Jonathan's front steps with Daisy's leash in hand, Colin bringing up the rear. The day had gotten away from her. After the hospital, she detoured to the center and found the new window installed. It hadn't come as a surprise when Olivia told her Mr. Whitley had already departed. A series of texts with her boss confirmed a new appointment on Monday afternoon. She had little doubt that she'd be looking for a job that same night.

From there, she'd showered. As she was at the door ready to leave, Colin arrived home from basketball practice. He'd insisted on coming and bringing Daisy to cheer up Izzy. Add another delay for his shower and a quick stop at Hollydale's newest gift shop, The Smoky Mountain Emporium, and that equaled too long away from Jonathan.

She rapped at the door ever so lightly, trying not to disturb any sleeping soccer stars. Jonathan appeared with his damp hair stuck up in all directions. She stifled a laugh. She could get used to seeing him like this. He was pretty cute, and she had a feeling she'd always believe that.

No longer could she use work or Colin or

her past as an excuse to hold back. She'd have to let down her guard and allow Jonathan access to her heart.

Daisy barked and raced into his house. "I know it might seem counterintuitive to bring a dog to someone who's injured—" Brooke smiled at Jonathan "—but she guards Colin and me whenever we're sick."

Colin stepped forward. "I insisted on bringing Daisy to cheer up Izzy."

Daisy suddenly propelled Brooke forward until the labradoodle stopped where Izzy rested. She circled the area in front of the easy chair once and then sat alert at the ready. Sure enough, Daisy was guarding the young girl.

Izzy stirred and then squealed with delight. "Daisy. You're here." Her soft speech affected Brooke, and she adjusted Izzy's blanket, receiving a loopy grin for her efforts. "Thank you. I feel better already."

That last sentence relieved some of her fears.

"Hey, squirt. Glad you're okay." Colin pulled a small stuffed animal out of his hoodie pocket. "This needs a good home."

Izzy reached for the toy dog with her free arm. "Thank you."

She smiled at Colin as if he hung the moon. Vanessa ventured into the living room. "Hey, Vanessa." Colin reached into his pocket once more. He turned back to Izzy. "I hope you don't mind, but I got something for Vanessa, too."

Maternal pride for her son's thoughtfulness skittered through her. Colin presented Vanessa with a smaller stuffed dog that resembled Daisy, while Izzy pressed her larger version of Daisy to her cheek and yawned.

"How about we take this into the breakfast nook so Izzy can get some rest?" Jonathan steered the three of them into the kitchen.

Brooke glanced behind her, but Daisy remained at her spot, guarding the patient. Vanessa rocketed for the refrigerator. "Can I have a soda?"

Jonathan hesitated before nodding. "Only one." He pulled out a red can and faced Brooke. "Would you like anything to drink?"

She shook her head, and Vanessa rocked on her heels. "Can Colin have one, too? I can show him the tree fort you built for me in the backyard."

Jonathan handed Colin a similar can. Vanessa yanked him outside, and Colin shot Brooke a look that told her she owed him big time.

Relatively speaking, she had Jonathan to herself, and not a moment too soon. He held out his arms, and she flew into his embrace, his solidness a firm reality, their connection substantial and magical. She broke away and led him to the table, scooting two chairs together until they touched. "What happened?"

He scrubbed his chin, and she thought she glimpsed a rather haunting look in his gaze. It was but a brief shadow before he exhaled and glanced at her with what looked like relief.

She reached for his hand and found she was still wearing her gloves. She stuffed them into her coat pocket. Then she stood, took off her coat and hung it on the back of the chair. Settling in once more, she grasped his hand in hers, hoping he could draw strength from her.

"I was the first officer on the scene."

Her bones ached for him. The memories, the flashback, the pain. "Jonathan."

He slipped his arm around her. Their lips met and her world came alive. Care, concern, love. All rolled into one. She couldn't hold back any longer. She broke away. "I love you."

Radiant joy spread over his face. "Brooke, you're the best thing to come into my life in such a long time."

"But I might have lost my job. Maybe a lot more, too." She loved helping kids like Emmie, teaching the GED class and planning groups like Mimosas and Masterpieces. "I walked out on Mr. Whitley when I found out Izzy and

Tina were at the hospital. Our meeting is now Monday afternoon at one."

His jaw dropped, and he drew her close, his freshly shaved cheek near her ear. "You did that for me?"

She separated from him and nodded. "Of course."

"You're amazing."

The look in his eyes was gratitude, and she remembered everything about his parents and how their work was the most important part of their lives. "I promise that I will always put my family above my work."

Hollydale and Jonathan were part of her family now. If he wanted her, that was.

His throat bobbed. "Brooke, I love you."

"Then again, if I'm let go on Monday, I won't be able to help you with your investigation anymore."

"You don't know, do you?" He pulled away and met her gaze. "The sheriff and I executed a search warrant at the home of the previous director when his son took off in his car. He crashed into Aunt Tina's SUV."

Chills wracked her body. "The former director's son is behind the fake ID scheme?"

Jonathan nodded and rubbed the fleshy part of her hand, breaking through the numbness that had settled into her. "He wasn't hurt in the crash. He was checked out and cleared at the scene. Now he's confessed and is awaiting his bail hearing." Jonathan launched into the rest of the story. "Once I figured out the keys were the missing factor, everything fell into place."

Keys? The blood rushed to her ears, and she gripped the table.

"Thank goodness you told him about the phone call." She hadn't heard Colin open the back door, but she turned and there he was, his hands in his hoodie pocket.

"What phone call?" Jonathan released her, and his face hardened to stone.

"Mom?"

"I was going to tell you about it last night, but with one thing and another…" Brooke swallowed, her breathing shallow. "A while back, someone called my office, and Colin answered. The person never identified themselves, but he asked Colin for the keys to the center. My son hung up."

How would Jonathan take this? Would he see this as a betrayal? A sign she still didn't trust him? One look at the harsh set of his mouth answered just that.

"I originally didn't tell you because you'd just accused Colin of trying to use a fake ID. I didn't want him exposed to the same assumptions and pressures I endured as a teenager. I was scared."

Jonathan scooted his chair away from her and stood. "My daughter was hurt in that accident." His voice sounded faraway, like it was coming through a tunnel. "I saw her, immobile in the back seat."

Colin moved toward the living room. "I'm going to take Daisy home while you and my mom work this out."

Was there a way for them to do that? Brooke had just told Jonathan she loved him, and now they seemed worlds apart. In a second, their bond seemed to have shattered like those Christmas ornaments on the tile floor of the supply closet. The same way her world had shattered when her mother hadn't supported her when Brooke told her she was pregnant.

She'd moved to Hollydale for a job, but had found so much more. Aunt Mitzi's kindness and encouragement, the camaraderie of great friends, and Jonathan's love.

"You helped me live again," he said.

There was an unspoken *but* in Jonathan's words. Everything she didn't know she needed had been at her fingertips, and now there was a chasm there instead. "But it's not enough," Brooke finished his sentence.

Ever since she'd read that pregnancy stick,

she'd had to maintain her composure. Grow up fast and take care of herself as best she could and a mother who partied and drank too much. Until now, she never dared risk everything out of sheer fear.

Some part of her held back in the community center's parking lot and last night in Aunt Mitzi's driveway, and now that mistake had cost her.

"I don't know. I need time to think." He leaned back against the counter and glanced away.

Brooke rose, her heart shattering into a thousand pieces. She'd lose her job on Monday, and she lost any chance of a future with Jonathan now. "I don't need time to know I love you. I can't imagine why you'd ever put your heart on the line for me. Not after you suffered one moment that took so much from you, and another, today, might have taken even more." She stopped, her voice cracking. She reached for her coat and threw it over her arm. "I'm sorry for not telling you sooner."

On her way out, she glanced at Izzy, still sleeping in the chair. The girl's trust had been slow in coming, unlike her father's. He seemed to trust Brooke right away. She'd had his love, and now?

She hadn't trusted him enough when she should have, and it was time to live with those consequences.

CHAPTER TWENTY-TWO

FORGET ABOUT RUNNING between raindrops. When the skies opened their floodgates like this, there was nothing to do but sprint to his squad car and stay dry. During his Monday morning shift, his first since the accident, vehicles had obeyed the speed limit, observing extra caution on this cold, damp day, as he monitored their speed with his radar gun. Worst of all, he'd done nothing except think of how he'd left things with Brooke.

Brooke. He felt pain at the silence between them over the weekend. Guilt struck him. She'd been carrying around the weight of the past and hadn't trusted him to help her. Then again, her mother and Colin's father had never supported her or allowed trust to flourish. It was understandable. Brooke had built a life for herself and Colin on her own, unlike him. When he'd started over, he had a support system that looked after him and his daughters.

Love was precious, once in a lifetime. If he was fortunate enough to have someone as terrific as Brooke in his life, was he throwing everything away because he had a genuine grievance? Or was he stuck on his pride once more?

He shook away those thoughts a good deal more easily than the wet chill invading his bones. He drove into town. Opening the door of The Busy Bean, he came close to bumping into Fabiana, who held her head high and passed by without saying hello, very unlike her.

Fabiana opened a leopard-print umbrella, and he held the door for Hyacinth, who passed him with a silent shake of her head. She huddled under the umbrella with Fabiana, and they hurried away. He hadn't progressed another step when his aunt crossed the threshold.

"Aunt Tina! Should you be out of bed yet?"

She popped open a black umbrella with a pink ribbon supporting breast cancer research. "You sound like your uncle. I'm feeling better, and I don't go back to work until next week. I needed to get out of the house, or your uncle and I were going to have words about how he's treating me like a delicate butterfly. You can't keep a good woman down. When you pick Izzy up from school, tell her I love her, and I'll drop by tonight."

She blew him a kiss. He'd started yet again

into the Bean when Mitzi and Betty ran outside. He stood back to let them pass.

Mitzi simply looked at him and exhaled a
deep breath. "I'm glad Izzy's on the road to re-
covery. As far as you and Brooke, I'm staying
out of it," she said with a huff. "If two people
can't tell they're meant for each other and see
how precious love is, far be it from me to interfere and put in my two cents to tell them otherwise. But I will say, Officer Maxwell, you can
get your hair cut at Chantal's from now on."

For Mitzi, that was strong language.

What did they want from him? He was the
one whose child was injured in a car accident.
Brooke had kept secrets, vital information that
might have helped him crack the case sooner.

*Because she hadn't ever been around people
who eyed her with anything less than distrust
and suspicion.*

She'd come to town, a blank slate, full of
enthusiasm for turning around the community
center. And she'd done just that, providing a
special place for encouragement and growth.
In addition, she'd kept her promise to him that
she wouldn't tell anyone, even Whitley, about
what was in that locker.

What had he done? He'd taken a picture of
her son and put him in a photo lineup. That

was his job, and he'd stand by that decision, but he could have been the one to tell her.

She protected her son by withholding the details of a conversation where neither she nor Colin knew the identity of the caller. Since Hinshaw had a stash of burners, Jonathan wouldn't have tracked him down.

And Colin had hung up as soon as he realized the caller had ill intentions.

His pride had kept him from speaking out when Brooke stood in the kitchen. He'd had all the clues in front of him and yet he hadn't followed up about Ray. And he didn't realize the importance of keys until it was almost too late.

"Jonathan." He glanced over at a small bistro table and found Mike talking to Aidan. "Just the person we wanted to see."

Should he stay or should he go to the center and check on Brooke? Her rescheduled appointment with Mr. Whitley was a mere half an hour away. She'd risked her job to be by his side.

Reciprocating wasn't just evening sides. She deserved his loyalty. It was the right thing to do for the woman he loved, the woman whose presence he was fortunate to have in his life and his kids' lives.

"I have to go."

"You got the job." Mike waved him over and pointed to the open chair.

Jonathan furrowed his brow and navigated his way to the table. "What are you talking about?"

"The detective position." Mike stood and clapped him on the back. "It's yours."

"Thanks for letting me know, but I have to be somewhere else. Let's discuss this later."

A weight lifted off his shoulders. He wasn't his parents, and he never would be, detective or not. He was simply plain old Jonathan. Well, not so old and not so plain, he hoped. At least not in Brooke's eyes, and that was all that mattered.

Someone tapped on his shoulder, and he turned around to find the owner, Deb, standing there with two disposable cups. "Just my regular blend, but tell Brooke her next cappuccino's on the house."

"How did you know?" He held up his hand and then accepted the cups instead. "Never mind. I don't want these guys to get the impression you'd make the best detective in town."

"Though I would." Deb smiled, and he returned her smile, his first since Brooke left his kitchen.

"Yeah, but I'll keep it our secret and give Brooke your message."

If he wasn't too late.

BROOKE PLACED THE last book into the box and dusted the shelf. She glanced around her office and willed herself not to cry. She'd been in bigger scrapes before and had always found a way through. This time, however, she'd also fallen in love.

How would she be able to stay in Hollydale and see Jonathan two, three or even more times each week? It had been hard enough being on the receiving end of glares of people she didn't care about. To see Jonathan upset with her because she'd kept the call to herself? That would truly be awful.

Somehow, she'd manage. She'd become attached to this town. The pumpkin patch had been her first real taste. Deb at The Busy Bean memorized how much steamed milk she liked in her favorite cappuccino, her reward on Saturday mornings when she walked Daisy downtown. She loved every minute of trying on bridesmaids' dresses with Lucie and Ashleigh and getting to know them better.

She'd find some job, any job, so she wouldn't break her promise to Colin that he'd graduate from high school in Hollydale. Aunt Mitzi had been kind enough to extend their living arrangements, even after Brooke told her about ditching Mr. Whitley and the probable consequence of that decision. Later this afternoon, she'd hit the pavement and apply for positions at every establishment in Hollydale. She wasn't too proud to work in Aunt Mitzi's salon or even at Mo's Gas and Bait Stop.

She took a deep breath and let it out, smoothing her wrinkled suit jacket that she hadn't bothered to iron this morning. Mr. Whitley would be here in a few minutes, and then she'd carry the boxes out to her car and start over. She'd done it before. She'd do it again.

But wait, was she giving in? She talked a good game about not quitting, and yet the boxes proved the opposite. She'd begun unloading the first one when she heard a commotion in the lobby. Brooke hurried out and found Mr. Whitley unbuttoning his gray overcoat with a circle of women closing ranks on him.

"Brooke Novak is the best thing to happen to this center, and I've worked here since it opened, so I should know." Betty waggled her finger at him.

"Brooke brings a melodious harmony to everyone who steps foot in the center." Hyacinth adjusted her sunflower scarf that topped her bright yellow coat with rainbow leggings beneath. "She cares about a person's artistic bent and every aspect of their well-being in constructing a total outer shell that matches the beautiful spirit…"

Fabiana tapped Hyacinth's shoulder. "A feisty spirit that would have been a perfect match for my Carlos, except she fell in love with a police officer instead."

"My nephew's not bad-looking. He's quite nice." Tina smiled.

Mr. Whitley raised his black umbrella and brought the tip down on the tiled floor of the lobby. "Ladies!"

"We're the Mimosas." Aunt Mitzi raised her chin high. "And you know why? Because Brooke listened to us. We needed an outlet for our creativity, and she provided that."

"The Matchmaking Mimosas," Fabiana corrected her before smiling in Mr. Whitley's direction. "I want grandchildren while I can spoil them rotten and send them home loaded up with sugar from my *tres leches* cake."

Brooke's heart swelled, and a tear slipped down her cheek. She wiped it away quickly. Who'd have guessed the teenager who had people whispering behind her back would have these shouts of love? These five wonderful ladies were standing up for her. She cherished each of them, and it was time to stand up for herself.

There'd never be a better opportunity than now. Heck, there might never be another opportunity, period.

"Look within yourself, Brooke Amber." Aunt Mitzi only called her that when she wanted Brooke to pay special attention. "Now's the time to meet your struggles. No more running away."

How did her aunt do that? Know what she was thinking and say precisely what Brooke needed to hear.

"Mr. Whitley, thank you for returning for the third time in the past week." She found her voice, and Hollydale helped contribute to that.

"Ms. Novak, you seem to have quite a few supporters." He gestured at the women, who were smiling and high-fiving each other.

"I'm *their* biggest supporter. They've given me strength to confront my mistakes and do what I can to fix them." She might never get another chance with Jonathan, but she deserved a chance to finish what she'd started at the center.

"And do you make that many mistakes?"

"Mr. Whitley, I think this conversation might go better in private. We can finish what we started last Friday."

"So you admit you were wrong to walk out like that?" He arched an eyebrow, his tone challenging.

"I admit nothing of the kind." She tilted her chin upward, the same way as Aunt Mitzi. "When a family emergency comes up, that will always take precedence. For a while, I was lucky to believe I might be part of Jonathan's family. Which I messed up, but that doesn't mean he's any less special in my life." She loved him, and the ache in her heart throbbed.

Tina came over and placed her arm around Brooke's shoulders. "Thank you, sweetheart." Tina squeezed before releasing her.

"Mr. Whitley, before we go upstairs, I want you to promise that you'll keep the Mimosas and Masterpieces art class going. These ladies helped me with the very successful Heartsgiving celebration, and they deserve this forum."

"I don't think you're one to speak about promises, Ms. Novak. When I hired you, I trusted you'd inform me of any wrongdoing associated with the center, and you failed in that regard."

"No, she didn't." Jonathan's assertive voice was loud and clear.

Brooke stared at him standing there with Izzy. Jonathan placed two disposable cups on Betty's desk. Mr. Whitley tapped his umbrella two more times on the lobby floor. "Excuse me? Have we met?"

"I'm Officer Jonathan Maxwell of the Hollydale Police Department. I asked for Brooke's cooperation and swore her to secrecy. It was an official request, if you want to get into the semantics." Jonathan wound his arm slowly around Izzy, carefully avoiding the purple cast. "In my time serving this town, I haven't met anyone as responsible and reliable as Brooke. When she makes a promise, she delivers on her word."

Brooke went over to Izzy. "Shouldn't you be in school?"

"The school nurse said I needed some rest and Daddy came and signed me out for the rest of the day. When Daddy said he was coming here, I asked if I could tag along. I wanted to see you. I didn't get much of a chance to the other day." She yawned and shrugged, then yawned again and chuckled. "Good thing I have, since I probably need another nap soon."

Jonathan gave his daughter a quick nod and let go. He stepped forward, snagging Brooke's gaze. He focused on her and her alone now. "Brooke, I know my wanting to control what I can't has led to some mistakes, but my feelings for you aren't a mistake. Life is too short not to act on something real, and what we have together is real. I didn't follow you out the door on Friday when you needed reassurance, and I'm sorry about that. I blamed you for someone else's actions. That was all wrong. I love you." He broke the gaze, hurried to Betty's desk and returned with two cups in his hands. "I come bearing gifts."

"And that will make everything better?" she asked. Her grin was her way of letting him know they were back on track.

"It's coffee." He grinned too and held one out to her. "Coffee makes everything better, especially when it's Deb's from The Busy Bean."

Mr. Whitley cleared his throat. "Ms. Novak, a word."

He motioned they should move away from the rest of the group.

"It seems as though you have a strong group behind you, Ms. Novak."

"Isn't that the point of a community center, sir? To bring the community together?"

Mr. Whitley pushed up his glasses to the top of his nose. "It is, and I'm as dedicated to the community as you are. You're not fired, Ms. Novak, but I expect to know every detail of what's happening from now on."

"Our weekly staff meetings are Friday mornings at eight. Betty bakes a sausage casserole that we all love and devour." Brooke raised her chin. "If you come and take an active role, you can have a corner piece. Then you can stick around and ask me whatever you want to know rather than asking others to pass you information."

A long pause followed. Perhaps she'd be repacking that one book after all.

"I'll ask our cook to make a kringle," he said. "It's a special pastry she only does during the holidays. I expect to start at eight sharp."

He strode toward the automatic doors and tipped his hat to the group. The doors parted for his exit, and a hush fell over the crowd until Mitzi tapped her watch. "This emergency meeting of the Matchmaking Mimosas is called on account of work. We'd best return to our jobs."

Betty smiled at Izzy. "I think we'll see if there are any leftovers from this morning's cooking class. A full stomach will help you rest better." She glanced at Jonathan. "If you don't mind?"

He smiled in return and shook his head. "You read my mind."

Brooke was so relieved. The distance between her and Jonathan that seemed like a million miles had now narrowed to only the few feet that separated them. They met in the middle.

Jonathan swept her hair off her shoulder. "I like your style. Actually, I like you."

"A minute ago, you said you love me. Now you only like me?" She let out a nervous laugh at her lame attempt at humor. It was hard to be funny when her stomach danced the dance of a thousand hippos.

"I like you enough to leave Mike behind when he offered me the detective position." Jonathan sipped his coffee.

Her heart leaped, and it was wonderful to have it beating strong once more. "You got the job? Wait, you walked out on Mike?"

"I told him and Aidan I had a pressing matter. Considering they both have strong relationships with their wives, they'll understand why I left and won't hold it against me."

She placed both coffee cups on a nearby table before stepping toward him, her promise on her lips but even more in her heart. She closed the gap and kissed him. A minute later, her favorite taste, coffee, lingered on her lips. "So that's what it's like to kiss and make up?"

He laughed and pulled her close once more. "I guess we'll have to fight every once in a blue moon. In the meantime, I'd like to kiss you, and often."

Kisses for every occasion, all of them cementing how grateful they were that they had found each other. Her heart swelled with love for this funny man who showed her life was more than a job and home was more than a destination.

Hollydale had once been her destination, but now its people filled her life with bonds and what she felt would be lifelong friendships. No longer was she the scared girl who couldn't stand up for herself when people whispered behind her back. Now she was the loved woman who stood up for herself, surrounded by the people who'd taken her in and shared their strength, not to mention their family, with her.

And she couldn't wait to end each day with those kisses.

EPILOGUE

THE NIGHT SKY twinkled with stars that were only half as bright as the faces surrounding him. The dipping temperatures meant a fire in Jonathan's recently constructed stone pit in the backyard and was perfect for Christmas Eve.

"Dad, what happened to hot chocolate by the tree?" Izzy grumbled and settled into a chair closest to the fire.

"It's our first holiday with Brooke and Colin." Jonathan assembled a s'more for Izzy, taking care to break it into chunks she could eat with only one hand. "And I built this pit with Colin's help. Thanks, Colin."

He handed the teenager the ingredients for him to make a s'more and he did so, using extra chocolate. Brooke smiled. "I think the fire pit is romantic and sweet."

"I like it, too." Vanessa licked the chocolate remnants off her fingers. "Can I have another one?"

"No. Too much sugar, and you'll never go to sleep." Jonathan hid his smile at the thought of her staying up since he'd planned on proposing to Brooke later tonight by the tree.

Though they'd only known each other two-and-a-half months, tonight was the perfect time. The few short weeks they'd been dating only confirmed what he knew in his heart. The tree lighting in the town square, Vanessa's holiday pageant, Colin's playoff game where he scored the winning basket at the buzzer— every day he'd fallen more in love with the woman sitting across from him. He loved how she made every minute count. Besides, any-one who could convert Mr. Whitley and Izzy to her side had to be someone special.

"Then is it too early to unwrap presents?" Vanessa sat on the edge of her seat.

Jonathan shook his head. "Let's enjoy the beautiful night. Izzy wants to finish her s'more. There'll be enough time for the two of you to open a gift before you go to sleep."

"Vanessa, you know we always get the paja-mas tonight. Tomorrow's the good stuff." Izzy set her paper plate with the rest of her treat on her chair.

Colin scarfed down his s'more. "Mom and I are bringing over our gifts to you guys in the morning. I'll warn you now, Mom takes pictures of everything." He licked his fingers.

"But Vanessa and I asked Brooke, and she said we can give these to Daddy tonight."

She reached under her chair and pulled out two wrapped rectangles.

"You didn't have to get me anything," he told them.

"We didn't *get* you anything. We made these." Vanessa jumped up and stood by his side. "Rip off the paper."

He opened the packages and found two paintings of connected hearts. Brooke came over and joined them. "This was their Hearts-giving project."

Misty-eyed, he held the canvases close to his heart. "Thank you, Izzy and Vanessa."

"Look closely at mine, Daddy." Vanessa plucked out the one that was hers and held it in front of him. The light from the fire was enough for him to make out the details.

"Why are there five hearts?"

"One for each of us, plus one for Brooke and one for Colin."

"You included Mom and me?" Colin's throat bobbed as Vanessa nodded and showed him the canvas.

Jonathan choked up at how his daughter had acknowledged what he'd almost lost. At least he'd come to his senses. Last weekend he'd asked Colin and Mitzi for their blessing. Mitzi even agreed he could come back to her salon, muttering something about no nephew of hers getting married with a mullet.

"Yoo-hoo! Is everyone back here?"

Speaking of Brooke's aunt, she and Owen popped around the corner, waving a present and bringing Daisy to enjoy the fun. "Merry Christmas." Mitzi glanced at Jonathan, then at Brooke's hand. She let out an exaggerated sigh and rattled the gift. "We brought the family a little something. Champagne."

"Thank you." Brooke ushered her aunt to her vacated seat and accepted Daisy, who slobbered on her with dog kisses as if they'd been separated forever.

Jonathan rushed to get Owen a chair, sitting him next to Mitzi. "Would either of you care for a s'more? We have more than enough to go around."

"Thanks, but I'm full of Ashleigh's country fried steak with all the trimmings. Owen's daughter can cook up a storm in the kitchen."

"Hello? Is everyone in the backyard?"

Aunt Tina and Uncle Drew entered the yard, laughing, with his uncle holding several containers in his hands. He pointed to the kitchen. "If now's a good time—" he sneaked a peek at Brooke's hand "—and it is, I'll put this soup in your freezer and be back in a few."

Daisy wriggled at the newcomers and traveled around the circle, waiting for people to pet her.

"Anyone home?"

Jonathan's eyes widened as Betty and Joe arrived. What was going on? He hadn't sold tickets for his Christmas Eve proposal. "Did you also hear about the s'mores?"

"No." Betty shook her head and looked at Brooke. "A little birdie told us..."

"About the new fire pit." Joe nudged Betty, who started nodding.

"Yes, that's right." Betty waved her hand as if batting away her comment. Even with only the light of the fire, the bright red of her cheeks matched her holiday sweater.

Jonathan rose and pointed to the shed. "I'll be right back with more seats."

"I'll help." Colin jumped up and accompanied him.

Jonathan located more chairs and handed one to Colin. "Here you go."

"What should I call you after this? Jonathan or Dad?" Colin's gaze met his, and Jonathan saw his own acceptance of their burgeoning relationship mirrored there.

"Brooke hasn't said yes yet, but you know you're family, right?"

Colin's chest puffed out. "It's nice to hear it out loud. I'm getting two sisters, too."

Good to know Colin saw things the way that Jonathan did.

No sooner had they arrived with two chairs for Betty and Joe than he rubbed his eyes as two more people appeared. "Fabiana? Hyacinth? What's going on?"

"On this most beautiful of nights, the family camaraderie of a fire pit and the munificence of our new community director led us here." Hyacinth beamed and held out some mason jars of fruit. "Besides, I thought a few jars of my delectable peaches would bring much joy tomorrow morning."

Fabiana held out a carrier. "Carlos missed his flight, so I brought you his *tres leches* cake. I hope you enjoy it."

"Thank you." His arms were full, and his pocket was heavy with the ring practically burning a hole through the fabric.

Joe rushed over and accepted the cake carrier. "I'll see if Drew's okay in the kitchen."

Jonathan felt everyone's gaze upon him. He didn't need to use his detective skills to figure out what had happened. Mitzi spilled his secret to the Matchmaking Mimosas, and they all dropped by to see the ring.

Except he hadn't proposed yet.

Brooke rose and picked up the mason jars. "You stay out here and enjoy your company." Jonathan laughed as Brooke appeared to be the only one not in on the secret. She reached up and patted her cheeks. "Do I have chocolate smeared all over my face? Everyone's staring at me."

"In the happiest sense possible." It might not be the time he'd chosen, but it was sweet with their children and the Matchmaking Mimosas nearby. He dropped to one knee and brought out the small box with the amethyst and diamond ring he'd selected for her.

She gasped.

"Brooke Amber Novak, when I followed a lead in my investigation to the center, I met an unforgettable woman who challenged me to wake up the part of my heart I thought was gone forever. Since you started your new beginning in Hollydale, you've helped cement friendships to the point where people drop everything on Christmas Eve to support you and be in your corner, just as you've been for them. You're humble and sweet and you put your entire self behind your promises. You're my passion, my love, my life. Will you marry me? Join our family? Or, we'll join yours?"

She nodded, and everyone cheered. He rose and swung her around. All assembled crowded around to congratulate them as he slid the ring on her finger.

Tonight was the first night of the rest of their future, one he looked forward to with a full and happy heart.

* * * * *

For more great Hollydale romances from Tanya Agler and Harlequin Heartwarming, visit www.Harlequin.com today!

HARLEQUIN SELECTS COLLECTION

19 FREE BOOKS IN ALL!

From Robyn Carr to RaeAnne Thayne to Linda Lael Miller and Sherryl Woods we promise (actually, GUARANTEE!) each author in the Harlequin Selects collection has seen their name on the *New York Times* or *USA TODAY* bestseller lists!

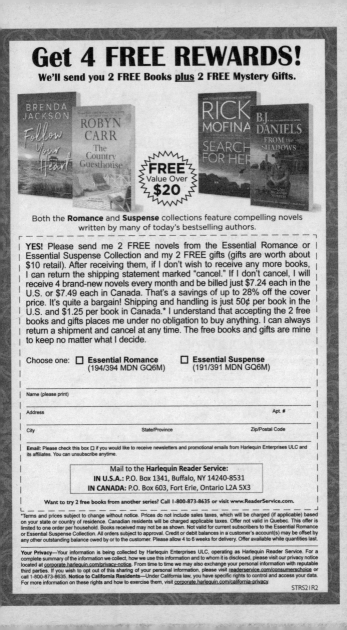

#395 A TEXAN'S CHRISTMAS BABY
Texas Rebels • by Linda Warren

Chase Rebel and Jody Carson wed secretly after high school—
then life and bitter hurts forced them apart. Now they're back in
Horseshoe, Texas, still married, but no longer sweethearts. Can
past secrets leave room for second chances?

#396 A SECRET CHRISTMAS WISH
Wishing Well Springs • by Cathy McDavid

Cowboy Brent Hayes and single mom Maia MacKenzie are
perfect for each other. Too bad they work together at the dating
service Your Perfect Plus One and aren't allowed to date! Can
Christmas and some wedding magic help them take a chance
on love?

#397 HER HOLIDAY REUNION
Veterans' Road • by Cheryl Harper

Like her time in the air force, Mira Peters's marriage is over.
When she requests signed divorce papers, her husband makes
a final request, too. Will a Merry Christmas together in Key West
change all of Mira's plans?

#398 TRUSTING THE RANCHER WITH CHRISTMAS
Three Springs, Texas • by Cari Lynn Webb

Veterinarian Paige Palmer learns the ropes of ranch life fast
while helping widowed cowboy Evan Bishop. But making a
perfect Christmas for his daughter isn't a request she can
grant...unless some special holiday time can make a happily-
ever-after for three.

Visit ReaderService.com Today!

As a valued member of the Harlequin Reader Service, you'll find these benefits and more at ReaderService.com:

- Try 2 free books from any series
- Access risk-free special offers
- View your account history & manage payments
- Browse the latest Bonus Bucks catalog

Don't miss out!

If you want to stay up-to-date on the latest at the Harlequin Reader Service and enjoy more content, make sure you've signed up for our monthly News & Notes email newsletter. Sign up online at ReaderService.com or by calling Customer Service at 1-800-873-8635.